The Street Life Series

IS IT PASSION OR REVENGE?

Also by Kevin M. Weeks

The Street Life Series:
Is It Suicide or Murder?

IS IT PASSION OR REVENGE?

Kevin M. Weeks

With Book Cover Artwork by
Matt Brumelow

Book Cover Design by
Marion Designs

Library of Congress Control Number: 2007908110
ISBN: Hardcover   978-1-4257-9736-2
               Softcover   978-1-4257-9712-6

1. Jackson, Teco (Fictitious character)—Fiction. 2. Troop, Hanae (Fictitious character)—Fiction. 3. The Paradox (Fictitious character)—Fiction. 4. Strictly Business (SB)—Fiction. 5. Young Black Mafia—Fiction. 6. Murders—Fiction. 7. Detectives and Law Enforcement Officers—Fiction. 8. Male Exotic Dancers and Night Clubs—Fiction. 9. Washington (D.C.)—Fiction. 10. Philadelphia (PA)—Fiction. 11. Conshohocken (PA)—Fiction. 12. Asheville (NC)—Fiction. 13. Atlanta (GA)—Fiction. I. Title.

This book was printed in the United States of America.

To order additional copies of this book, contact:
Xlibris Corporation
1-888-795-4274
www.Xlibris.com
Orders@Xlibris.com
41408

DEDICATION

Dr. Billy Nichols

THE STREET LIFE SERIES:
IS IT SUICIDE OR MURDER?
2006-2007 YEAR IN REVIEW
EDITOR'S CHOICE

"Weeks has a very accessible prose style, which makes the book just plain fun to read."
Judge: Writer's Digest 15th Annual International Self-Published Book Awards

"We advise all urban lit lovers to read The Street Life Series. Entertaining, Engaging, Authentic and a WINNER!—JUST IN! This book is dangerous and real!"
Reviewer: Heather Covington, critically acclaimed literary television hostess, national best selling author, and Founder of YOUnity Guild of America

"Kevin Weeks is brilliant in his deliberate and calculated steps to captivate his audience with The Street Life Series."
Reviewer: James M. Lisbon, Founder AMAG/Awareness Magazine

"If you dig Donald Goines novels and you were a fan of New Jack Swing then you are gonna roll with this Book with ease . . . . Weeks is a very sharp writer and has a promising future with his sense of timing with characters."
Reviewer: "mistermaxxx," Amazon.com Top 50 Reviewer

Author Note's

Adult Fiction

Parental Advisory: Contains Adult Situations

SPECIAL ACKNOWLEDGEMENTS

*G*od, You blessed me with a host of people, who make my new career, new goals, and new accomplishments worthwhile. *René*, you have been a true blessing in more ways than one. *Signe Adderley*, I'm glad that I can make you laugh again. I love you mom. *Anthony Weeks, Trezonna Weeks, and Denise Weeks,* thanks for the words of encouragement. Apostle *Annyebelle Neal*, auntie, you went above and beyond by taking that long trip from Philly to Atlanta to see me. Our counseling sessions are the mortar for my new strong foundation. Thank You. *Hazel Blackwell*, you are the best grandmother in the world. *Mercedes Weeks, Chanell Weeks, Kevin M. Weeks, Jr.*, when I think of you all, I reach deeper within myself to succeed. To my little cousin, *Gabrielle Weeks,* you hold it down in West Chester. I'm very proud of you for reaching a higher level of education. *Valerie Griffin, Avis Griffin and Latisha Lee*, thank you and your family for all of the support.

Heather Covington, I am honored to be a member of Diamonds, Silver, and Gold (Disilgold). Thank You. *Xlibris Corporation*, I must say that you support your authors well. To the Ladies of *OOSA*, you conducted the first book review of my debut novel and included me in the OOSA article titled *Authors on Lock*. Thank you. I will never forget. To *Shunda Leigh and the Booking Matters* staff, you made the first public premiere of *The Street Life Series* possible. Thank You. *Troy Johnson*, speaking with you was indeed inspirational.

Yolanda Diamond and Samuel Howard, my prayer is that the writing tips I share with you are as beneficial as the invaluable writing techniques that I receive from my literary mentor, *Ryan D., Pen American Center*. In addition, here's to *James Lisbon*, Founder of *Awareness Magazine*, who mentors youth every day in the field of publishing. Bro, one day I'll be able to do more than donate books.

Shouts out to my *Philly peeps*. But most of all, shout out to my homeboy, *Tyrone Chestnut*; yo homie, stay focused and keep your head up. I thank you for each and every long talk on the big yard. As I wrote the second novel in *The Street Life Series*, this shout out is for all of those souljas who put up with me: *Paul Harrison*, I thank you for the book review. *Romeno Johnson "Cutty"*, keep the faith and remember it's for Romena Johnson and Aeeril Johnson, your Lil' Cuttys. *Khalil Muhammad*, here's to your life's philosophy of one God, one love, and one mind. *To my family and supporters*, thank you for the kudos and believing in me. Thanks to the *United States Postal Service* for delivering my manuscript safely. If I didn't mention your name, please understand that there isn't enough paper to acknowledge you all.

A king will arise in his time. Thank you all. See you on the freedom side.

par·a·dox:

An apparently true statement or group of statements that leads to a contradiction or a situation which defies intuition.

> # I despise a snitch.

"Paradox." *Wikipedia. www.wikipedia.org*

CHAPTER 1

When the back door cracked open, the Senior Hotel Manager of the Comfort Inn saw a shadow which resembled a tall man wearing a trench coat and a teardrop dress hat. Then she heard footsteps; and in a flash the shadow was gone. She was not fazed because parking was behind the building. When the wind hit her face, she crossed and rubbed her arms to keep them warm. After she straightened the cross on her necklace, she pushed her windblown hair behind both ears. The manager looked at her Timex gold tone watch. "*The garbage truck will be here soon.*"

Due to the overcast, the back of the hotel was very sombrous. At two o'clock in the morning, everything was quiet as usual. At the far right of the back door, only one light was working. She made a mental note to call maintenance. The dumpster reeked of beer; and a sudden sound startled her. Picking up a scrub brush, she threw it at the dumpster. A face, with a black mask around the eyes, popped up. "Largate de aquí animal cochino, cochino!" She screamed as the filthy raccoon came out of the dumpster at her command. As the bushy tail vanished in the woods, all that was left were sounds of crickets chirping in a distance.

When she turned back to put the trash into the dumpster, she noticed the soles of shoes on a person lying on a discarded box spring. When she told him that he needed to leave, the person never moved. So the manager picked back up the scrub brush and tapped him on the feet. There was still no movement. As she stepped closer to get a full view of his total body, she thought he looked familiar and knelt down beside him. His face was pale and she screamed, "Ayudenme aquí esta una persona muerta! Alguien llame a la policía por favor!" No one responded to her cry for help; so she ran back into the hotel to dial 911.

Within the hour, Linda Hubbard, the Lead Crime Scene Investigator (CSI) snapped pictures as Detective Marcus Brown, who was known as Swoosh, walked under the crime scene tape to get a good look. He saw hotel guests from inside looking through the open curtains. Swoosh waved hello to a police officer who was stationed on Branch Avenue for traffic control. Because the police officer stopped directing traffic to acknowledge Swoosh, an impatient driver honked his car horn and yelled, "Hey! What's going on over there?" Bystanders chattered about the possibilities of what led to this event, because they loved to see the police in action.

The Prince George's (P.G.) County police assisted the D.C. detectives in securing the perimeter, because the Comfort Inn was on the borderline between D.C. and Maryland. As Linda's red hair blew in the wind, she walked the grid with her camera as the crowd witnessed the white sheet being placed over the body. Linda put numbered tags near different objects and took pictures of her findings. From her peripheral, she noticed a tall male coming in her direction.

"Hello Linda."

Linda's green eyes sparkled as she looked up from her camera and said, "Hey Swoosh. This one is pretty bad." She immediately noticed Swoosh's haircut. His brunette hair with blonde highlights was cut short on the top and the sides but long in the back. Linda never told Swoosh, but she always thought he looked like a younger version of Richard Dean Anderson.

"So what do we have?" asked Swoosh.

"Well, it looks like strangulation."

"Male or female? What is that?" asked Swoosh pointing to a piece of cloth as he pulled back the sheet.

"It's a male; and from what I can see, it's a white G-String around his neck with something tied to it."

Swoosh put his right hand on his forehead and began to rub softly. Linda said, "Oh, here you go rubbing your head. Do you have to do that at every crime scene?"

"I sure hope we don't have a serial killer."

"What makes you say that?"

Pointing towards the G-String, Swoosh said, "Well that's a note tied to it; and once it's cleared, we'll see what it says."

"Have you called Trooper?"

Swoosh looked at Linda not wanting to answer her question. "No, not yet."

"What are you waiting for? I think Trooper will want to see this."

"She is a workaholic. She needs to rest this weekend. Don't you think?"

"Trooper is one of our best detectives. We need her here. She sees things you even miss." Linda said with a smirk.

With the car door opened and his left leg extended out of the car, Swoosh called dispatch to connect him to Trooper's home phone. Linda glanced over at Swoosh and realized that the size of the police car was not comfortable for his height. Once, Swoosh told her that he played basketball for Notre Dame and that his teammates gave him the nickname Swoosh. Even though he was scouted by the NBA Development League, his passion was to become a homicide detective. People thought he was out of his mind when he turned down the NBA; however, the unsolved murder of his younger brother was a major driving factor for him choosing a police career over basketball. He felt authorities dropped the ball on his brother's case; and he was determined to be the detective in whom families could depend.

Trooper picked up the phone and said in a groggy voice, "This better be good. It's 4 in the morning."

"Good morning partner. Sleeping well?" asked Swoosh.

"Don't PARTNER me; and yes, I was sleeping well until the bat phone rang."

"I think you want to see this."

"What is it? Can't you handle this until I get in on Monday?" Putting the pillow over her head, Trooper really wanted to let this one pass.

"The team is asking for you specifically," said Swoosh.

Twenty-six year old Detective Hanae Troop was the quick-witted one on the force with an 85 percentile rank in closing cases. She leveraged her Criminal Justice Degree from Duke University in solving crimes. As a result, her first police partner nicknamed her Trooper because she was the epitome of the type of detective that the force wanted in their Homicide Division. Trooper said, "Alright, I'm on my way."

As Trooper traveled at high speeds throughout D.C., her police car's blue flashing lights were in full blast. Upon arrival at the crime scene, 5 different news crews tried to bum-rush the vehicle; however, Swoosh towered over them and was able to push back the camera man who was in Trooper's way. Almost falling down, the camera man yelled, "Hey man watch the camera!" Right then and there, the reporters knew that Swoosh meant business; and they cleared a path. Swoosh pointed to a P.G. County cop and screamed, "Put them farther back!" The noise from the crowd was giving Trooper a headache.

"You look good for just waking up," said Swoosh.

Trooper said a curse word under her breath.

Swoosh asked, "What did you say?" His compliment was genuine; however, Trooper believed otherwise. Swoosh never understood how a woman could always look as if she were going to a photo shoot, even near the break of dawn. Never requiring makeup, Trooper's milk chocolate skin was flawless. She always wore her hair bone straight and pulled back into a long ponytail. At this time of the morning, she wore a beautiful pink and blue silk scarf tied around her head.

Trooper ignored his question and asked, "What do we have?"

"A black male, age in his mid-twenties, 5' 8", and strangled. It doesn't seem to be a robbery. He still has on an Italian suit, Stacey Adam shoes, an expensive gold necklace, and an authentic Movado watch. In his waist pouch, there is $300 in $1 bills and $100 in larger bills."

"What is that?" asked Trooper pointing towards an object marked #1.

"You would never believe me if I told you."

"Try me," said Trooper kneeling down.

"It's a G-String."

"You have got to be kidding me. Is that a note?"

"That it is; and I wanted no one to touch it until you got here."

Trooper put on latex gloves and picked up the white G-String, which appeared to be brand new. "Here, put this G-String in an evidence bag. He is wearing nice cologne. That's Drakkar Noir. Did he have any I.D.?"

"No," said Swoosh, who reached for gloves and an evidence bag.

"Who called this in?"

"The manager of the Comfort Inn Hotel. She is a wreck."

"Where is she? And what's her name?" asked Trooper looking around the perimeter.

"Over there; and her name is Mrs. Garcia," responded Swoosh as he pointed to a P.G. County police car.

"Gather all evidence. We've got this one, partner." Trooper walked over to Mrs. Garcia, the manager of the Comfort Inn, and asked, "¿Habla usted inglés?"

"Si," responded Mrs. Garcia.

"Do you mind answering a few questions? I promise not to keep you long."

"The officer already took my statement," said Mrs. Garcia, whose face was red from crying.

"I see. Well, do you mind if I ask you one more question?" asked Trooper.

"I'm tired. Can I just go in and call my housekeeping staff to come into work? I gave them the day off because business is always slow a few weeks after Memorial Day on this side of town. I want to go home. Plus, I need to go and reassure my guests that the hotel is secure and safe now." She said with a sense of urgency.

"Have you ever seen the victim before?" asked Trooper.

" . . . Now I remember. A few months ago on Valentine's Day, it was my 30th wedding anniversary. My husband and I were working together at the front desk that day . . . ." She said sobbing and Trooper passed her a handkerchief. Ms. Garcia crossed her arms over her chest and continued, "This same handsome young man, whom I found tonight, registered for a one night stay. He told my husband to take me home and to make passionate love to me. Then this young man made me blush. He told me to let him know how my husband performed; and if I wasn't pleased that he would come back to the hotel and give me my very own private lap dance. Of course, I laughed. In fact, the young man pulled out a CD and gave it to my husband. He told my husband and me to listen to a song by . . . What's the singer's name? 12 Play is the song . . . by . . . by? . . ." She asked wiping the tears from her eyes.

"By R. Kelly?" asked Trooper.

With a pleasant memory of the victim, Mrs. Garcia smiled and said, "Yes, by R. Kelly. You should have seen the look on my husband's face; and I've never seen him that jealous before. In fact, that was the best sex I've had with my husband in years." She said and chuckled.

"Ookaay, that should wrap it up . . . . Linda, see if you can get a name from their files and see if her husband still has that CD case so we can dust it for prints," said Trooper.

Swoosh yelled, "Troop! It's all clear. Come see this note."

Trooper was in deep thought as she walked back to the edge of the woods to get a better visual of the perimeter. *The victim is extremely built. Maybe he goes to a nearby gym. How did he get behind the hotel building? His body was carefully positioned as if the killer cared how he was found. There is makeup on the left side of his breast pocket and lipstick on the collar of his shirt . . . . He gives lap dances . . . . There are $300 in $1 bills . . . . "*

"Troop! Heellooo. Troop, come back to earth. The note . . ."

"Oh yeah, I was just thinking."

"How did you calm our witness down so quickly?" asked Swoosh.

"She needed to reminisce. What you got?" asked Trooper reaching for the note.

"Take a look."

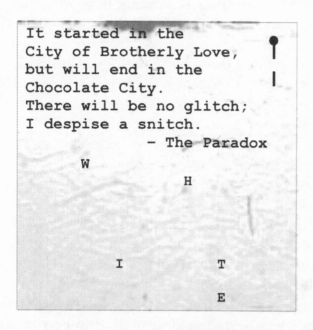

"This is going to be interesting. Well Paradox, where are you going to lead us?" asked Trooper pulling out a Snickers bar.

"Who is Paradox?" asked Swoosh, who never understood how Trooper maintained her hour-glass figure eating Snickers.

"The killer."

"Where did you come up with that name?"

"Didn't you see the name on the note?"

"Oh yeah, now I see it. We need to find The Paradox before there are any more murders," said Swoosh.

Trooper agreed and decided to go into the hotel and speak with the hotel clerk. A black male uniformed P. G. County police officer stepped aside as Trooper walked into the lobby. She smelled the newly installed gold carpet. The blue clothed sofa and 2 gold and blue striped chairs were in a U-shape configuration. The live potted trees surrounded the furniture and made the seating area look cozy. The Front Desk Clerk greeted Trooper with a smile and asked, "May I help you?"

"Were you working when the body was found?" Trooper asked the Front Desk Clerk.

"Yes." She said putting away some hotel receipts.

Handing the clerk a business card, Trooper said, "I'm Detective Hanae Troop. I need you to answer a few questions."

The clerk looked down to read the card and said, "Okay."

Trooper pulled out the grim Polaroid picture and asked, "Do you recall seeing this man checking into the hotel tonight?"

"No, from our records there were only 3 women who checked in."

"Were you working on Valentine's Day? Did a detective by the name of Linda come in and get that registration printout from you yet?"

"She requested it. I haven't had a chance to print it for her yet. Let me get it for you now. You know, as a matter of fact, I do recall him making Mrs. Garcia laugh that day."

"Give her a statement form," said Trooper to the police officer who was still by the door. Then Trooper looked at the Front Desk Clerk and said, "Oh yeah, don't leave until we tell you to." In an instance, Trooper did a spin on her heels to recheck the lobby and noticed the cameras in two corners. "I need to see the tape from those two cameras." Trooper said to the clerk.

The clerk's face turned berry red. Her boss told her days ago to call the surveillance company. There was no question that the contents of a tape would be beneficial to the police. She moved her lips to respond to Detective Troop; however, the words would not come out, because she was going to be fired for sure. The cameras were broken.

CHAPTER 2

Teco Jackson woke up feeling no breeze coming through the bedroom window of Apartment 276. Not having to go into work today at the Children's Clothing Store by Melvin, Teco was lying in bed and contemplating how he would spend his day. For sure, cooling off was a top priority. Since he heard laughter and water splashing, Teco imagined that there were lots of people out by the swimming pool.

Sitting on the side of the bed, he rubbed his eyes to gain focus and saw the pool area was indeed full of gorgeous women, young and old. One thing he loved about living at the Rosewood Village Apartments was the fact that there were lots of females, whom Teco affectionately called skimmies.

After moving from Philly to D.C., Teco finally turned away from a lifestyle of huge money and drugs. Even stealing cars no longer gave Teco the rush and pleasure he once found while living in West Philadelphia. Teco couldn't believe that settling down with his girlfriend, Rasheeda Igrubia, was finally providing him with a sense of home, which he never experienced before. He also knew that Rasheeda was trying her best to get him to stop smoking weed. As he reflected upon his 26 years of life, he now acknowledged that hopping from bed to bed, though physically fulfilling was risky. Nevertheless, Teco decided that he would go socialize with the twelve or so women who were already at the pool.

Yvette, Candi, and Toi were putting on sun block when Candi noticed Teco coming through the pool gate. Candi tapped Toi on the shoulder, which caused Yvette to turn around in Teco's direction.

"Girl, look at this fine ass brother with the toothpick in his mouth," said Candi.

"Damn . . . His arms are huge," said Toi.

"Girl, he wearing those black bikini swim trunks with them red and yellow stripes. Look at all that body oil on that six pack. When he see me, you know he gonna get hard. Don't he see these kids out here?" asked Yvette.

"Now Vette, you know he ain't gonna lust over your flat ass," said Candi; and Toi laughed.

"As soon as he gets in the water, I'm going to see if he wants to play," said Toi.

"Don't nobody want to play with your hot ass either," said Candi; and Yvette laughed.

"As soon as his towel hits that lawn chair, I'm going over there and introduce myself. Y'all just mad because he smiled at me first," said Toi.

"Yeah, yeah, whatever," said Candi.

As Teco strolled over to an empty green and blue striped lounge chair, he put his red terry beach towel down. He walked to the edge of the pool and dangled his foot into the water to test the temperature. A few kids were playing a water game causing water to splash onto Teco. "Marco! Polo! Marco! Polo! Marco! Polo!" Therefore, he backed up to watch the kids play. Then he heard laughter and turned to his left. Three fine women were walking in his direction.

"Hi, my name is Toi; and these are my girls, Candi and Vette."

"Nice to meet you," said Teco nonchalantly.

"How long have you lived here?" asked Toi, who was stepping into the pool.

"You work out?" Candi asked reaching for her romance novel.

"Your accent is funny. Where you from?" asked Yvette licking her lips.

"I'm from Philly," said Teco. They were throwing so many questions his way that he was trying to decide who to answer next.

"You don't talk much. Do you?" asked Candi.

"Give the man time to talk," said Yvette.

"Don't mind them. You want to swim?" asked Toi.

Out of no where came this real sharp tall pecan tanned brother with broad shoulders. This dude walked as if he were gliding on air, really smooth. Candi, Toi, and Yvette, who were initially trying to get Teco's attention, immediately walked away. Teco couldn't believe how the women were lined up to give this guy hugs. *Who the hell is that? Okay . . . I see . . . playing hard to get doesn't work in the Chocolate City. So much for swimming with Toi . . . "*

Even though there were no more females on Teco's side of the pool, Teco was actually digging this dude's style, until he stared at Teco too damn hard. *"What the hell is he looking at me for?"* As this brother walked towards him, Teco was on point for any drama.

"What's up? My name is Charles. Everyone calls me Chuck. You live around here?"

"Yeah, why you asking?" asked Teco, who gave Chuck dap.

"The ladies tell me that they like your style. Have you ever thought about being an exotic dancer?" asked Chuck.

"A while back, a skimmie asked me did I dance at parties. I haven't given it much thought since then."

"You can make a lot of money by dancing."

"I don't know about this dancing thing."

"Look, let's go to the club and you can see for yourself what it's like; and you'll see how all the women will throw themselves at you."

"What club is this?"

"Club Classic, across from Andrews Air Force Base."

"I'm not going to give you an answer about this dancing thing, because I have to see first."

"Can you get out tonight so we can go to the club?"

"Sure I can," said Teco as he observed a tall sophisticated woman in a black tailored suit walking through the pool gate. He immediately noticed the bulge of a gun protruding from her right side. "She is overdressed to be taking a swim. Don't you think?" Teco asked and removed the toothpick from his mouth.

"Sure is. Damn she fine," said Chuck.

Detective Troop walked up to the group of women who were standing by the pool and asked, "Do you know Charles Mobley?"

"Why?" asked Toi.

"I'm investigating a homicide and I need to ask him a few questions."

The group of women dispersed leaving Trooper standing alone. Chuck said, "I'm Charles Mobley. What's up?"

"May I ask you a few questions?" asked Trooper.

"If you call me Chuck."

"Chuck, were you at the Branch Avenue Comfort Inn on Valentine's Day?"

"Yeah. I hosted a party there that night. Why?"

"I have the hotel's registered list of guests; and your name is on the list. I'm trying to find out the name of an unidentified man who was murdered last night. He was also at the Comfort Inn on Valentine's Day. Well, you are not our victim. Here is my card; and if I have any more questions, I'll get back with you."

"I'd like that. So Detective, do you get out much?" Chuck asked in a player voice.

◊◊◊◊◊

There was a slight summer breeze and a quarter moon as Teco knocked on Chuck Mobley's door wearing a pair of Gucci jeans and a black silk shirt.

Chuck looked at Teco and said, "Man, we aren't going to the IBEX."

"What? I can't dress like this?"

"No. Look, come with me." Teco followed him into a bedroom that looked like it was a fashion designer's showroom. There were clothes and costumes on racks all over the place. Chuck picked out an outfit for Teco to wear and said, "Try this on."

Teco went into the bathroom down the hall and shouted, "Chuck! These pants are too long."

"Don't worry about that. Give me the pants and I'll hem them." Once Teco put on the altered pants, he agreed with Chuck. Teco looked dapper.

Within the hour, they pulled up to valet park; and Teco saw a line full of luxury cars. The gold trim around the roof of Club Classic's building immediately impressed Teco. Through the window, he could see the VIP room, which appeared to be in a glass bubble with smoke tinted windows that set it off. The main thing to catch Teco's attention was the fine ass women of all nationalities. If he didn't know any better, he would have thought he was at a United Nations Women's Convention.

As a skimmie passed Teco, he asked, "You see that ass on her?"

"That's Vickie," said Chuck.

"You know her?"

"Yeah, she's a regular here."

As they went through the front door, Chuck was able to walk right pass the bouncer. "Yo, only male dancers get in free tonight," said the bouncer to Teco.

"I'm with Chuck," said Teco.

The bouncer turned to Chuck and asked, "Is he with you?"

"Yeah Big June, this is a new dancer. Let him in," requested Chuck.

"My bad, you can go in," said Big June.

Teco liked the respect that dancers received. Once he passed the palm trees, all the lights in the club hit Teco. The only club he ever went to was the After Midnight Club in downtown Philadelphia; and it was nothing like this. Club Classic was more lavish and full of wall to wall women. Every female in the club displayed money in their hands. He was totally amazed.

Toi approached Teco and broke his train of thought. "Excuse me; Chuck wants you in the VIP room . . . ." She said pointing to the glass bubble. " . . . Before you leave, have you decided to be a dancer?"

"Yes, I have," said Teco.

She squeezed his ass and said, "Damn you fine. Are you dancing tonight? I want to see you sling that beef."

"No not tonight. Sorry baby," said Teco.

"Well here's your tip for being so fine." She gave Teco a $10 bill. "What's your stage name?" asked Toi.

Teco looked around the room. He saw a drink menu on the table and the first drink listed was called Rising Sun. "I'm sorry, what did you say?" asked Teco shifting the toothpick to the left side of his mouth.

"What's your stage name?"

"Rising Sun."

"I like that. You can rise on me any time."

Teco was starting to like the dancer's life already. The limelight was looking good to him. Plus, he could make more money dancing than he made in retail. As Teco went to the VIP room, Chuck motioned for him to take a seat.

"How you like what you see?" asked Chuck.

"It's alright man. All these fine women are bumpin'."

"Would you like a drink?" asked Chuck.

"Yeah, let me get a Cognac, no ice."

The waitress took their order; and just as she left, she winked at Teco. Paula Abdul's song "Opposites Attract" pumped through the speakers; and the blue, red, and yellow lights with a bright strobe light brought a high intensity to the place that made you want to jam. The brass railings around the dance floor were shining from the lights sparkling over them. The stage was huge. Teco saw the steps leading down to the dance floor, which looked like an empty orchestra pit.

The waitress came back with the drinks and asked, "Who's Rising Sun?"

"I am," said Teco.

"Toi told me to tell you that your drinks are on her. You must have it going on."

"Why you say that?"

"Because Toi don't break for nobody. Keep that to yourself."

Chuck looked at Teco and asked, "Rising Sun? Where did that come from?"

"Toi asked me if I decided to dance and I said yes. She then asked me my stage name, so I said Rising Sun."

The show was about to start; and the M.C. walked on the stage with the microphone in his hand. "Ladies! My name is G-Rock and laaadies! Are you sexy women hot and ready to see some beeef?"

All the women in the club screamed at the top of their voices, "Yeaaah!"

"Do we have any birthday bunnies in the house?" asked the M.C.

"Yeaaah!" screamed the women.

"Ladies, put your hands together for our first dancer. Laaadies! Here is Slick . . . Nic . . . The Ruuuler!" The women shouted and waved money in the air. H-Town's song "Knockin Da Boots" played through the speakers. This tall curly blond hair and blue eyed dude came from behind these double doors. He walked to center stage with a smooth erotic stride. His blue, black and yellow sequence two-piece suit sparkled off of the lights. As he lip-synced to the song, his body moved in a sensual circular motion. Slick Nic was doing a great job of seducing the women in the crowd.

"Yo, Chuck!" shouted Teco, because the music was blasting. "Why they call this dude Slick Nic The Ruler?"

"Man, you ain't gonna believe this!"

"What?" asked Teco.

"This white dude is twelve inches long!"

Teco said in amazement, "He's huge." Then Teco felt himself, not knowing if he could hang as a male exotic dancer.

At the front of the dance floor women lined up to tip Slick Nic. Just as the slow song ended, there was a BOOM. At that moment, Slick Nic snatched off his break-away pants and ripped off his top. That's when Teco saw the G-String that matched Slick Nic's outfit. Teco said, "Damn . . . . What the hell is he wearing?"

"That's what you'll have to wear," said Chuck.

"I don't know about that shit," said Teco.

Slick Nic danced around the dance floor. As he moved, he held a twelve inch ruler up to his body to show the ladies that he was indeed twelve inches long. As he danced around the club, he began to look like a money tree. Teco observed how smooth Slick Nic was to kiss the women on the cheek after they tipped him. Some women even allowed him to smack them on the ass with his ruler. Other women would feel all over Slick Nic's buffed frame and ruler.

"I can do that." Teco enjoyed entertaining women.

As the music ended, G-Rock called another dancer's name. "Teco come with me," said Chuck. They started walking towards the back of the club through some double doors that led down a narrow set of stairs. At the end of the hallway was a large room where male dancers were seated while wearing either a towel around their waist or just wearing a G-String.

"What's up Chuck?" asked Black Heat.

"What's up man? I would like for you guys to meet one of my new dancers, Rising Sun."

"What's up, Rising Sun?" they asked in unison.

Black Heat spoke with authority as if he were the head dancer of the crew and asked, "Have you danced before?"

"No, not yet. Is it hard?" asked Teco.

"No, but there are some things which you'll need to learn first," said Black Heat.

"Like what?" asked Teco.

"Do you know how to beef up?" asked Black Heat.

"What the hell is that?"

When Teco asked this question, everyone started to laugh; so Teco laughed with them. One guy pulled out a six-inch black piece of elastic.

"Man that looks like the elastic that goes around the bottom of sweatpants. What do you do with that?" asked Teco.

"When and if you dance, you'll find out."

Teco looked at them as if they were crazy and asked, "Can you tell me now?" Learning from past experiences, he didn't like going into anything blind.

Black Heat demonstrated how the black piece of elastic was used during a performance. "It's a dancer's version of a cock ring. At first it will be painful until you get used to it; however never tie it in a knot," said Black Heat.

"Teco we've got to jet," said Chuck.

"Nice meeting you guys," said Teco.

On the way to another club, Chuck looked at Teco and asked, "So what do you think about dancing?"

Teco never understood why men went to male exotic dance clubs, but now he knew. With all of these alluring women in one spot, he felt as if he were in Victoria's Secret heaven.

CHAPTER 3

Teco tried to slip into the apartment unnoticed. When he entered, Rasheeda was sitting on her favorite brown floor pillow eating some Edy's Butter Pecan Ice Cream. When Teco shut the door, she put the spoon and bowl down on the end table, turned the television down with the remote control, and stood to her feet with her hands on her hips. "Where the hell have you been; and do you see what time it is?" asked Rasheeda. Her body language said even more.

Teco moved close to her and tried to charm Rasheeda by putting his arms around her. He softly planted sweet kisses on her neck. "Ah Baby, come here and let me show you who I love. You missed Rising Sun?" asked Teco in a seductive tone.

"Rising Sun? Who is that?"

"Me. That's my stage name."

Rasheeda was starting to blush and to squirm in Teco's arms. "Boy, I ain't playing with you. Where you been? It's 4 in the morning." As Rasheeda and Teco sat down on the sofa, she had déjàvu.

They stared into each others eyes; then Teco broke eye contact and said, "I met this guy name Chuck at the pool yesterday." Before Teco could say another word, a bright smile came over Rasheeda's face; and Teco didn't understand why she was so excited.

"Who Charles?" asked Rasheeda.

"You know him?"

"He works at Club Classic with Yvette and Toi. Lately he's been hanging out with this new girl named Candi. All the women around here know him. He can sling that—"

Teco stared at her with a look as if to say, *"Watch your roll and you better calm down."* He said, "Chuck invited me to check out Club Classic since I've never been there."

"Oh, that was nice of him." She said looking at her freshly manicured nails.

"Baby, I need to ask you a question." Teco said taking a deep breath.

An inquisitive look came over her face and she asked, "What?"

"Check this out. What do you think about male exotic dancers?"

"I think they are sexy; and the way they move, mmm . . . I think—"

"You think what!" Teco exclaimed looking intensely into her eyes.

"Nothing, nothing." She said with a smirk on her face as she picked back up her ice cream and sat back down.

Joining her on the floor, Teco asked, "What do you think if I became a dancer?"

She gave him a long stare and burst out into laughter. "You? A male dancer? Come on now." She said dismissing his thought of being a dancer. Teco stood to his feet and took her laughing at him as a challenge. Rasheeda was still laughing until she saw his ticked facial expression. Then she asked, "Baby, you're serious aren't you?"

"Yes I am; and I think I'll do well as a dancer. So what do you think?" asked Teco.

"As long as you don't cheat on me, I don't have a problem with it. I know a couple of male dancers who are married. Now, how about a shower?" asked Rasheeda. Just as Teco lifted her into his arms in order to carry her over the threshold of their bedroom, she said, "Wait, wait, let me put down my ice cream." The rest of the night Teco gave her his undivided attention and put them both to sleep.

The next morning in the apartment parking lot, Teco saw Chuck who asked, "What's up man?"

"Nothing, just enjoying the morning dew. I've been thinking about the dancing thing and want to know when I can get started?"

Chuck smiled and said, "Okay, first you need a manager. If you would like, I'll be your manager."

"So how do I get my first gig?"

"First you have to meet the club owners. If they like what they see, they'll put you on the roster. The better you are, the more you'll get paid."

"Have you managed dancers before? You sound like you know the business."

"Of course I know the business. Remember how the bouncer gave me mad respect last night?" asked Chuck. Teco did notice that and liked the respect just the same.

◊◊◊◊◊

Detective Troop sat at her desk looking over the case file and waiting for a report from Linda to identify the body. Chatter of other officers was loud because of the huge open cubicle area. Trooper ruled out all male guests at the Comfort Inn, except one. She was waiting for a finger print match from The Department of Motor Vehicles (DMV) and was anxious to start interviewing people who knew him. There were so many questions. *What's the deal with the G-String? How does this tie to Philadelphia? What does the puzzle mean?* As she waited, she stared at the huge picture frame of all fifty state law enforcement patches with state seals. The phone rang bringing her back to reality.

"This is Detective Troop."

"Trooper, it's Linda. I think you need to come down here to forensics."

"I'm on my way." Trooper holstered her gun, which she affectionately called Sunshine, and headed for the basement. At the entrance of the forensics lab, Trooper put on a white smock. She immediately noticed that Linda's eyes were glued to the digital microscope camera. "Hey Linda, what's up?"

Linda turned down the Bose CD player so that she wouldn't have to talk over the music by En Vogue. "Hello Trooper. First, I want you to see these slides of the victim's wounds." Next to the CD player was a small remote, which Linda picked up and clicked a button. On the screen appeared the victim pale as ever. "What this confirms is that this was indeed strangulation. See these markings? They are consistent with the G-String straps. So, in this evidence bag is your white G-String murder weapon. Now look under the microscope." Trooper put her eyes on the eyepiece. On the glass slide were two pubic hair samples. Linda continued, "The pubic hair on the left is the victim's. The one to the right has the characteristics of female hair."

"Are we able to get DNA?" asked Trooper.

"Sure, plus we also collected vaginal fluids off of the victim's phallus."

"Are you saying The Paradox is possibly a woman?"

"Well, you have the makeup on the shirt, the lipstick on the collar, female pubic hair and vaginal fluids. It's circumstantial. The way The Paradox carefully placed the victim on the mattress says they might know each other. The girlfriend or wife knows about the rendezvous and waits for him to get into a compromising position; then she strangles him. That says it might be a crime of passion. Or The Paradox stages the crime scene to look like a female kills the victim. The note says, 'I despise a snitch.' So, it could have started in Philly as it says; and our victim was a snitch on something he saw. So The Paradox waits until the best opportunity and strangles him. You tell me detective. Is this a crime of passion or revenge?"

◊◊◊◊◊

One week later, Teco was practicing his dance moves in the living room with the music blaring to Gerald Levert's song "Baby Hold On To Me." He closed his eyes and dropped to the floor. His tight ass went around and around, then up and down like a wave. When Teco opened his eyes, all he saw were Rasheeda's shoes. Then he rose up off of the floor.

"Teco, what the hell are you doing?" asked Rasheeda, as if she didn't know.

For a moment, he was lost for words and didn't know how to explain himself. "Baby, I was practicing. So don't laugh. I'm for real. Sit on the sofa and I will dance for you. You tell me what you think."

"Now you talking . . . If you're not good, then I won't tip you." As Teco started to dance for her, she really liked the way he moved his body. When he brushed up softly against her, she reached into her purse and pulled out a $20 bill. She was ready to make love to Teco right then and there. However, he was more in tuned to perfecting his moves.

"How was that?" asked Teco.

Fanning her face with her hand, she said, "That was hot!"

"Chuck told me about a few places where I can get outfits to wear for my first performance. I'm going to check them out.

"Can I go with you?" She asked reaching for her fake Burberry purse, which was on the coffee table.

Within the hour, they were at J. B. Productions. Male and female mannequins displayed jazzy outfits; and Teco was excited as he entered the store. Pictures of dancers were posted on the walls. Outfits with rhinestones and fringes hung on several racks and ranged from $150 to $500. There were different colored capes, shirts, pants and hats. Teco liked the silk and satin fabrics the best. G-Strings were $10 to $30. Two styled G-Strings were on display. The nose G-String was made with a nose like pouch. The regular G-String was cut like a man's bikini. When he saw a sign that read 9 inches or better, he definitely knew to avoid that section.

Teco didn't have a lot of money to get his outfits. He walked around the store over and over trying his best to find a price which wouldn't kill his pockets. Having at least 2 costumes and 3 to 4 G-Strings were essential for getting started. He pulled out his wallet and counted $80. He checked all of his pockets and found 1 quarter. When Rasheeda saw the distressed look on his face, she said, "I'll give you the money and you can pay me back once you get all those tips. How about that?"

The cowbell on the front door to J. B. Productions startled Teco. As he turned, he couldn't believe his eyes. There was the gorgeous Detective Troop, who walked in the store and stood at the front checkout counter. Rasheeda saw that Teco was admiring her a little too long and said, "Teco, I know you are not going to lust over that woman in front of me."

"No baby, I saw her at the pool the other day. She was investigating a murder."

"Word?" asked Rasheeda. Teco moved in closer to see if he could hear what was being said.

"Hello, I'm Detective Troop. We are investigating a homicide; and we have in our possession a white G-String with your label stitched inside." Trooper showed the tall thin lady with blond hair a Polaroid picture.

"Hi Detective Troop, I'm the owner Cindy Lewis. Yes, that's a part of my signature collection."

"Who would normally buy your collection?" asked Trooper.

"Well, women buy for men, men for men, men for themselves, male dancers—"

"Back up. Did you say male dancers? Do you sell these money pouches also?" Trooper showed her another photo.

"No Detective. That looks like fine Italian leather." Cindy Lewis said looking closely at the picture.

"Do you know where I would find one like it?"

"Saks Fifth Avenue perhaps. Why?"

"It might just be a coincidence. Your brand of G-String is sold to dancers and our guy had a money pouch with a large sum of $1 bills," said Trooper looking around the store.

"Sorry, I can't help you detective."

Trooper saw Teco and said, "Hello. I remember seeing you at the pool with Charles Mobley. I'm Detective Troop." She extended her hand out to him.

"I'm Teco Jackson. How did you remember that?" Giving her a firm handshake, he gazed into her eyes.

"Well, people say I have a photographic memory. Your accent is different. Where are you from?"

"West Philly." Immediately Teco noticed that Detective Troop raised her right eyebrow.

CHAPTER 4

Teco's first club performance was at The Mirage on M Street in Southeast D.C. This area is in the hood and down the street from the Navy Yard. Teco couldn't believe that the White House was only five city blocks away. Many of the buildings were made of cobblestone and built in the early 1900's. The new McDonald's on the corner looked odd in an historical district. When he drove up, Teco admired the electronic billboard sign which read, "The Mirage" in vibrant colors. As Teco walked into the club, there was a square indoor sign with lights around it; and the word "Mirage" illuminated in blue lights. He liked the illusionary reflection of a lot of lights endlessly going into the wall.

The Mirage was much bigger than Club Classic. Women were all over the place and stopped Teco 10 times before he reached the dressing room. The D.J. was pumping Frank Ski's "Do Do Brown" as the dancers dressed for the show. None of these dancers were at Club Classic when he went with Chuck a few weeks ago. Teco could hear the M.C. announcing for the ladies to give Dr. T, who was the first dancer, a big round of applause. Teco was up next.

Trooper and Swoosh walked into The Mirage and headed straight to the bar. The bartender asked, "What are you having?"

Swoosh showed him a photo and said, "We're on duty. Do you know this man? His name is Jeffrey Barnes."

The bartender looked at the DMV photo. "Sure. His stage name is Polo. The manager is pretty ticked at him right now though."

"Why's that?" asked Trooper.

"He hasn't been to work in a while; and he draws a huge following. When he's not here, a lot of women don't show up at the club."

"Are you aware of a Valentine's Day party that he attended this year?" asked Swoosh, pulling out his inhaler because the smoke from the bar was causing him to cough.

"Yeah, I was there. I worked the cash bar."

"Was he there with a female friend?" asked Trooper, who looked at Swoosh with concern. She knew Swoosh's asthma flared up in smoke filled rooms.

"Let's see. Candi use to hang out with him a lot."

"Is Candi here now?" asked Trooper.

"No, she stopped coming here since Polo has been a no show. She thinks Polo dropped her for another woman. So, Candi's hanging out with some other dancer now."

"Does Candi have a name?" asked Trooper.

"I don't know it. Why you asking so many questions?"

"Hate to tell you, man. Jeffrey was murdered. We are trying to find out as much about him as possible," said Swoosh after taking 2 puffs from his inhaler.

The microphone made a screeching sound causing Trooper to look towards the stage. The M.C. said, "Laaadies, I want you to put your hands together for our newest dancer. Here's Risssing Sunnn!"

The music blasted to Babyface's song "Whip Appeal;" and Rising Sun walked out on stage wearing a red teardrop hat and a black trench coat. He took stage center and the women in the audience screamed. After tipping his hat over his eyes, Rising Sun twirled the hat up and down in his hands like a magician. Then he threw the hat into the crowd with a Michael Jackson signature move. All the ladies went wild. In one smooth move, Rising Sun untied the belt and dropped the coat, revealing his baby oiled six pack and red suspenders. With his left thumb, he pulled down the right suspender; and with his right thumb, he pulled down the left suspender. Crossing the suspender straps in front, his body gyrated to the music like a whip. The ladies held out hundreds in $1 and $5 bills. When he released the suspenders, his pants dropped to the floor.

A few women screamed for him; and one lady yelled, "Where's the beef?" When Rising Sun looked down at his body, he realized what the lady was saying because there was nothing holding up his G-String. After he left the dressing room, the G-String was packed. Rising Sun couldn't figure out what happened. Then the sound effects went BOOM during the climax of the song. He went up to one female to get a tip. As she felt his G-String, she burst out into laughter and said, "Rising Sun, yeah right. More like rising pinky." He believed at that moment that all the people outside of the club could hear the women laughing inside. When his set was over, Rising Sun rushed off of the stage. *"I ain't with this bull."* In the dressing room, he only counted $5.

Though Rising Sun was trying to camouflage his tips by folding the money several times, another dancer came up to him and asked, "Man, what happened? First timers usually get at least $50 to $75."

"I have no idea," said Rising Sun throwing the money up in the air, because there was no way to hide the fact that his performance tanked.

"You either beefed up wrong with the elastic or you are small."

"I had to have beefed up wrong because I'm packing." Rising Sun said defensively.

"My real name is Jimar Wilson; but everyone calls me Legend." He said remembering the first time he performed; and there was no one to help. Legend added, "Come with me tomorrow. I have seven parties to do. I'll let you dance at my shows to get some practice. I can't pay you; however, the tips that you make you can keep."

"Okay that sounds cool." They exchanged numbers so that Legend could pick Rising Sun up from the apartment.

On the next day, Teco was ready for the parties that Legend lined up. Time seemed to always fly on Saturdays. After taking a shower and getting his things together, the doorbell rang.

Legend was on time. Teco gave Rasheeda a kiss on the forehead before he left. Once he was in the car, Teco asked, "Legend, who is your manager?"

"I don't have a manager. No dancer has a manager. We are our own bosses. The money you make belongs to you. Why?"

"Chuck is my manager. I pay him 15% to line me up gigs."

Legend laughed out loud and asked, "Did you sign a contract?"

"No."

"Well, get rid of him. He can't do anything for you."

When they arrived at the first party, Legend verbally instructed Teco on the tricks to beefing up before a performance. Then he gave Teco some pointers on how to keep the ladies' attention. Before the last party, Teco pocketed $200.

As Legend drove Teco to the next gig, Legend said, "I noticed how well you danced today, because you are a quick study. You don't even look like the same dancer who made just $5 last night." They laughed.

"Thanks man," said Teco recounting his tips.

"Are you interested in making more money?" asked Legend pulling into the Eighteenth Street Lounge back parking lot.

"Hell yeah. How?"

"I book a lot of shows out of town. You'll work them with me," said Legend getting out of the car.

"It's that easy? No convincing club managers?" asked Teco walking with Legend to the front of the building.

"Nope. They know I only recruit the best talent. Consider, it done."

As they entered the building, the restaurant was on the lower level of the club. Teco noticed that there was a large crowd out for this party; so Teco decided to change into his performance outfit. On the way to the dressing room he saw Toi, who was giving him a sexy look and licking her highly glossed lips.

Shortly after Teco was introduced to Toi at the Rosewood Village Apartments swimming pool, Teco heard some women at the complex saying that Toi was amphierotic. By Toi's sexual undertones, she was acting as if she finally found her man. "Excuse me Rising Sun. I need to ask you something," said Toi, who was walking beside him.

"Sure, what's on your mind?"

"Do you do private parties?" She asked stopping to get his full attention.

As expected, Teco also stopped and asked, "How many women will be there?"

With an alluring smile and a provocative gesture, she said, "Just me. And if you are as pleasurable in person as you are on stage, I'll pay you $400 for the evening."

"Hold up. I'm not a male prostitute." Teco started to pinch himself to see if this was really happening. This was the first time he turned down a beautiful dimepiece and money in the same sentence. This episode with Toi felt like a dream.

"Well consider the $400 not as payment but a large tip."

"I never mix business with pleasure. Sorry baby."

Toi kissed Teco on the cheek and said, "I'll help you practice and perfect your dance moves. If you change your mind, let me know. Here is my cell number." She passed him her card; and Teco walked away.

He was in a daze because in the past he would have been all up on her. As he worked his way through the crowd to get to the dressing room, Teco put his bags down and immediately headed to the D.J.'s booth. Through a large window, Teco scanned the room.

When he found Toi, she was sitting at a table alone and having an apple martini. He liked the fact that she created a style of her own. Her black hair was short and naturally curly. Though she was well endowed, her pink blouse left much for the imagination. However, the short black skirt displayed her mocha legs, which glistened from the club lights. Seeing her lick her highly glossed lips made him imagine tasting the apple flavor. He still couldn't believe that he walked away from her so easily.

The last woman he let go was Gail Indigo Que, whom everyone called GQ. Teco was attracted to GQ when they both were members of the Strictly Business (SB) Crew in the Mount Airy area of Philadelphia. However, he respected GQ too much to treat her like a sex toy. The night they came face to face, Teco tossed and turned trying to decide if he should tell GQ how he felt about her. That's probably why they were oil and water when they were members of the SB Crew. Sexual tension is powerful. Bashi Mujaheed Fiten, the SB Crew boss, was right from the start. Unfortunately, GQ murdered Bashi; and Teco could never forgive her. Everything turned out for the best. Since then, he turned his back on a life of drugs and fast money. So letting Toi go was probably another good move.

◊◊◊◊◊

The Philadelphia Women's Penitentiary was operating business as usual. In the C-Block, GQ sat in her cell hating the color blue. She was located in an area which housed 20 women, 2 to a cell. C-Block was painted powdered blue with royal blue bars. The table and chairs were blue. The T.V. room was blue. The only thing that wasn't blue was the floor, which was painted gray. There were women playing cards while other women listened to music. To take her mind off of her surroundings, GQ picked up the newspaper, "The Philadelphia Inquirer." The headlines read, "D.C. murderer claims link to Philadelphia." She found out a while back from word on the streets that Teco was in D.C. The only thing she could vividly remember from the trial was the look on Teco's face after the judge gave her 25 years to life.

When GQ was first locked down, no one could talk with her because she was filled with so much anger. Initially, she worked out alone, read, or listened to her music. She never allowed anyone to get close to her. Finally her roommate Chi Chi reached out to GQ by hooking her up with a job in the law library. That's when GQ started to look into her own criminal case during her free time. She found out that there were some flaws in her indictment, which she continued to fight since the jury read her the verdict for killing Bashi three years ago.

"Gail Que, get your pretty ass up! You have an attorney visit. Get dressed in your blues!" yelled the Corrections Officer, who thought the C-Block smelled like an eau de toilette factory. She never understood why women in prison wanted to smell good every day even though there was no place for them to go.

GQ grabbed the yellow envelope with her legal work, which was under the mattress. She looked over to her cellmate who was still asleep. GQ wanted to thank her again for introducing her to this Appeals Attorney, whose reputation was upstanding. At first, GQ didn't trust him until he showed GQ that she could come from under her court imposed sentence.

Attorney Michael Hamesath smiled as GQ entered the interview room. Even he couldn't deny that she was one of the most beautiful women he knew. She resembled the Supermodel Iman and the women from Somalia, Africa. For a brief moment, he wanted to touch her silky brown hair and to caress her sienna smooth skin. Because of her long supple legs, he thought for sure that she was a ballet dancer at some point in her childhood. Every time they met, her eyes appeared to be a different color. Sometimes they were hazel, or light-blue, or even almond-blue in the light. Attorney Hamesath regained focus, motioned for her to take a seat and asked, "So Gail, have you been studying the cases that I gave you?"

"Yes I have; and there are six total cases overturned for the same reasons as mentioned in the motions that you have submitted for me."

"That's right. So are you ready to fight this thing out in court?"

Fighting was all GQ knew how to do in order to survive on the streets. She fought her way to the top leadership position in Bashi's SB Crew. After Teco, a.k.a. Homicide, took GQ's position; she fought to get her spot back. Now serving a life sentence because of the snitch Teco, GQ looked at her attorney and said, "Hell yeah, I'm ready to fight." Then she slammed her fist on the desk.

CHAPTER 5

D etective Brown, whom everyone called Swoosh, decided this part of the job was the hardest of all. As he opened the car door, he could smell freshly cut grass. To his left, there was a guy with a high powered blower clearing the street. The Glass Manor apartment complex looked dated. The buildings were tan with weathered brown roofs. Swoosh walked up to the murder victim's last known address and knocked on the door.

"Who is it?" asked someone from inside.

"It's Detective Brown from D.C.'s Homicide Division." At least 5 deadbolt locks released. The young man cracked the door open and looked at the shield. "May I step in please?" asked Swoosh.

"Not until you tell me what this is about."

Swoosh opened the folder under his arms and asked, "Do you know Jeffrey Barnes?"

"Yes, he's my brother . . . . Ma!" He opened the door for Swoosh.

Coming down the short hallway was an elderly woman. After she reached the living room, Swoosh said, "Ma'am, I'm Detective Brown. I've come here to ask you to come downtown with me."

"Is it Jeffrey? I keep calling his apartment and he doesn't return my calls. It's not like him. He is a good young man. Never been in trouble a day in his life. I'm so proud of him. He makes a great living in the entertainment business."

"Ma'am I'm afraid it is about Jeffrey."

Detective Brown drove them both back to the precinct. "Ma'am, can you please wait here in this room?" He walked down the hall. "Trooper, I have the victim's family in Room 2."

"Alright Swoosh, I'll be right there." Trooper made a call down to Forensics. "Linda, any news on the DNA results?"

"Let me check . . . . Yep, Twyla Burke is a match. It says her last known residence is Conshohocken, Pennsylvania and that she has a record." said Linda.

Trooper reached for a pen and paper. "What's the spelling of the first name?"

"T as in Tom, W as in William, Y as in Yolanda, L as in Larry, and A as in Andrew."

"Got it . . . ." Trooper dialed the police station operator. "Please connect me to the Conshohocken Police Department in Pennsylvania."

The phone rang four times before a receptionist picked up. "Thank you for calling CPD. How may I direct your call?"

"The Robbery-Homicide Division please."

"Please hold ma'am."

Soft music played before a deep voiced man picked up. "Robbery-Homicide Division. How may I help you?"

"This is Detective Troop out of Washington, D.C. May I speak with your lead detective?"

"Detective Troop, he's out in the field. May I transfer you to his voicemail?"

"Sure, that would be fine. Whom am I speaking with?"

"Detective Melender."

"Thank you," said Trooper as she wrote his name down. The phone went into the voicemail box of Detective Paschall. Trooper left a message and headed to Room 2.

Standing in front of the two-way window, Trooper stared at the mother for a few minutes. Swoosh thought it would be best for a female to tell Mrs. Barnes. Trooper took a deep breath and entered the room. The look on Jeffrey Barnes brother's face was abysmal. He and his mother knew that things were not good. Tears were in their eyes. Trooper thought, *"I've got to be strong and hold it together."*

"Hello, I'm Detective Troop. I have to tell you—"

"Is my baby dead?" asked the woman with her hands shaking like crazy over her mouth. No matter how old a person is mothers will always see their child as their baby.

"Yes ma'am, we need you to identify your son."

"No! No! Why, why, why?!" cried out the woman as the young man put his arms around his mother to console her.

Trooper wanted to know more about Jeffrey; however, now wasn't the time to ask. At the present, her only person of interest was Twyla Burke. *"Did they have a lover's quarrel and Twyla snapped? Or was he murdered because he was a snitch on something that happened with Twyla in Philadelphia? Is it a crime of passion or revenge? I have to find Twyla."*

Trooper asked, "Ma'am, will you please come with me?" Mrs. Barnes and her son followed Trooper to the elevator. In the basement, they eventually faced large glass double doors.

◊◊◊◊◊

In the Rosewood Village Apartments parking lot, Teco looked around to see if Rasheeda's car was out front. To his relief it was not there. Over the last few weeks, he was working a different club every night and getting home between the hours of 3am and 4am in the morning. Rasheeda no longer supported him as she did in the beginning. She didn't know that Teco was saving to buy them a second car and a new home. He was averaging $250 to $500 in tips each night. At this rate, he would have the down payment they needed. He unlocked the apartment door. When he saw the living room light was on, he knew immediately that Rasheeda was home. He closed the door and dropped his bags. His eyes opened wide when he pulled out the tips for the night. He counted $1,500; and his ego soared.

Rasheeda came into the living room with her hands on her hips uttering curse words. "Where the hell have you been?" Not giving

Teco a chance to respond, she continued, "Your ass is sleeping around so much that you no longer have time to be with me."

"Rasheeda, please not now. And where the hell is your car?" asked Teco trying to switch the subject.

"It's down the street and don't try to check me. All y'all dancers ain't no damn good. And if you're not going to be my man like you were before you started dancing, then you need to leave."

"Rasheeda, baby listen . . ."

She stormed out of the room and started to throw Teco's clothes out of the front door.

"Rasheeda it's not what you think. I've been dancing my ass off for us and—"

"You a damn lie. Get your shit and leave now." Rasheeda held the door open revealing a pile of clothes on the ground.

Teco saw the neighbors through the window. *"Nosey ass neighbors."* Rasheeda refused to hear him out, even though she invested a great deal in him. He knew that he was a better man, because she was the first woman to convince him to clean up his life and his language. Now what was he going to do?

"Well, I'll let you cool down and I'll be back tomorrow." He said hoping she would reconsider.

"The hell you will. I'll have a restraining order completed before the sun can come up. I've had it."

"If that's how you feel, then fine," said Teco with a stern look. "I have to use the bathroom before I go." Teco went into the hall bathroom and locked the door. He pulled out a flathead screwdriver from underneath the sink. Taking out the screws to the vent, Teco removed the cover and reached for his blue bank zipper bag. When he did not touch it, he panicked. Then he felt from a different angle; and there it was. He screwed the cover back on and wiped his hands together to get the dust off. Teco unzipped the bag and was relieved to see that the $10,000 was inside.

On his way out of the apartment, Rasheeda was still holding the door open for him. *"His ass will be back because he has no where to go."*

◊◊◊◊◊

At the precinct, Trooper and Swoosh sat at a folding table in a 10x10 room, which provided the best lighting because of the high gloss white walls and florescent lighting. This room was known as the "Think Tank," because its primary purpose was for inspecting evidence. They were looking over the pictures of the G-String murder weapon and the victim. Jeffrey's mother told them that he did not have any enemies and that he was D.C.'s number one performer.

"Trooper, I think it's time to check out some of these clubs."

"Yeah, I think you're right. Would you like to go undercover?" asked Trooper with a smirk.

"And do what?" asked Swoosh with raised eyebrows.

"Dance of course. Laaadies! Put your hands together for BIG SWOOSH!" Trooper burst out into laughter.

"Oh, you think that's funny? You don't think I can do it?" Swoosh stood up and did a poorly executed dance version of the moonwalk. Trooper pulled out a quarter and slid it across the table. When Swoosh saw the quarter, he stopped dancing and put up his middle finger. He headed for the door and said, "Trooper, I'll pick you up at 10 o'clock. We are checking out Club Classic first."

The phone on Trooper's desk rang three times before she realized that there was a call. She pushed the speaker phone button.

"Detective Troop, I have Detective Paschall on the line."

"Put him through."

"Hello, this is Detective Paschall."

"Hello, I'm Homicide Detective Troop. I'm working on a case; and a name came up as a resident of Conshohocken. I need your help."

"Sure, I am happy to help. What's the name?" asked Detective Paschall picking up an ink pen.

"Twyla Burke, female."

"Is that Twyla with an 'i' or a 'y'?"

"A 'y'."

"Give me a minute Troop, if it's alright to call you that."

"Call me Trooper. That's what the whole division calls me."

"Wow!" exclaimed Detective Paschall.

"You know this person?"

"Well not exactly. Do you have a few minutes for me to tell you about the Burke family?"

"Sure, I'm all ears. Do you mind if I record this conversation?"

"No, please do. The entire Burke family is into the street life, real heavy. They run their drug deals from West Philadelphia to Conshohocken. Trooper, are you still there?"

"Yes Detective, I'm here," said Trooper doing a computer map search of the area.

"The Burke family owns lots of strip malls, car lots, and strip clubs. Their main cash flow is drugs and prostitution. This Twyla Burke is the daughter of the queen of a prostitution ring called Special Touch. While other drug dealers sell hand to hand on the streets, the Burke family usually sells at their family businesses. So it's extremely hard to prove anything. Even though they are into the street life, they are seldom on the physical streets. Do you see what you're dealing with?"

"I do; go on." After Trooper found a detailed map, she hit the print key and turned her total attention to Detective Paschall.

"At 17 years old, Twyla was arrested for stabbing a female who was sleeping with Twyla's boyfriend. After Twyla's release, we haven't seen her since. She is well trained and positioned to replace her mother in the family business. Because Twyla is such a beautiful and strong black woman, she has a way of charming men. They give her any and everything she wants. Twyla has a sex addiction. And after one man finds this out, word gets out fast. You want to find Twyla? Then look in a location where there are a lot of attractive men. By the way, she changes aliases like she changes designer shoes."

"Can you send me a mug shot of Twyla?"

"Sure will Trooper. I can't send it right now, but will send it to you as soon as I can."

"And Detective Paschall, thanks for your help."

"Any time."

Trooper hung up the phone and leaned back in her chair trying to figure out Twyla Burke's reason for moving to D.C. and how was Jeffrey Barnes involved. Trooper retrieved the recording of the conversation so that she could study it; then she headed home to get ready for tonight. She was going to a club.

CHAPTER 6

Candi sat at the bar watching the dancers come into Club Classic. She needed a date for the Classic After-Party. Though she tried her best to control her sexual desires, the line-up for tonight's show was simply delightful. Her mother told her that she needed to settle down in order to run the Burke family businesses and that a future mistress of the house doesn't sleep around. Well, Candi watched handsome men treat the women in the house absolutely like princesses. Her mother ran a business where women prostitutes were to be respected. If a man got out of line, he was banded from the house. So, Candi's life was not a life of physical abuse as many would suspect. Candi was taught that sex is an art. Men who frequented the house gave Twyla the nickname Candi because her mother forbade them to touch her gorgeous daughter. Twyla's friends teased that her nickname represented the real meaning of "eye candy." Twyla moved to Washington, D.C., because she wasn't ready to take over the family dynasty. In fact, she wasn't using her given name Twyla Burke, because she didn't want anyone, not even her family, to find her.

Outside of Club Classic, Swoosh and Trooper pulled up into the parking lot listening to the taped interview with Detective Paschall. When Swoosh found a good parking spot, they alerted the local P.G. County police that they were there and that they were investigating the G-String murder.

Trooper looked into the visor mirror in order to reapply lip gloss to the edge of her bottom lip and worked her lips together for the final touch. She usually wore jeans or khaki slacks. Tonight she wanted to blend into the crowd; therefore, she put on a nice black cocktail dress. Trooper felt wonderful and was going to enjoy the evening. The line was not long to get into Club Classic. A male dancer of the club walked past Trooper and said, "Hello gorgeous."

Trooper returned his hello with a sensual smile. The compliment made her feel very sexy, taking her back to her teenage years. Because she was the most popular girl in high school, many people thought she was as they say, "stuck up." Hanae Troop was the captain of the women's high school basketball team, president of her senior class, football Homecoming Queen, voted "Most Likely to Succeed" and valedictorian. The school administrators told the students that Hanae couldn't run for Prom Queen, because they wanted to give other girls a chance to win. Hanae always wanted to be #1 at everything she did, which some people took as being conceited. She never wanted to go out and party with friends; and as an adult, the Blue Shield Pub didn't count as going out either because she was always with the boys from the force. Even going to the club tonight was business. However, she was going to pretend as much as possible that she was not working; and seeing the half naked man who was currently on stage was absolutely doing the trick.

"You can close your mouth Trooper," said Swoosh. As they wended their way through the crowd of women at the bar area, Trooper walked right past Candi.

"Where is the manager's office?" asked Trooper.

"Up the stairs to the left," said the bartender, who was pouring beer into a frosted glass and nodded in that direction.

Trooper found her way to the manager's office and knocked on the door. No one answered. On her way back down the steps, an Italian man who looked to be a model straight out of GQ Magazine asked, "May I help you?"

"Sure, if you are the manager."

"I am the club owner. For you beautiful, you can have as much of my time as you want." He said with a seductive look.

Trooper didn't know whether to smile or be offended. However, she knew that women kept the club jam packed every night and that the owner was compelled to make every woman feel beautiful in order to get them to return night after night. "You're the one I need to talk to," said Trooper as she showed him her badge.

"How may I help you officer?" He asked with a more sincere facial expression.

"I'm Detective Troop from the Homicide Division. Do you know Jeffrey Barnes, a.k.a. Polo?"

"Yes, I heard the very sad news."

Trooper thought for a moment that she saw a tear in his eye. Then she pulled out her pad and pen. "Can you tell me about him?"

"He dated my ex-wife. At first I thought your visit had something to do with her. She's always pulling stunts." Hanae looked at him with skepticism, as if he were trying to get his ex-wife into trouble. The owner continued, "Polo was a very good dancer; all the women loved him."

"Can you think of anyone who might want to harm him or any of the other dancers?"

"Well to be honest no one comes to mind. Polo is, I mean was, the number one ranked dancer in all of the clubs in this area."

"Do you know of anyone who may seek revenge for something that happened?"

"No."

"Any old girlfriends that might—"

"Detective Troop, most of the dancers don't have girlfriends. Dancers are known to draw a large crowd of women. Girlfriends or wives don't like that particularly well."

"One last question, do you know Twyla Burke?"

"No. Should I?"

"I guess not. I'm just asking. Thanks. If you can think of anything please give me a call," said Trooper, passing him her business card.

"Detective, I hope you stay and enjoy the show."

Ebony Wood, who was dancing when Trooper first walked into the club, finished his set and went to the bar for a drink. He sat on a barstool next to Candi, who felt as if she found her date for the evening. Candi smiled at Ebony Wood and said, "You did great up there tonight."

"Oh really? So what was your favorite part of my act?" asked Ebony Wood, who wanted to see if she really paid attention to his performance.

"When you made your body wave like a snake wrapped around a woman."

"So you really were paying attention." He said with a big smile.

"Of course. Can I buy you a drink?"

"Only if you tell me your name." Ebony Wood decided at that moment that this woman was by far the most beautiful woman in Club Classic.

"You can call me Candi. What are you having?"

"I would like a Heineken and what would you like to drink?"

"I bet that you would be thirst quenching." Candi said licking her lips.

"So is that an invitation or are we playing a little game?"

"You tell me. Want to go to the Classic After-Party with me?"

G-Rock walked up to the microphone and said, "Okay laaadies, we have to continue our special show for you tonight." As he talked, he placed a wooden chair at center stage. The lights went to a dark red and green, which illuminated the chair only. G-Rock continued, "Laaadies, I need one of you sexy women to come on the stage for our next dancer. So which lucky woman wants to come up?"

Trooper was leaning on the back wall by the front door tripping off the fact that so many women wanted to be on stage with the next dancer. Hands were up all over the club. Toi was working as a waitress and walked past Trooper with an empty brown round tray. Trooper said, "Excuse me—"

Toi looked back at her and said, "Hold on, I'll be right back." Then Toi rushed off to tend to her previous customers.

G-Rock pointed to a petite fine ass female to come onto the stage. During rehearsal, Rising Sun told G-Rock that he needed a smaller sized woman for his grand finale. When she stood up all the other hands went down. She smiled at her friends and headed to the chair. The strobe lights flashed sporadically as the music started to play Gerald Levert's song "Baby Hold On To Me." Behind the curtain, Rising Sun heard the women screaming rampantly.

"Laaadies put your hands together for Risssing Sunnn!" The crescendo of the song was timed to perfection as he walked up to the female who was seated in the chair. Rising Sun leaned over to whisper into her ear. "Just relax and enjoy the show."

"Please don't embarrass me." She said.

Rising Sun smiled at her and said, "I'm only here to pleasure you." He started to slow dance in his erotic style. Trooper's undivided attention was all his.

This was the first time Trooper really looked at Rising Sun. *"Damn, he's kind of cute. The way he moves is quite desirable. I wonder does he have anything to work with tonight."*

Toi saw the intrigued look on Trooper's face and said, "Yeah girl, he drives me crazy too. What can I get you to drink?"

Trooper looked at Swoosh and said, "I'm going off the clock. There is nothing else I can find out tonight. You agree?" asked Trooper.

"Sure, you need to relax. I'll call it in that we are officially off duty," said Swoosh as he fingered his loose hair back behind his ears and put a peppermint toothpick into his mouth.

"Okay, I'll have a Tequila and lime," said Trooper.

"Girl, we have a better drink with the Tequila, orange juice, and grenadine on the rocks."

"And what do they call this drink?" asked Trooper as she was trying her best not to take her eyes off of Rising Sun.

"Tequila Sunrise."

"Okay, let me have one of them; and I still want the lime."

The female on stage became skirmish while seated in the chair. Rising Sun softly took her hands and placed them on his sculptured chest exactly to the lyrics, "Hold on, hold on." The crowd cheered. Even Trooper smiled. The positive levels of serotonin started to flow through Trooper's body, reaching parts that haven't been touched in a long time. Rising Sun bent over and planted a kiss right on the woman's lips before he snatched his break-away pants off. As Trooper looked down at his G-String, she imagined that she was the woman sitting in the chair. *"Rising Sun definitely has more than enough to work with tonight. That answers my question."*

He moved his hips to the right, then to the left. The contents of his G-String followed suit right in front of the petite woman, who blushed. Rising Sun did this popping move as he walked closer to her; and right on cue with the beat, he straddled her. She didn't even see it coming. The women in the audience screamed, "I'm Next! I'm Next!" He came so close to her body that her most natural response was to put her hands on his waist. The light crew did a special effect with the mirrors and lights which gussied up the stage for Rising Sun's finale. Directly from her lap he did a back bend and landed on his feet. The women screamed and cheered. Then Rising Sun escorted her back to the table with her friends, kissed her on the hand, and exited stage right. He admitted to himself that this dance routine was much better than the one he practiced when he lived with Rasheeda.

When Toi came back with Trooper's drink, Toi asked, "Do you see that fine brother who is sitting at the bar? . . . the one with the wrestler's body and broad shoulders?"

The young man acknowledged Toi and Trooper with a polite nod. "Yes," said Trooper.

"Well, he says your drink is on him."

Trooper picked up the drink and tipped it his way and he smiled. "Excuse me. Do you have a few minutes?" Trooper asked Toi.

"Sure what's up?"

"I'm officially off duty; however, can you tell me about Polo?"

"Not really. He was one of those egotistical dancers and you couldn't tell him shit."

"Did you and he ever—"

"Hell no." She said jerking her head back. "I like brothers like him." Toi pointed to Rising Sun who was mingling in the audience. Toi continued, "But my girl use to sleep with Polo until she caught a VD from his ass."

"Is your friend here tonight?"

"No, she went into the Air Force a year ago."

"Okay thanks. If you hear anything, here is my card."

Trooper observed Rising Sun. There was a line forming to speak with him; and she wanted to get in line; however, she thought it best that she didn't.

Back at the bar, Ebony Wood asked Candi, "Why don't you just skip the After-Party and hang out with me?"

"Only if you are my night cap for the evening," said Candi smiling.

"I like. Give me a few minutes to get my bags."

Ebony Wood went into the basement. Rising Sun asked, "Ebony, you leaving already?"

"Yeah man. Before I dip out, you got a business card handy that I can get? I have a private show to do this weekend. That back bend you did from the chair was tight. I would like for you to show me how you perfected that move, if you don't mind."

"Sure, my cards are in my bag. I'll be right back." Rising Sun returned with a business card and handed it to Ebony Wood.

Trooper observed everyone in the club. Everything seemed so normal. The atmosphere was blissful as if every patron was having a time of their life. She saw the first male performer of the evening join a female at the bar; then the two of them headed out the door. Within a few seconds, the guy who bought Trooper the drink walked towards the door to leave as well. Trooper said, "Thanks for the drink."

"Sure, no problem. Tonight you were my eye candy." He said and winked at Trooper. Before she could respond, he was gone.

CHAPTER 7

A major Shriners Convention was coming to town; and housekeeping at the Red Roof Inn on Central Avenue needed to clean rooms quickly before today's guests arrived. The guest in Room 201 was the last to checkout. Even though this was the tenth time the front desk tried to call the room, there was still no answer. With only one housekeeper to clean 12 rooms, the hotel manager was concerned that the rooms would not be ready on time. Head of Housekeeping radioed the front desk and said, "I can't wait any longer on Room 201; I'm going into the room."

The little green light flashed as she removed the plastic key card. She couldn't believe what she saw next. Two cans of whipped cream were on the table; and condoms were all over the floor. On the pillow of the bed was a pink G-String. She put on cleaning gloves and put everything into a clear trash bag.

By lunch time, she reached Room 205. With the room darkening curtains drawn closed, she hit the light switch. The person lying in the bed startled her. "Housekeeping!" She shouted. The man did not move. "Housekeeping!" She went closer to the bed and realized that the person's eyes were open; however, he was not breathing. She ran out of the room, grabbed the hand held radio on the cart and shouted, "Call 911! There is a dead man in Room 205!" Her heart was pounding and her hands became sweaty.

Within the hour, the P.G. County Forensic Unit combed the room. In the victim's pocket was a business card, which was placed in a zip lock bag. The P.G. County Lead Detective called the D.C. Homicide Division. "Hello, this is Detective Adams. We have reason to believe that the killer you call The Paradox is at it again. We also have a business card from the pants pocket of the victim that reads 'Rising Sun, Male Exotic Dancer' with contact information on it. Is it possible for you to come to the Red Roof Inn on Central Avenue?"

"We are on our way," said Trooper.

Pulling into the hotel parking lot, Trooper parked the car and pushed the trunk release button. She wished she could spend the rest of the day at the park, because the weather was perfect. While Swoosh squeezed out of the car, she retrieved latex gloves, blue paper shoe covers, and a Mag flashlight. In the second floor hallway, Trooper and Swoosh put on their protective gear and entered the room. The room was extremely crowded with law enforcement. Trooper pushed through and said, "Excuse me, I'm Detective Troop from the D.C. Homicide Division. Where is the P.G. County Lead Detective?"

"Over there," pointed the photographer.

Trooper walked over to a short thin man and said, "Hello I'm—"

"I know who you are Detective Troop. I'm the one who called you in. Let me show you what we have." He passed her the evidence log, which she reviewed thoroughly. Trooper headed to the bed with a puzzled look on her face.

The Medical Examiner was zipping up the body bag. "Hold up," said Trooper.

"What is it?" asked Swoosh putting his right hand on his forehead and rubbing softly.

"I do remember this guy. SHIT!" exclaimed Trooper.

"Do you know this one?" asked Swoosh.

"He was at Club Classic last night. He was dancing when you and I arrived at the club. Damn, this means that the killer could have been there with us as well. The crime scene is staged like The Paradox's work; however, something's missing on the evidence log." Trooper walked out of the room to find housekeeping. The hall was clear. Trooper asked the P.G.

County Officer who was guarding the door, "Where is the lady who called this in?"

"Downstairs in the lobby. She is scared to death," said the Officer.

Swoosh said to the Medical Examiner, "The log says that there's some fluids on the victim's phallus. Can you rush the results from the lab to me ASAP?"

Before Trooper went into the lobby, she scanned the crowd. The housekeeper was sitting in a chair and guarded by three police officers in the atrium. "Hello, I'm Detective Trooper. I need your help." The guests from the convention filled the area and appeared to be watching the entire investigation unfold. "Ma'am, do you mind if I get a hair sample from you?"

"For what? I didn't do anything wrong." She said with grave concern.

"We have to eliminate all workers who may have been in Room 205, so we can find the person who did this."

"Yeah, I guess." She said as her right knee shook uncontrollably.

"Okay, tell me what happened when you started to clean on the second floor."

"I started in Room 201. This room was messed up like a freak show."

"What made it so?"

"Well, there were whipped cream cans and condoms all over the room. The only thing clean in the room was a pink G-String. I vacuumed—"

"Where did you put the trash?" Trooper asked with a sense of urgency.

"It's still on my cart, but I heard an officer say that they were going to take all of the contents on my cart away and look for more evidence."

Trooper dashed down the hall, almost knocking over several convention attendees. When she saw the exit sign, she ran up the stairs to the second floor. The cart was gone. She ran down to Room 201 and realized the door was locked. Swoosh came from around the corner of the hall, as he did a final walk-through of the second floor. Trooper yelled, "Get this door open! And call CSI back here, because we have a secondary crime scene! And I want the trash from this room! Now!" Swoosh smiled at Trooper, because she always amazed him on how she pieced together crime scenes.

As housekeeping opened the door, a police officer brought Trooper the clear bag of trash. The pink G-String was sitting near the top. With gloves on, Trooper reached inside. Her gut feeling was right. There was the note.

"Damn!" exclaimed Trooper.

◊◊◊◊◊

GQ was sitting in the television room in the Philadelphia Women's Penitentiary. She was waiting for the authorities to come and take her to court. "We have some breaking news," announced the News Reporter on television. "Good morning, I'm Rosalind Cole with Channel 5 Fox News. I'm here at the Central Avenue Red Roof Inn. There's been a string of murders within the Washington D.C. and Maryland area that are said to be tied to a connection in Philadelphia. I'm here with the Lead Detective Troop." Trooper stepped into view from the left of the News Reporter. "Detective Troop, do we have any leads on who may be responsible for these murders and is this the work of one person?" asked Rosalind Cole.

GQ was on the edge of her seat when she heard, "Gail Que . . . Gail Que, I said get your pretty ass up. Time to go to court," said the Corrections Officer.

GQ's heart raced the entire time from the television room to the courthouse, which was full of police. In the courtroom, her attorney sat to her right going over paperwork. The smell of polished wood filled the room. GQ closed her eyes to pray; and then she heard, "All rise, Judge Kipped presiding."

When she looked up, Judge Kipped said, "Gail Indigo Que, I'm sworn by the Federal and State of Pennsylvania to make sure that the court's rules and procedures are enforced according to the law. Everyone that comes before this court or any court in this district of the City of Philadelphia must be given an equal protection of the law." Sweat was forming under GQ's arms. The appeals process was long and tedious; and she couldn't believe that this day was finally here. The best thing going for her was the fact that Teco Jackson was soon going to be out of the picture. The judge's voice snapped her back into the present. "I really believe that you should do more time in prison for the crime and what involvement you may have had in the brutal death of Mujaheed Bashi Fiten. However, the law is the law. Due to a fundamentally flawed indictment by the D.A.'s office the charges of murder have been vindicated. Does the D.A.'s office have any objections?"

"No Your Honor," said D. A. Brown with an agitated look on his face. He turned to GQ and saw her breath a sigh of relief.

The judge continued, "The charges of escape and the assault on a police officer still stands. You are to remain in the custody of the Department of Corrections for the rest of your time, which is now fourteen days. Court dismissed."

"Yes! Yes!" exclaimed GQ, who didn't pass out this time. She turned to see if her family was there. Her big smile dropped, because no one was in the courtroom to support her.

◊◊◊◊◊

The national news was now covering the Washington D.C. murders. The District Attorney was adjusting the microphones on the platform stage, as the evening News Reporter stated, "In a few minutes, we will be hearing the latest update on the D.C. murders. There are two black male victims, who were both male exotic dancers in the D.C. and Maryland area. The police will only release that they are pursuing a person of interest. So far, they are being tight lipped, which means that they don't want the killer to know what they know. One thing I do know is that someone always leaks information to the press. Stay tuned for more information momentarily . . . ."

In a Southeast D.C. dilapidated residence, which was built in the 1960's on MLK Avenue, The Paradox was seated in the small cramped kitchen. The vegetable print wallpaper was peeling away from several sections of the wall. Even though dishes were stacked in the sink as well as on the green Formica countertops, the scent of steak and potatoes was the most pleasant aspect of the room. Listening intently to the News Reporter, The Paradox's sewing machine needle was moving 4500 stitches per minute through the fabric. Vaagglum! Vaagglum! Vaagglum!

When The Paradox saw Detective Trooper, the volume was turned up on the television with the remote. "I am D.A. Alexander. I have with me today a host of people who will update you at this press conference. First, I want to introduce you to Detective Hanae Troop . . . ."

The Paradox was fixated on the press conference and cut the extra thread from the imitation J.B. Productions label stitched on the G-String. There was a loud thud noise by the back door, which startled The Paradox. Grabbing the 45mm gun, the Paradox looked out of the window and noticed 2 young boys climbing over the wooden fence. Seeing the football in the hands of the younger brother, The Paradox breath a sign of relief and placed the 45mm back into the kitchen drawer.

Reaching for scissors and cloth, The Paradox thought, *"Well Detective Troop, after this next kill, I think I'll send you a gift."* The delusional and vindictive killer believed all actions of these crimes were supported by the laws of the street life. The Paradox pushed the pedal to the sewing machine and finished making the yellow G-String. *"After I finish my work here in the Chocolate City, I'll head back to Philly. Snitches get more than just stitches."*

◊◊◊◊◊

GQ walked back into her cell, beaming with joy.

"So girl what happened," asked her roommate Chi Chi, who was sitting on her bunk.

"I'm out of this concrete jungle in 14 days." Reaching into her locker, GQ pulled out a bag of potato chips.

"Did you hear about those sexy men in D.C. getting murdered?"

"I know about it."

"They say it's tied to Philly. Didn't you say that snitch Teco is in D.C.?"

"Yep, that he is," said GQ popping potato chips into her mouth.

"Didn't you hear a rumor that Teco was a lip synching artist or something like that?"

"Why you asking me all these questions?"

"I want to know if you got anything to do with it? Looks like someone keeps getting the wrong snitch to me." Chi Chi said with her arms folded.

"You don't know shit."

"Well, your future is more important than revenge."

GQ sucked her teeth and said, "I'll be right back. I need to call my fam." She walked to the phone with the biggest smile ever. Other inmates asked her what happened in court as she went into the blue phone room. All of a sudden everyone on

C-Block was hopeful. She wanted to tell them that every case is different, but she didn't want to burst their bubble. She picked up the phone to dial her sister.

"Yo, what's up sis?" asked Gwen, who was just getting out of the shower.

"Girl I gave it back to them. What happened to my fam being in court today?"

"We didn't get up on time; and by the time we would have gotten there, court would have been over." GQ felt that Gwen was lying and hiding something from her. Gwen continued, "When do you get out?"

"In 14 days."

"What? You lying girl."

"Nope. Check this. I need you to handle something for me," said GQ leaning against the royal blue phone room door.

"What's up?"

"I need you to go on the computer and do a people search for Teco Jackson in Washington, D.C., but don't tell no one."

"Gail, why are you still tripping off of that low life snitch?"

"Look! Just do this for me; and hold on to the info for me."

"Just move on with your life."

"I'm handling my business. You handle yours."

"Sis, you don't have to do anything when you get out. I got your back. I'm sitting on a quarter of a million and your attorney's fees are paid. I'll give you half of what I have." Gwen was trying to convince her sister to leave Teco alone.

"What do you mean by my lawyer fees are paid?"

"Your man, Travis Delgado, and I paid him to take your case for the low-low."

"What does Travis D. have to do with this? Have you been screwing him behind my back?"

"Travis D. and I have been moving shit out here for you, so that you won't have to look back. That's why I need you to leave Teco in your past."

GQ's face displayed total confusion, trying to figure out what Gwen meant by moving shit. Gwen never hustled a day in her life; and GQ refused to go back into drug dealing. *"If Gwen does have money for me, I need it for . . . "*

"Gail! Are you still there?"

"Yeah, Yeah, I'm here. Look, let me holla at you later."

When GQ returned to her blue cell, she laid down on her bunk trying to figure her sister out. Chi Chi didn't know if GQ was mad at her for probing about Teco; so Chi Chi tried to change the conversation. "Girl, what are your plans when you get out?"

GQ said, "With my new look, I'm going to follow my dream to be a fashion designer. I want to model my own clothes." She knew that she would have to relocate to New York. She wanted to take Gwen with her; however, she didn't know if Gwen would leave Philly. There was something about GQ and Gwen that no one in the SB Crew knew but Bashi; and Bashi was 6 feet under.

"What will you call your line?"

"GQ Fashions by Indigo or Indigo by GQ."

"Both of them names sound tight."

Deep in inside, GQ was on a mission to find Teco. *"Why did Teco and Lisa turn on me? This shit ain't over yet . . . . "*

"Gail, Gail you listening? Can I tell you something?"

"Sure, you know we can talk."

"Look, these pussies gave me a life sentence which means that I'll die in here. You have been given another chance to be somebody and make something out of yourself. Don't go back out there and fall into the same bullshit. Take what you have learned in here. My nana use to tell me, 'A person's character is defined by their enemies. Chi Chi, the street is your enemy.' She would say." Tears rolled down Chi Chi's face.

Then GQ reached over and gave her a sister hug and said, "Girl, turn that Keith Sweat tape on."

CHAPTER 8

T rooper sat at her desk looking at the computer display and searching on all kinds of keywords. The last 12 hours flew by as she tried to put the case together. She did the sniff test. *"Damn, I need to go home and shower."* However, she refused to leave until the information came in from the crime lab. *"Why was Rising Sun's card in the victim's pants?"*

Now there were 2 persons of interest, Twyla Burke and Teco Jackson. Both were from the Philly area. Maybe the term Rising Sun would give her a clue about the connection between the two of them. She entered "Rising Sun" in the search field. Within a few seconds the word "Match" flashed on the screen.

"Yes!" shouted Trooper. She clicked on the link. The page read, "Rising Sun, a cocktail drink also known as Tequila Sunrise." She pushed away from her desk and exclaimed, "Shit!" Then the telephone rang. "This is Trooper."

"Hey, this is Linda. I'm faxing you the findings on the victim from the Red Roof Inn; and you were right. It's the same DNA from the first murder. It's Twyla Burke."

"What about the condoms?"

"This is strange. The condoms had no vaginal fluids and no spermatozoon. Get this. The cans of whipped cream were full." Trooper's mind was racing. She flashed back to both crime scenes.

"Trooper! Trooper! Are you with me?"

"Yes, yes I'm here. Did we get an I.D. on the victim?"

"Yes, his real name is Robert Anderson out of Falls Church, Virginia."

Trooper's special gift to solving cases was the algorithms she calculated in her mind. Her brain processed information better than a search engine. She noticed a new email in her inbox. There was a picture of a teenage girl. The information at the bottom read: Twyla Burke, age 17, black female, 5'4", brown eyes, black hair.

"Linda, I'm on my way home. If you find out anything new, please call me."

"Okay, get some rest."

Trooper was about to exit the building when she heard a very authoritative voice. "Detective Troop! Don't you go out that door. I need to see you in my office ASAP," demanded her superior, Captain Wicker. She turned around with a folder in her hand and headed to his office. Trooper knew that her commander would ask about her progress with the G-String murders. She wasn't even close to making sense of this case. The Paradox really knew how to stump her, which bothered her a great deal.

As she walked through the door, the Captain stood up. He was a stately black man, who looked like he had a few to many beers over the years. "Detective, tell me what's going on with the G-String murder case." He said.

"Sir, we're doing the best we can with what we—"

"Trooper, I don't want to hear that bureaucratic bullshit. You're the best detective I have and I don't care how you do it. Close this case. I have all kinds of wild hairs up my ass and unless you have some tweezers—"

"Sir, as a matter of speaking, I do—"

"Trooper, don't play with me. Today's not a good day to be a freaking comedian! Where is your partner?"

"He's speaking with our second victim's family."

"Have a seat and fill me in," bade her egotistical boss, who took a seat in his burgundy leather chair. Behind his desk on the wall were 8 shadow box frames with his medals. His desk was cluttered with paperwork. Everything in his office looked worn and dingy, except for a new picture frame of his homely looking wife. Trooper moved to sit on the black vinyl sofa with aged cracks. Then she opened the case folder.

◇◇◇◇◇

. . . *"Homicide you didn't have to snitch on me. You know we could have ran this shit on our own. I didn't kill Bashi. I didn't like how you use to sleep with all those women either. You never asked me out,"* said GQ to Teco, *whose alias was Homicide when he lived in Mount Airy. "GQ, you know it would have never worked out. You knew that . . . Whoa! Whoa! Put the gun down; please GQ. Put the gun down,"* said Homicide.

"You sent me to prison; and I tried to tell you that I didn't kill Bashi. You got on the stand and told them that I killed Bashi. You know I would have never hurt him. So now it's your turn to feel what it's like to get burnt, you low life snitch."

"Wait! Wait!" Homicide stepped forward and pushed the 9mm to the side and kissed GQ very passionately. As she returned the embrace, the gun fell out of her hand and hit the floor. POW! The bullet ricocheted across the room and hit Homicide in the heart . . . .

"Oh Shit!" Sweat was all over GQ as she rose up out of her cell bunk and awoke from the nightmare. She gained focus. GQ looked over to Chi Chi, who was sleeping like a baby. They talked all night about their time as cell mates, because today was GQ's big day. Heading to the shower, GQ needed to calm down. After getting dressed, she packed her things.

This morning seemed as though everything was on time. Breakfast was on time; and count was on time, which was very unusual. GQ came back from chow and realized that Chi Chi was not in their cell.

"Gail Que, let's go," shouted out the Commanding Officer (C.O.).

She got off the bunk and grabbed her things. Because Chi Chi was at her detail in the Law Library, GQ left Chi Chi a nice card and a letter. Before she turned to walk away, GQ looked at the blue cell one last time, making sure that she remembered the vivid visual.

Intake was a different world within the penitentiary. "Come with me, Ms. Que," said the same C.O. GQ looked around to see if her estranged mother was in the room. Being addressed as "Ms. Que" was a new experience since her incarceration. GQ was taken to a small room with a window like slot. "You can wait here," said the C.O.

Within a few minutes, GQ was handed a box with her Gucci white sweat suit and sneakers inside. Gail was so full of ebullience that she couldn't stop smiling, displaying her perfect white teeth. After GQ put on her civilian clothes, the C.O. asked, "Can you tell me your full name please?"

"Gail Indigo Que."

"Your birth date?"

"July 16."

He asked a few more questions; and then gave her a piece of paper to sign. GQ picked up the pen. The C.O. continued, "Okay Ms. Que, you are free to go after they fingerprint you."

When GQ walked through the lobby doors, there stood her boyfriend, Travis Delgado and her attorney along with Gwen. GQ embraced her sister who also wore the same Gucci white sweat suit.

"You looking fine as ever. What's up baby?" asked GQ.

"You, with your fine ass self," said Travis D. GQ and Travis D. kissed like never before.

Gwen's smile left her face, when GQ and Travis D. seemed to not let go of each other.

"Okay, you love birds. This isn't the love nest," said the attorney. "Gail, these are your parole papers. You have 48 hours to see your Parole Officer."

"The judge didn't say anything about parole. I have plans to—" GQ said.

"It's not forever. Just finish six months clean and I'll see what I can do. Okay? For now, I need to run. Call me."

"I'll call you tomorrow afternoon," said GQ.

"Let me get that bag for you. Today is GQ's day," said Travis D.

◊◊◊◊◊

Swoosh walked around the club looking for people to speak with in regards to the G-String murders, while Trooper talked to the owner at The Mirage.

"Do you mind if I show you a picture?" asked Trooper.

"No . . . no . . . no, I don't mind," said the Club Owner, who thought Trooper looked brow-beaten.

Pulling out a black and white mug shot, Trooper asked, "Have you seen this woman?"

He took the mug shot into his hand using his right index finger and right thumb. Trooper observed that he tried to gain strabismic control as he looked at the picture. "No . . . no . . . I can't say that I have. Detective, we don't allow ladies this young in our club." He handed Trooper back the mug shot.

"She wouldn't look this young now. This was when she was 17." Trooper carefully pinched the top right corner of the mug shot.

"Detective, I would know this beautiful . . . Wait . . . wait . . . there is a young lady who comes close to looking like this picture. She is one of our customers named Candi."

"Is she a regular here?"

"Well, she . . . she . . . she comes around quite often to see the guys."

"Is she here tonight?"

"See . . . see . . . tonight isn't a ladies get in free night. So she will probably be at another club tonight."

"Can you tell me the name of the other clubs where male dancers perform?" After the owner gave Trooper the other club names, she asked, "Do you mind if I ask around about Candi?"

"Detective, I don't want my employees and party goers running off; so . . . so . . . so please be light."

As she walked down the hallway, she stopped for a second and pulled out a small zip lock bag, slipped the mug shot into it and wrote on the bag, "The Mirage Owner #1."

Trooper and Swoosh walked the entire club for two hours asking questions and getting prints from the stack of the Twyla Burke mug shots they brought to the club with them.

"I think we have what we need. Let's go to the precinct," said Trooper.

Neither said a word on the way back. Trooper was in deep thought about each conversation at The Mirage. She couldn't wait to sign into to the AFIS (Automated Fingerprint Identification System).

The precinct computer room contained the most up to date systems in the industry. There was a raised floor to accommodate electrical and air conditioner wiring. Before entering the room, Trooper put on a lightweight jacket, because the year round temperature of the room was always cold. Swoosh followed Trooper to the front of the room. The computer desks were arranged in a classroom configuration; and they sat at the first desk on the left side. Trooper swiveled in the computer chair as she talked to Swoosh about fingerprints.

"How do you know so much about prints?" asked Swoosh.

"I did a study of my own to understand how finger prints work. See in 1965, Marcello Malpighi recognized patterns in fingerprints and named them loops and whorls. Sir Francis refined the printing method of recording prints in 1892," said Trooper.

"You're kidding right?" asked Swoosh slapping his forehead with his hand.

"No I'm not. Pass me that first zip lock bag. See, whorls, loops and arches are still the basis for fingerprint matching and identification. As you know, everyone has a unique fingerprint, which makes us different."

"No shit. No two people can have the same print? Not even twins?" Swoosh asked sarcastically.

"Swoosh, you always playing. Now you are going to have to hear the rest of the story." Swoosh rolled his eyes while Trooper continued, "Sir Edward Henry, an Inspector General of the

British Police worked on a fingerprint classification system for years. Oh! Here we go!"

"Okay, who is this?" asked Swoosh.

"This is . . . the . . . owner from The Mirage." She answered as she read the information.

"Is he clean?"

"Well, he does have a few stars on his arrest record."

"Is it anything that can help us?"

Trooper reviewed the electronic file and said, "No, nothing that would be helpful to us. Hand me the next mug shot."

"What about this guy Rising Sun?"

"First we have to find him. I have a feeling he will be at Club Classic next week."

"Why do you think he'll be at Club Classic versus another club?"

"Well, he was there last Thursday night; and he was more popular than the other dancers. I saw his face when he received all of that money. Trust me. He will be back."

CHAPTER 9

"Yes, I'm still performing tonight. I can't believe it's Thursday either. The week went by fast. Hold on for a minute," said Teco to the club owner. Then he placed the cordless phone onto the upside down blue egg crate, which was used as a makeshift end table. Through the peephole there was a man in a full black body jumpsuit.

"May I help you?" asked Teco.

"We have a delivery for a Mr. Teco Jackson."

"Who is it from?"

"It's from Thompson Furniture."

"Come in sir." A distinct echo sounded in the 2 story foyer. Teco's pristine all brick Colonial townhouse in Georgetown was stunning and spacious. The delivery man saw a grand spiral staircase; however, his attention was immediately drawn to the smell of bacon and eggs coming from the gourmet styled kitchen.

Teco liked having legitimate money to settle down. An enormous master bedroom was now his haven with an adjoining sitting room, where he practiced his dance routines. He couldn't wait to finally sleep in a bed of his own.

"When do I get the furniture that's on backorder?"

"It's all here sir." Teco's left eyebrow went up in astonishment. It's amazing what $10,000 in cash can do, which was the cost to furnish his entire residence. The open floor plan on the main level included a kitchen, dining room, and a living room. Near the back door, was a half bathroom and laundry room. On the second floor were 2 bedrooms and 2 bathrooms.

The delivery man flagged the other workers to start bringing in the furniture, while Teco went back to the telephone. "Hello . . . I'm sorry. My furniture arrived. Can I call you back? . . . Okay. Peace."

The delivery men put runners over the tan carpet. As they started bringing the furniture into the home, Teco admired every piece with a smile. The last items were the 64 inch black Sony, an Italian leather sectional and oak end tables.

Before Teco went into the kitchen to have his breakfast, he sat down on the sofa to reflect on his accomplishment as a first time home owner. He wished that his dad could see him now. His father, Rico Jackson, died of lung cancer when Teco was 16 years old. Because his parents were divorced, Teco use to live with his father; and his sisters lived with their mother.

Except for when he was boosting cars, Rico was a great parent. He attended as many of Teco's school and sports events as possible. Whenever his dad was locked up, Teco would rebel and get into trouble for petty crimes. The last year of Rico's life, he and Teco made a joint agreement to stay clean. Teco leaned back onto the sofa to reminisce about his last vivid memory of his father.

. . . *Teco was hanging out on the corner with 5 guys from the hood. He was the youngest in the group. Out of no where five cop cars bum rushed the corner. The police jumped out of their cars throwing all of them onto the hot hoods of their police cars. Teco couldn't take the heat from the hood and raised his hands; however, a tall cop grabbed Teco's arms forcing Teco to put his hands back onto the scorching hood. Sheer fear was in his heart; however, he knew he was in the clear.*

One cop talked about an armed robbery at the Cheltenham Square Mall. The older guys in the group yelled that they hadn't been to the mall in days. When the police saw that Teco didn't match the description of the suspects; they let Teco go. However, they cuffed the other guys to take them to the precinct for a line-up.

When Teco ran into the house, he screamed, "Dad! You wouldn't believe what happened today!"

Rico was in the kitchen cooking Cheeseburger Macaroni for their dinner. "What son?"

"These guys on the corner robbed a store at the Cheltenham Square Mall."

"Teco, I told you to stop hanging out on that corner."

"Dad, I had nothing to do with it. If I still ran with them, I would be down to the police station now."

Rico said, "Son, see it for what it is and see it for what it's worth." . . .

The telephone rang snapping Teco back into the present. "Hello."

"May I speak with Rising Sun?" asked a male voice.

"That's my stage name. If you don't mind, how did you get this number?"

"From the owner of The Mirage."

"Who the hell is this?" Teco asked in an irritated voice. He didn't understand why the owner would give out his personal information to a stranger.

"Hey man, it's Legend. Remember, the dude who got you started with those 7 parties?" As Legend spoke, Teco was headed for the kitchen to reheat his breakfast in the microwave.

"Oh yeah, what's up?"

"I'm calling to let you know that I have a gig in Asheville, North Carolina. Are you interested?"

"Yes, I am. How much does it pay?" He asked putting his left index finger over his lips.

"$700 plus tips."

"Okay, I'll do it," said Teco reaching into the microwave to retrieve the hot plate.

"I'm glad you accepted, because I've told them about you."

"So what's the date?"

"This weekend. We'll fly to Greenville, South Carolina and then rent a van to Asheville."

After eating the late breakfast, Teco went to his bedroom and took a nap. When he woke up, he couldn't believe the time.

The red digital display on the clock read 4pm. As he dressed, Teco envisioned driving up to valet park at the IBEX in his new Benz. His black Sports Sedan Benz came with black leather seats and black interior wood trim. The feature he liked the most was the powerful audio subwoofers, which provided the sound quality he needed to review his performance music. He knew he would shine at the club. *"My own place . . . car . . . and a little money . . . I'm set."*

On his way out of the house, he grabbed his cell phone. While driving on Peppermill Road, he received a page and checked the number. *"What does she want?"*

"Hello, may I speak with Rasheeda?" asked Teco.

"Just a minute," said Yvette. When Rasheeda kicked Teco out of her apartment, Yvette moved in as her roommate. Teco heard 2 clicks. "Teco, you still there?"

"Yes, I'm here."

"Hold on, let me get her."

Teco waited for a while. Rasheeda said, "Hello, I've been trying to call you." She was in the kitchen putting uncooked hamburger patties and hot dogs on a tray. Rasheeda pulled out the punch bowl to make her favorite fruit punch.

"What's up?"

"You know I miss you baby. We need to talk." She said with her hand on her hip.

As he heard water running in the background, he thought, *"Here we go with the bullshit."* Then he asked, "Do you miss me or the sex?"

"A little of both to be honest," said Rasheeda; and Teco couldn't help but laugh.

"I can't come over right now. I need to run some errands before I go to the IBEX."

"Do you want me to come get you?" Dishes were clattering in the sink.

"No thank you, I have my own car now," said Teco.

"Oh really? Why don't you come over before you go to the IBEX."

"I'll see you around 7pm."

"Teco, don't stand me up. I need to talk with you."

"Okay. I need to run." As Teco drove to J. B. Productions to pick up some new G-Strings, he thought, *I really wonder what Rasheeda wants with me? Most likely some money . . . Speaking of money, I need to buy me a safe. Damn, I hope she's not pregnant.*

At 6:45pm Teco pulled up to Rasheeda's building. He smelled grilled hamburgers; and when he looked up, she was sitting on the balcony. A group of grade school kids were playing tag in the parking lot; and Teco wondered where their parents were. As he got out of the Benz, Rasheeda's mouth dropped open. Teco's stride was smooth. His head was in the clouds as he walked up the stairs; and today, the sky was clear blue.

"Hey baby," said Rasheeda.

"What's up?" asked Teco ignoring the baby shit.

Rasheeda leaned forward for Teco to give her the passionate kiss that she always received when he arrived home. Teco breezed past her as if he didn't notice her advances. However, he did check out her stomach to see if there were any signs of pregnancy. Her fine ass figure was the same.

"So, what can I help you with?" asked Teco.

She liked his Ralph Lauren single-breasted pinstriped suit from the Black Label Collection. However, she thought his Aviator style sunglasses were over the top. "I've been wondering if you are still mad at me?"

"No, Rasheeda, I put that all behind me."

"What about me? Am I behind you as well?" She lifted a clear plastic glass with the red drink. The aroma of the food was making Teco hungry.

"Well to be honest, you called the shot."

"I know I did; and I'm sorry for that. I was upset because you became a well known dancer. All I hear at the Hair Spa is 'Rising Sun this and Rising Sun that.' You should hear what women want to do with you."

With a slight smile, Teco said, "Rasheeda, that's a part of the life of a dancer. A lot of ladies dream of having this dancer or that dancer." He picked up a white paper plate, a hot dog, a hamburger, and barbeque chips.

"You know that 2 dancers have come up dead and stinking. I don't want that to be your ass. Can you see that I care about you?"

"Yes, Rasheeda, I can see that and I—"

"What hotel are you staying at?" She asked just as Teco took a bite of the hot dog.

Teco hesitated for a few seconds in order to chew the food. "Why do you ask?"

"Teco, you don't have to live in a hotel. Both dancers died in hotels. You are not safe. You can move back in with me until—"

"Until what? I already have a place of my own. But thank you any way." Teco reached for the punch ladle and poured Rasheeda's spiked punch into a plastic glass.

Rasheeda's eyes widen as her temperature began to rise. She was starting to feel as though she was played. Standing to her feet with her arms crossed over her chest, she asked, "With who? And what woman are you using now?"

Teco took a swig of the drink and said, "To be frank, I live alone." He glanced at his timepiece and knew it was time for him to jet. He said, "Here is the money for the outfits you bought me a while back. If you need to borrow some money or need help with something, let me know."

She watched the man who once filled her every desire walk towards the door, as if he were on a modeling runway. When he opened the door, Rasheeda said, "Wait Teco! Wait!" She was hoping for another opportunity to make him change his mind. Rasheeda continued, "Can you give me a ride to the club?"

"Sure, I'll give you a ride. However, I can't bring you back home when the club closes. I will not be staying that long." He knew this was more of her games.

"That's fine. I'll get Yvette or Toi to bring me home. Just give me 20 minutes."

Teco responded in a perturbed voice, "I can't be late."

"You will be on time, I promise. Come to the bedroom while I get dressed and we can continue our talk."

"No, I'll wait in the car." In the Benz, Teco turned on the tape of Keith Sweat's song, "How Deep is Your Love," which he was going to dance to tonight. He increased the volume and looked at the dark clouds overhead. He hoped the rain held off until morning, because most of the ladies wouldn't come to party during bad weather.

Minutes later Rasheeda hopped into the car and turned down the bass. "Okay, I'm ready." She said.

Teco started the engine and turned back up the bass. She was really testing his nerves. At first, they rode with just the music playing. As he pulled onto Pennsylvania Avenue, Rasheeda asked, "How much did your place cost you?"

"Not much. Why?" Teco adjusted the rearview mirror.

"I didn't know you had enough money to get your own place and a car. I must say that you do have a nice ride." She smelled the clean leather and felt the wood console. Then she placed her hand on Teco's right leg.

"Thank you." For the rest of the way to the IBEX, he played Go Go music by Rare Essence. When Teco pulled up to the front door to valet park, heads turned in his direction.

People wanted to see who would step out of the Benz. Whenever he was at clubs his dancer personae immediately went into character. Ten ladies gathered around Rising Sun as he emerged from the car. Because the ticket booth sold dancers' photographs at the front door, pictures and ink pens came from purses in order for him to sign his autograph. That's when Rasheeda realized the Aviator sunglasses gave him a Hollywood look for the crowd.

Tonight was college alumni night with ladies from Howard University, Georgetown University, and Baltimore University along with other surrounding colleges. Money was always good on college alumni night. "I'll holla at you later Rasheeda," said Rising Sun as he got deep inside the club.

There were three floors of the IBEX club. Dancers performed at the top level. The main floor was for Hip Hop and House music; and the lower level was for Go Go music lovers. Rising Sun could smell weed as soon as he hit the top level; and Salt-N-Pepa's remix to "Push It" was blasting through the speakers. His head bobbed as he sang, "Baby, baby, baby, baby." He clocked-in and found out that he was first to perform. This was good because he wanted to leave without Rasheeda.

Before he could put on his performance shoes, Rising Sun heard, "Laaadies put your hands together for Risssing Sunnn!"

The stage manager cued the lights to go to black and the dry ice machine to fill the stage with fog. Rising Sun took center stage. The music to Keith Sweat's song, "How Deep is Your Love" started and a single spotlight revealed Rising Sun in the haze. The Ladies cheered. He grabbed the brass railings around the stage as he made his body wave. Then he moved his pectoralis major muscles to the beat of the music. Ladies were jumping up and down with money trying to entice him to come over so they could touch his chest. He smiled in an inveigling manner.

"Laaadies, do you want to take Rising Sun home?"

"Yeaaah!" yelled the women.

"Rising Sun, you have some excited ladies over here!" exclaimed the M.C. pointing to stage left. "How about let's show some love to the beautiful quiet lady in the hot pink who is sitting all alone?" The D.J. did a smooth transition to the song "Make It Last Forever" by Keith Sweat; and five body building bouncers held back the savaged crowd. Rising Sun felt like he was at a Rock concert.

Rising Sun established eye contact with the lady in the hot pink cocktail dress. He looked at her as if she were the only woman in the room. She was calm and showed no excitement as he danced his way over to her table. The white spotlight followed him; and the women in the crowd were wildly screaming his name requesting that he come to their tables instead. His gaze never left the quiet woman. As he reached over to kiss her cheek, Candi tipped him a $100 bill and whispered something in his ear that no one else could hear.

CHAPTER 10

On Thursday night, Trooper walked into Club Classic and flashed her badge. "Is the owner in?" The bar was packed with men; and ESPN Sports News was on every TV screen in the club.

"Yes, he is in his office. I'll call him down," said the bartender. He pulled a black Motorola Walkie Talkie from his back pocket and called the owner's office. "He'll be down in a minute."

Swoosh joined Trooper, where they sat at the bar for five minutes. The smoke caused Swoosh to go into an asthmatic attack. Trooper asked, "You okay?" Swoosh reached into his pocket and pulled out his Albuterol inhaler and nodded.

The owner of the club approached them. Trooper asked, "Do you remember me? I have some more questions."

"Let's go back to my office." He said with an Italian accent.

The stage was empty with no signs of movement. Trooper finally realized that the music, lights, and dancers provided the magic to make the stage come to life. To her surprise, she was disappointed that there was no show tonight.

After ascending the stairs Trooper continued, "Do you know Teco Jackson, a.k.a. Rising Sun? Also, I now have a mug shot of Twyla Burke. Do you recognize her? I thought a mug shot might jog your memory." As Trooper asked the questions, Swoosh's pad and pen where in hand in order to jot down the responses.

"Rising Sun yes, the other name no."

"Do you know what club he is dancing at tonight?"

"Tonight is college alumni night at the IBEX; and most dancers are there. Is Rising Sun a suspect?"

"Well . . . we just want to talk with him," said Trooper turning to leave.

As Swoosh and Trooper were driving over to the IBEX, Rising Sun was still charming the ladies after his set. He noticed a crowd of people from the lower level of the club rushing up the stairs to leave out of the building. The only time people rushed like that was during a fight. Watching the crowd, he was content until he heard bullets over his head, which caused him to duck. When he turned around, he could have sworn that he saw a lady who looked like GQ. His heart was racing; so he jetted outside. All of the dancers' cars were already lined up at the curb. The valet attendant threw him the keys across a crowd of people. When Rising Sun saw the panicked look on the woman's face, he yelled, "Hop in!" Before she could close the door, Rising Sun took off. Everyone in the parking lot heard the tires squealing, saw the smoke on the pavement, and smelled rubber burning. As he drove out of the back parking lot entrance, Rising Sun passed the police who were rushing to the scene as if they were on a high speed chase.

As Swoosh tried to turn into the front entrance of parking, he asked, "What the hell?" The entire block appeared to be gridlocked; and Trooper was ready to jump out of the car right then and there. Women were running to their cars in high heels. Swoosh thought there was going to be road rage right before his eyes. Drivers were throwing up middle fingers and horns were blaring.

"I wonder does this have anything to do with The Paradox?" asked Trooper.

Swoosh picked up the radio and said, "This is B1-T1. My 10-20 is the IBEX at Georgia Avenue Northwest." Trooper opened the car door before Swoosh put the car in park.

There were a few seconds of static and radio traffic. Then the female dispatcher said, "B1-T1, that's a copy."

Police Officers took three hours to clear the club. "Partner, he's not here. Witnesses say that he did dance here tonight and left with a beautiful woman. No confirmation on who the woman is. Now what?" Swoosh asked Trooper, while scratching his head.

"Well, let's find the owner. We need to find out who Teco Jackson left the club with," said Trooper. They spoke with the owner for an hour. Since he offered no pertinent information to the case, Swoosh and Trooper decided to leave with the CSI team.

Back at the office, Trooper walked down the narrow starch white hall and heard the echoes from her black penny loafers. Just as she reached the evidence room, her cell phone rang. "This is Detective Trooper."

"There is a package for you that just came in," said Swoosh who was back at his desk.

"Who's it from?"

"The mailroom says it's addressed to 'Hanae Troop—Homicide Division'."

"Okay, I'll be up in a few."

She walked through the steel double doors of the evidence room. Trooper reached for the log book in order to sign-in and said, "I need case numbers 70028010 and 70028019." The clerk looked up at Trooper; and then he looked at her name on the log. "I'll be right back."

"Thank you . . . Ronald."

"How did you know my name?" As he walked backwards, he almost tripped over the trash can.

"I read your name on your badge," said Trooper.

He regained his footing and walked away with a smile. When he came back with a brown box with the numbers labeled on the side, he said, "Detective Troop, can you sign here please? This must be returned before 6pm."

"Sure Ronald."

"You seem to be very pragmatic."

"I want people to know that I take my work seriously. You seem to be the same way yourself."

"I really am." Not knowing if his timing was right, he decided to leap way out of his comfort zone. He continued, "Maybe we can do lunch some day."

"I'm very busy; however, I may be able to squeeze in a few minutes for coffee next week." Ronald saw this as a personal meeting; however, Trooper always knew that networking was a good thing and that it wouldn't hurt to get to know him better.

Ronald was now showing all of his pearly white teeth as Trooper turned to leave, "Call me when you can go; and coffee is on me." He said.

Trooper walked back down the narrow hall and sat the brown box down on her desk. Then she went a few feet away to the mailroom to retrieve her package.

The mailroom clerk said, "Hello Detective, I have your package right here." To his left, the clerk pulled the package off of the top shelf.

"Has it been cleared?" Trooper asked with a concerned look on her face.

"Yep, I cleared it myself." The clerk said with pride.

"Okay thanks."

As she walked back to her desk, she realized that the package was extremely light. Trooper sat the small package next to the evidence box on her desk. She pulled out her keys and cut through the tape. Pulling both flaps open very carefully, she looked inside the package; and there was a white letter envelope. She held the envelope to the light which showed a few squares the size of business cards. Opening the envelope, she saw the colors of the squares.

Swoosh walked up to her desk and asked, "What's in the box?" She gave him the envelope. "What are these silk squares for? Is there a letter with it?"

"No . . . not yet." Trooper put on a pair of plastic gloves from a box on her desk and pulled out each piece of fabric from the envelope. The colors were white, yellow, pink, red, brown and black.

Trooper opened the evidence box and pulled out the log sheet. As Trooper signed the sheet, Swoosh placed the zip lock bag with the Twyla Burke mug shot photos inside.

◊◊◊◊◊

Friday morning came quickly. Teco thought about all of the people he needed to contact before going out of town. He wanted to make sure that the club owners knew he wouldn't be in this weekend. First on his list was Legend; and then he decided to call Toi, because she told him if he ever changed his mind about kicking it with her to give her a call. For some reason, Toi stayed on his mind.

He located Legend's number on his Caller-ID. The phone rang twice before a female picked up. "Hello."

"Yes, this is Teco. May I speak with Legend please?" There was silence for a few minutes.

"Teco, what's up?" asked Legend.

"Nothing, just waking up, and you?"

"Getting some last minute things done. Can you be at my place by 3?"

"Sure I can. That's why I called you. What are the directions to your place?" Teco realized he knew the exact location of Legend's subdivision.

"Oh yeah, the female you spoke with is my sister. She likes you. So don't be taken aback if she's all in your grill this weekend—"

"One thing I don't do is mix business with pleasure."

"You didn't let me finish. She's my road manager."

"Oh, I see. Thanks for the heads up. I'll see you at 3."

"By the way, turn on Channel 5 News. What you see is going to trip you out. It's probably a good thing that we are leaving the city this weekend."

While Teco was at his townhouse turning on the television, Trooper was at her residence when the telephone rang. Exhausted from the long days and nights at work, she really wanted to turn over on the sofa and let it ring. "Hellooo," said Trooper trying to gain focus by rubbing her eyes.

"Hanea! Hanea!" No one called her by her first name unless she was in trouble.

"What? I'm here. What?"

"Get up partner and turn the T.V. to Channel 5. You've got to see this," said Swoosh.

Trooper sat up. "I'm reaching for the remote now. Hold on. Do we have another victim?"

"No, just look."

The News Reporter said, "We're here in Washington, D.C. at the U.S. Capitol lawn with almost 7,000 families and friends holding signs and protesting. They want male and female exotic dancing to be banded . . . ."

"Oh Shit! Swoosh, where are you?" asked Trooper jumping to her feet.

"At the office and you know who wants to see you."

"Yeah, I bet. Swoosh, get out of there and meet me at the Capitol in 30." As she put on her khaki pants, her right foot twisted in them almost making her fall to the floor.

Within a few minutes, she was in her car with the lights flashing. Even the D.C. Traffic Cops looked frustrated. Taxi drivers were blowing horns. Many pizza delivery shops resorted to using Bicycle Carriers. The sun was beaming; and the humidity made the air stuffy. The government's bureaucracy was one thing, but the roads where another. Trooper hit every street pot hole. Her neck was getting tense.

Trooper's thoughts were centered on The Paradox. *I wish this rally wasn't going on. The families of these dancers have the right to scream for justice. With the powers to be a stone's throw away, where else would they gain national attention? There is no place like this in the entire nation for political visibility. Will The Paradox show up?*

As she parked, she heard the crowd shouting, "Get different careers! Stop showing your rears! Get different careers! Stop showing your rears!" Shoulder to shoulder, the protesters made it difficult for anyone coming late to the rally to maneuver through the crowd.

Trooper looked to see if there was a crowd gathering in support of the dancers; however, there were none. The temperature was reaching 100 degrees. Because the air was musky, Trooper didn't know how much longer she could smell people who needed to go home and take baths. Relief was all over her face when she saw Swoosh, who found his partner quickly. They flashed their badges through the crowd making their way towards the platform to get a better view.

The police posted up on the outer perimeter giving the protesters protection and making sure things didn't get out of hand. The Paradox was right beside Trooper and Swoosh. The Paradox led the crowd in a new chant, "Stop the Killer! End this Thriller! Stop the Killer! End this Thriller!" Then Trooper and Swoosh reached the platform area. The Paradox felt a real boost of power for everyone's support of the rally. Up and down in the air, The Paradox's sign read, "NO ★ EXOTIC ★ DANCERS ★ NO ★ KILL." Putting down the sign, The Paradox picked up a Canon digital camera. Click! Click! Click! Click! Click! Pictures were taken of Trooper, who stared at the camera. For a moment, The Paradox felt recognized.

"What does the boss want with me?" asked Trooper, who was getting annoyed at the person who was taking pictures of her.

"The same as always, an update on the case," said Swoosh, who began to rub his forehead. Trooper pulled out a Snickers bar and moved to a different vantage point. Swoosh looked around to see if anyone stood out. To him, they all did.

"What did you tell Captain Wicker?" asked Trooper.

Swoosh looked at his partner as if she were crazy. "Do you have to ask?"

"It doesn't hurt to ask. I want to know what you said . . ."

The camera kept clicking until there was no more film. The Paradox moved to the edge of the U.S. Capitol lawn. *"This rally is too boring, let's take it up a notch."* The Paradox pulled a spider out of a tiny container from inside the camera bag and tapped the lady to the right and said, "Excuse me, you have a crab spider on your shoulder."

The woman yelled, "Help! Help! I'm going to die! I'm going to die!" She flicked her shoulder and the spider flew onto a man's head. The man looked like he was doing an African dance and exclaimed, "Ah Shit! Get this damn thing off of me!" The crowd went berserk. With limited room to move, people trampled on each other. Trooper tried to see what the commotion was all about. At that moment, she looked in the direction of the screaming and recognized someone she previously saw at Club Classic. Trooper tried to push through the crowd, but was penned in; therefore, she hopped up and down trying to get a better view.

The Paradox followed a group of people who were rushing to exit the U.S. Capitol lawn. Moving with the flow made it real easy to reach the car, which was several blocks away from the confusion. A Ticket Officer pulled up next to The Paradox's car to check the meter.

"Is there a problem sir?" asked The Paradox.

"Is this your car?" asked the Ticket Officer.

"Yes, it is."

"Well you're right on time."

"Yes, I am. Have a good day officer."

"You too."

From a distance, the Ticket Officer barely heard, "Stop that car! Stop that car! Get the tag number!"

The Paradox rushed into the car and slammed the door, hit the car in reverse and spun off. Trooper reached the Ticket Officer out of breath. When Trooper looked to the Ticket Officer for answers, there was no tag number because there was no parking ticket.

CHAPTER 11

As Teco cleaned his crib, he was thinking of ways to hype his stage performance. He recalled a dancer who used a contraption called a finger flash, which made fire come from his hand. Cutting the vacuum cleaner off, he pulled out the phone book to find a theatrical shop. When he located one, he inquired about other stage props they sold. Teco identified something that fit him well. In order to insure he was at Legend's house on time, he left one hour early to swing by the shop in Landover, Maryland.

After Teco was packed and ready, he got into the car and called Toi on her cell phone. "What's up girl?"

"Who is this?" asked Toi, as she put clothes in her suitcase.

"Rising Sun. You told me to give you a call."

"What took you so long? I've seen you perform a couple of times and you know how to touch me without lifting a finger." Her stance relaxed; and she felt aroused by the sound of his deep voice.

"Is that right?"

"You called to give me my own private party?" She asked digging his player spirit.

"No baby, I have to be out of town a few days. I wanted to see if you and I could get together next Friday night."

"Sure, call me. I'll have my tips ready," she said as she closed the suitcase.

Within the hour, Teco pulled into the driveway of Legend's crib in Kettering, Maryland. The yard was well manicured. In this neighborhood, the 3 story brick house floor plans were all the same; however, the exterior trim colors were different.

Neighbors were out either washing their cars or working in their yards. When Teco saw the curtains open, Legend's sister looked out of the window. "Whose Benz is that?" She asked.

Legend came to the window to look with her. "That's Teco, Lil Sis."

"Who is Teco?"

"Rising Sun, so you behave." They watched Teco put a blue cover over the car. Then Legend's sister went up to her room to freshen up to greet Teco. She believed that her DKNY Be Delicious perfume would do the trick.

"What's up Teco?" asked Legend. Teco stepped into the house and admired the elaborate home sound system, which was playing Kenny G's "Breathless" jazz album.

"Nothing man . . . Just chilling and ready to rock North Carolina."

Legend showed him where to put his bags. "I want you to meet my sister." She came down the stairs on cue; and Teco's mouth dropped wide open. Legend continued, "Teco, this is my sister Toi; and Toi, this is Teco."

Teco didn't know whether to be excited or to be cool. He decided to play it cool. "I thought you were a waitress?"

"I have a couple of gigs. I enjoy being a road manager the best of all." She said licking her highly glossed lips.

"Legend, I thought you said you didn't have a manager," said Teco, trying to put things together.

"Toi lines up my out of town gigs. I don't have the time to do it myself. You two know each other?"

"Not officially. Nice to meet you," said Toi.

"Yes, likewise," said Teco, who didn't understand the somber look on Toi's face; however, she was disappointed that Teco didn't show any excitement to see her.

◊◊◊◊◊

The two crime notes were on Trooper's desk. She saw the words white and pink. *"Why is The Paradox giving me colors?"*

She turned her focus to the computer display. *"There has to be something that I'm over looking. I know this Twyla Burke is aware that she's wanted for questioning. Is she still in town? Let me do a nationwide search for similar killings of any male exotic dancers."* Trooper entered several combinations of keywords and there was no match. "Shit!" exclaimed Trooper. *"I know this didn't start here in D.C.; so there has to be something."* She sat back in her chair. Things seemed to be going no where. She issued an APB (All Points Bulletin) for both Twyla Burke and Teco Jackson. Trooper wanted them in for questioning; and she wanted them now. Then she called Forensics. "Hey Linda, it's Trooper. About the victims in the G-String murders, can you tell me about how they died again? I mean in detail." Linda and Trooper worked together for the last two years. At times, they acted like sisters.

"Okay, let me pull the two cases up." Linda pushed a few keys and continued, "They were killed by Ligature Strangulation."

"Are they consistent with contusions or abrasions?" asked Trooper.

"Well, first you need to understand what occurs when a victim is strangled with the ligature technique."

"Please explain," said Trooper as she entered the words "ligature killings" in her keyword search.

"You have manual strangulation, which occurs when someone applies pressure to the victim's neck with a body part like a hand and constricts the airway. Then there is ligature strangulation, which occurs when someone tightens something around the neck. Trooper, all ligature strangulations are homicides."

Trooper wanted to say sarcastically, "No shit," but she decided against it, because she needed Linda's help. "Is this why the victims had bruised skin tissue around their necks?"

"Something like that. If the ligature is soft, there may be no marks; otherwise there may be a mark."

Trooper restated their conversation. "So in the G-String murder case, the G-Strings were the ligature and caused abrasions on the victims' necks, which shows how fiercely and successfully the victims struggled against the attacker . . . . Linda, one last question, do you think the attacker is a male or female?"

"Trooper from the look of the abrasions which show strong pressure, I would say a male or a female who works out everyday or lifts weights."

"That's what I thought myself," said Trooper who ended the call. The search on the words "ligature killings" came back with a hit. The article was titled: "Dying for Pleasure: Autoerotic Asphyxia." Trooper stood up and paced back and forth. "This is the craziest thing I've ever heard of."

"What did you say?" asked Swoosh, who came into the room and sat at his desk.

"I'm just going over a few things," said Trooper.

"Okay, hit me."

"We have to analyze the perpetrator's psyche. As you know, there are 3 categories of offenders: organized, disorganized and mixed."

"Why do I always feel like I'm in a remedial class when I'm with you?" asked Swoosh laughing. When he saw the serious look on Trooper's face, he said, "I think he is a mixed offender."

"Why?"

"Because a mixed offender leaves behind mixed messages at crime scenes. The Paradox is showing signs of planning and some sophistication as we put this puzzle together. Plus, I think he or she has violent fantasies."

"Couldn't The Paradox be a disorganized offender? After all, he or she appears to attack with sudden violence. The crime scene is messy and chaotic. Remember all of those condoms and whipped cream cans? Plus, The Paradox left the body at the scene."

"Yeah, but the condoms and whipped cream seemed staged to me. What about an organized offender? After all, The Paradox is showing control; and he or she took the time to prepare and write the note as well as buy the G-Strings. Each crime scene looks like a dress rehearsal for the next victim."

"I know that we will figure it out. Well, I heard your APB on the radio. I've found out Teco Jackson's new address; and I'm headed over to his house. Do you want to come along?"

◊◊◊◊◊

When Candi opened the door to leave her apartment, she saw lightning flash in the distance. So, she turned back into the foyer to grab her black umbrella. Because Candi grew up in the hood, she was always aware of her surroundings. When she was 12 years old, her mother enrolled her in self-defense and weight lifting classes, where she learned to always be on guard when out alone late at night.

Two guys from the apartment complex were sitting on the hood of a car engaged in deep conversation. A black cat crossed her path and she thought for a moment that she should just stay home for the evening. A few yards away she saw an unrecognized black Town Car. Because the windows were tinted, she couldn't make out the driver.

On the way to the Royal Palace Club, the Town Car still appeared to be tailing her from a distance. Her heart was racing; however, she knew the valet attendant at the club would valet park her car, which provided her some security. Upon arrival, red and blue lights illuminated the stucco building of the Royal Palace. After paying the valet attendant, Candi stepped onto the red carpet, which covered the area from the sidewalk to the club entrance. Everything was so peaceful outside. She wondered if anyone was inside the club.

When the bouncer opened the door for Candi, the music was bumping, which startled her. The club was packed with distinguished looking patrons. She looked up and saw a vintage crystal chandelier and 2 grand staircases, one to the left and another to the right. Shadow was on stage dancing to Barry White's song "Sweetness." Shadow was by far one of her favorite dancers. She liked his fresh explicit approach to dancing. Once she sat down at a private table, Shadow immediately saw her.

Candi was known to be a great tipper and he was going to make sure she left the club happy. During the bridge of the song, Shadow danced over to her table. His chest was bare; and the only thing he wore was a red necktie and a red G-String. Candi grabbed his necktie and pulled Shadow close to her and said, "You sling that thing as if you know what you are doing."

In character and with a deep Barry White voice, he said, "Believe me I do and I go real deep."

She touched the outside of his G-String; and Shadow asked, "You like the feel of that?"

"Is it all you?"

"Well, it's only one way to find out." Shadow kissed her on the cheek and moved to the next female. Candi chewed on her strawberry daiquiri straw watching Shadow move his hips in a circular motion. When he reached the far end of the club to another group of women, Candi got up and walked to the bar area where she could have a better look at the back of his G-String. She was disappointed because $1 bills covered most of his tight ass. When Shadow saw that Candi moved to the bar, he danced his way back over to her. He was surprised there was no tip from her yet. Shadow said, "You're giving me that enticing look again; I guess you didn't have enough and want some more. Huh?"

"Don't ask questions. Just work that body like a pro," said Candi.

"Oh shit, I like the way you talk. I guess you like to be in control." The ladies in the club were screaming for Shadow to come back over to their side of the club. Dollar bills were in the air like branches on an old pecan tree. The white spotlight, which was following Shadow across the room, turned red. On cue, Shadow turned to face the ladies and went into a split. The women cheered.

When he got back up, he turned back to Candi and asked, "Are you doing anything later after the show?"

"Well that depends if you tell me if it's all you."

Shadow took Candi's hand and slid her hand into his G-String to show her the answer. As her hand came back out, he looked down and there was a $100 tip. Shadow asked, "So does that mean that we're on for tonight?"

"I'll meet you outside after your set. Now go make that money." He liked the fact that she knew his role was to cater to all the women in the club. He was now the #1 dancer and the ladies asked for him by name. What he didn't know is that Candi enjoyed fantasizing about how he would move in bed. She couldn't wait to sleep with Shadow tonight.

Two hours after his show performance, Shadow held Candi's black umbrella as he escorted her to the front door of the Quality Inn hotel. Rain was pouring down; and they kept stepping into mud puddles because the parking lot was being resurfaced. Walking into the lobby drenched, he enjoyed watching her bare chest through her soaked white blouse. The effects from the rain put them in a primitive mood; and the sparks began to fly before the hotel room door closed.

After the fourth round, Shadow returned from the bathroom and fell backwards onto the bed. Candi liked the way the mattress and the pillows bounced, almost in slow motion. Shadow didn't know if he could hang with her any longer. She straddled him and moved her hips back and forth. He was trying to figure out a smooth way to ease out of the hotel room.

"Shadow, would you be upset if I left early?" asked Candi.

Not wanting to show any signs of relief, he said, "Damn Candi, we just got here a little over an hour ago. Do you have to jet so soon?"

"I need to go and get ready for work tomorrow. Maybe we can hook up later at my place," said Candi, who saw that he didn't have the stamina to continue. What Shadow didn't know was that Candi didn't have to work because she lived off of a family trust fund.

When she climbed out of the king size bed, Shadow reached over to touch her soft ass. Candi gave him a seductive smile on her way to the bathroom, where she freshened up and combed her hair. When she emerged from the bathroom, there was a zip lock bag in her hand. Shadow wanted to see what was in the bag; however, she held it in a way that prevented him from getting a good visual. Candi put the zip lock bag into her purse and turned to leave the room.

"I don't get a kiss before you jet?" asked Shadow.

"Yes, you can have a kiss." Candi walked over to the bed, planted a sweet little kiss on his lips, and left out of the room.

Shadow went into the bathroom to take a quick shower. As he stepped out to towel dry, there was a soft knock on the door. "Hold on Candi. I'm in the bathroom!" He shouted putting a white towel around his waist. On his way to the door, Shadow looked around the room to see what she left behind that would make her come back to the room. Sitting in the chair by the heater were Candi's earrings. He picked them up and opened the door.

When he saw a person standing there wearing a black mask, Shadow's eyes got big. Before he could say a word, Shadow was hit with a Black Cobra stun gun, pushing 600,000 volts into his whole body. The electrical charge instantly immobilized him causing a loss of balance and muscle control. The blast knocked Shadow to the ground. As The Paradox dragged Shadow back to the foot of the bed, the white towel came from around Shadow's body. Then he was handcuffed.

Putting water into a plastic cup from the bathroom sink, The Paradox went to the foot of the bed and threw the cold water into Shadow's face. "Huh, huh, huh," murmured Shadow, who began to gain focus of his senses. Wondering why he was on the floor, Shadow tried to pick himself up; however, he couldn't move because his hands were bound. Shadow asked, "What the—" The Paradox struck him in the face and then put on latex gloves. Shadow moved around in an impetuous manner becoming very rabid. "I've never done anything to you . . . . Why are you doing this to me? Why? Why?" asked Shadow who was trying his best to break free. When he saw a zip lock bag with a yellow G-String inside, Shadow became hysterical.

With force, The Paradox placed the yellow G-String around Shadow's neck. Shadow began to kick as The Paradox applied more pressure. As Shadow became less and less resistant, his body went limp. The Paradox carefully attached the note to the G-String and placed it on the pillow. This was the first time The Paradox became uneasy after a kill. On the way out, The Paradox unknowingly stepped on the white towel and left the room.

CHAPTER 12

Swoosh and Trooper pulled to the curb of Teco's townhouse. There was no car in the driveway and all of the blinds were closed. Trooper hit the release on her crimson and cream umbrella and rang the doorbell. There was an inpatient look on her face as they waited for several minutes knocking on the door. Then they heard, "Calling all cars to the Quality Inn near Wisconsin Avenue, we have a reported 10-27-1."

"Shit!" exclaimed Trooper who ran to the car and threw the umbrella in the backseat. Swoosh squeezed behind the driver's seat and turned on the blue lights. Traffic was clear; however, rain made driving visibility extremely poor. Swoosh knew that this police case was going to draw more attention to the homicide department.

When they arrived, there were 5 police cars on the premises. The Front Desk Clerk directed them to the room. As Trooper looked at the crime scene from the doorway, she asked Linda, "Is The Paradox becoming infuriated about something?"

"This doesn't look good," said Linda.

"No homicide looks good if you ask me," replied Swoosh. "Don't look now but you know who is coming in 5, 4, 3, 2—"

"Detective Trooper and Detective Brown, I need to see the both of you outside now!" yelled Captain Wicker.

Trooper said, "Sir, we're in the middle of a crime scene, and I just—"

"Detective Troop, you are this close to being pulled off of this case." He said holding his index finger towards her face and glaring at her with sheer frustration.

Trooper told the CSI team to carefully handle the white towel with the shoe print; and she walked carefully out of the room not to disturb any evidence. They followed Captain Wicker to the far end of the floor, so no one could hear him. "Detectives, you both have been ignoring my request to meet, which shows me that you have no regards for WHO I AM! I directly told you to report to me the findings of this case." Sweat was popping from his forehead.

"Sir, we are doing all that we can to solve this case. You're not out here in the field day in and out coming up with dead end leads. I am. Now if you don't mind, I have a crime to solve and—"

"Detective Troop, you are good at what you do; however, you're not showing any progress. If you don't have something to me by Friday, I'm giving the case over to the Feds. Let me break it down for you. WE ARE LOOKING BAD! Now go solve this case. You are dismissed."

Walking towards what seemed to be a road block, she knew that this crime scene must be the missing link. Was she overlooking something right before her eyes? Or did she need to turn on the high beams to see the clues on the road? "Shit! Shit! Shit! Shit!" She exclaimed as she pumped her right fist into the palm of her left hand.

"Calm down," said Swoosh, who was rubbing his forehead.

They walked back into the room. Linda was aligning numbered cards next to objects and snapping pictures.

"Where is it?" asked Trooper.

"#1 on the pillow," said Linda.

Trooper walked over to the pillow and saw the yellow G-String with the note attached. Before she could ask, Swoosh passed her the plastic gloves.

```
W
   P        H          I
             I      K
                 E
                     Y
       I        L  T  W
 L
       O N         E

               - The Paradox
```

"This is really ticking me off," said Trooper, who reached for her radio. "We have a 10-27-1. BOLO for Twyla Burke. I repeat; be on the lookout for Twyla Burke."

"Good. Now that we have notified the department of the homicide, let's head back to the clubs tonight," said Swoosh.

"How do we even know this guy was a dancer?" asked Trooper.

"Check out item #3 that Linda marked in the bathroom," said Swoosh.

Trooper stepped to the doorway of the bathroom and saw a red necktie and a red G-String on the floor.

The alarm clock in the Asheville North Carolina Marriott read 4:30pm. Teco woke up drained from the flight and the drive from Greenville, South Carolina to Asheville. The late Friday night performance at the Platinum Plus club was exhausting. The women in Asheville acted as if they were at the theatre, because they wanted encore after encore. He needed to get up out of the hotel bed because he wanted some water. Before his left foot touched the floor, the phone rang. "Hello," said Teco in a sleepy voice.

Legend asked, "Teco, where you been? I've been calling you all day."

"I was knocked out man."

"Are you dressed yet?"

Teco looked down at himself, "No, why?"

"Look, get dressed and meet me in the lobby. It's time to go back to the club."

Immediately, after Teco put the phone on the receiver, the phone rang again. "Hello."

"Teco, are you dressed?" asked Toi.

"No, why are you asking?" He was still sitting on the edge of the bed.

"I was just letting you know that I'm ready to smoke a joint. So once you get dressed come to my room."

"Baby girl, I appreciate the invite; however, I've been clean for almost a month."

"Don't you remember the feeling and how good the sex was when you smoked?"

"I have to get dressed for a show." Letting his answer hang in the air, Teco stood up to stretch. "I'll see you in the lobby."

Toi hung up the receiver and was sitting at the desk in her hotel room not knowing what to say next. This was a big let down because she thought Teco was warming up to her advances.

Just as Teco reached the lobby, Legend looked at his watch and said, "We better get going to the club. Where in the hell is Toi?" Teco looked up to see if he could see Toi coming out of her room, since the lobby was open all the way up to the top floor. The only thing he saw was the Housekeeping staff cleaning rooms. When a few toddlers ran through the lobby, Teco saw Toi walking down the lobby hall.

He could tell by the look in her eyes that she never lit up that joint, which was a major turn on for him. When she stood beside Teco, he playfully put his arm around her neck and she laughed. "Baby girl you know, you are alright with me," said Teco.

As they walked to the car, Teco remembered the days when he sold drugs hand to hand in West Philadelphia and Conshohocken for the SB Crew. He witnessed how drugs turned crack fiends into vagabonds and how sexual relationships were devalued as a result. His SB drug boss, Bashi was a great person and taught Teco about the finer things in life. Since GQ killed Bashi, Teco finally decided that he wasn't going out like that. Today doing the right thing felt good. At first, Teco quit smoking weed for Rasheeda; but today, he officially quit smoking pot and doing drugs for Teco.

◊◊◊◊◊

Now that GQ was living in the free world with Travis and Gwen, she needed to get a new hair style to go with her vogue look. GQ wanted to look her best for Travis. So, she decided to go to the beauty shop where Bashi's old girlfriend, Tammy, worked as a stylist. As GQ drove in Gwen's Acura Legend down Ogontz Avenue, the neighborhood looked the same. She felt her heart beating strongly because she didn't know how she would be received by the people in the salon. Returning from prison back into society was a very difficult transition. Though Gwen and Travis D. were there for her, GQ felt as though she was starting her life over from scratch. When she reached the shop, GQ parked in the front. When she looked in the driver's mirror, her hair looked a hot mess. Walking up to the receptionist desk, she asked, "May I get my hair done today?"

"Sure, we accept walk-ins. Go downstairs and have a seat. The next available stylist will do your hair."

As she walked down the steps, she remembered the last time she and Teco, a.k.a. Homicide, rode together after leaving this same salon. The entire basement was remodeled. Each stylist station was equipped with a long mirror and black shampoo bowl. The walls were yellow and the trim was black. GQ must have been looking around too long, because all eyes were on her once she took a seat. She tried her best not to think about Homicide or Tammy.

A stylist asked, "Yeah girl, can I help you?"

"Yeah, I need a relaxer and a cut," said GQ rubbing softly across her hair.

"Okay, we got you. It will be just a few minutes," said the stylist, who was cutting her current client's hair with the precision of the Master Stylist, Tippi Shorter. All the women stared at GQ and many were whispering. She picked up an Ebony Magazine to see if she could find a hair style she liked. When all the attention seemed to be off of her, GQ looked over the edge of the magazine and saw Tammy putting hair spritz on her client. GQ was trying to decide what she was going to say to Tammy in the form of some explanation as to why she was out of prison. However, GQ didn't know where to begin. No one would believe her any way. GQ closed her eyes and prayed, "Lord, please help me through this. I need—"

"Excuse me. Hey girl . . ." The stylist tapped GQ on the arm in order to lead GQ to the styling chair.

When GQ looked up, Tammy was gazing at her. "Do I know you from somewhere?" asked Tammy spinning her client around in the chair to look into the mirror.

"No, I don't think so," said GQ who walked past Tammy's station.

When GQ sat down, the stylist frowned as she felt GQ's brittle hair. "Child, when was the last time you had a deep conditioner?"

"It's been a long time." When the stylist began to apply the relaxer, GQ closed her eyes and allowed herself to relax. Feeling her neck against the shampoo bowl felt awkward; and GQ slowly readjusted to the curve of the sink. While GQ sat under the dryer, the stylist noticed that GQ was asleep. The hour flew by; and before she knew it, GQ's hair was now shoulder length and cut into a long layered haircut. Looking into the mirror, GQ shook her head and her hair flowed freely from side to side.

Tammy said, "That's a tight haircut. Look's good on you. It's something about you. Damn, I can't put my finger on it." GQ's heart started to beat fast again. She tipped her stylist well. Tammy continued, "Girl, you sure we haven't met somewhere before?"

Playing it off as if she was trying to figure out where they might have met before, GQ said, "I'm sorry but—"

"Tammy, you think you know everybody," said GQ's hair stylist. So GQ took the clear shot and walked up the steps to leave. As she stepped onto the curb, GQ heard cat calls for the first time in years. This extra male attention encouraged her to walk as if she were modeling her own line of clothes. She smiled at them as she started the car.

GQ knew she was getting back into the swing of things when the turn onto Williams Avenue came so naturally. As she came up to the old SB crib, she slowed down to give Bashi some thought. While avoiding Conshohocken, she continued on to Main Street in Norristown where she reflected back on the day that Homicide beat the shit out of Trey because of money Trey owed Bashi. Then GQ turned into the St. Patrick's Cemetery.

"May I help you ma'am?" asked the middle-aged cemetery groundskeeper.

"Yes you can. I'm looking for the lot of Mujaheed Bashi Fiten," said GQ.

"Just a minute." The groundskeeper pulled out a large book and thumbed through the pages with the precision of a librarian. "Okay, Mujaheed Bashi Fiten is in lot 317 north end."

"Can you please show me which way that is?"

"Sure I can," said the groundskeeper coming from behind the counter and walking with crutches because one leg was missing.

"Oh, I'm sorry. You didn't have to move."

"No don't be. I get around just fine; and it's no bother." They went outside and he pointed to where the north end started. "The lots are in sequential numbers. So it will be easy to find. It should be on the left side of the road."

"Thank you kindly." She drove what felt like a city block until she saw 317. As she stood at the tombstone, GQ said, "Hello Bashi, you have some beautiful roses here." There were fresh blue roses at his grave site. She knelt down and took a deep whiff, because red roses were the only color she knew. However, the blue rose smelled exactly the same. She stood up and saw that no one was around.

"Bashi, I'm sorry that I missed your home going ceremony. I really wanted to be there. During that time I was running for my life because . . ." Tears ran down her eyes and her mascara began to streak. " . . . because I was accused of killing you. I . . . I tried to talk with Homicide when he got out of jail." She paced back and forth in front of his grave, stopped to face the small tombstone, and said with conviction, "I told you that he wasn't good enough to protect you and SB. In fact, he put me away for life; but you know me, I bucked up out of that. Your spirit must have been riding with me." Her sinister look was undeniable. "Don't worry; I'm going to get his ass. Then I'll find out who did this to you." She said pounding her hand in her fist. When she thought she heard footsteps, her look softened and she said, "After paying Homicide back, I'll put the street life behind me. I promise."

GQ bowed her head with her eyes closed and sobbed. She felt someone walk up and hold her right hand; however, she was too afraid to open her eyes. In GQ's heart she was hoping the person was Gwen. When the person spoke, she knew immediately who it was. The voice said, "I knew you would be here. I've been trying to find you for months. I didn't know how to get added to your phone list or how to get your address." The person held GQ's hand a little tighter. "About 6 months ago, I heard word on the streets from a reliable source that you didn't kill Bashi; however, you were at the house when he was murdered. Don't you remember anything that happened that day?" GQ cried out loud and wiped the tears from her cheeks; however, she still couldn't find the courage to look up. The person continued, "GQ, I believe you didn't kill him." At that moment, GQ looked up and saw Bashi's old girlfriend Tammy; and they embraced each other for the first time as mutual friends.

The groundskeeper drove up in a golf cart and said, "Hi Tammy, the blue flowers you put on Mr. Fiten's grave are beautiful. I think they will last longer than the purple mums you put out last time. I was just checking in on this beautiful young lady to see if she was alright. She's been here a while now."

"Yes, I'm fine. Spending time with friends." said GQ.

◊◊◊◊◊

For the rest of the weekend, Legend could see the chemistry between Teco and Toi, who learned that playing a subtle approach worked best in getting to know Teco. Even though Teco earned $2,500 in tips over the weekend by entertaining the women at the club, Teco gave Toi his undivided attention off of the stage.

At 5 o'clock in the afternoon on Monday, Legend, Teco, and Toi pulled up to Legend's crib. Teco pulled the cover off of his Benz and removed the things out of Legend's SUV. As Teco popped the trunk, Toi walked up beside him. When he looked into her eyes, she gave him the most sensual kiss he received in years. He explored her mouth with his tongue and she reciprocated. Legend saw a car a block away and cleared his throat. Toi and Teco let go of the embrace.

A pearl toned Lexus pulled up behind Teco's Benz. As he looked to see who was in the car, Toi walked to speak to the driver and bent over in the car to kiss the person in the car on the cheek.

"Tyler, can you back up so one of our dancers can get out?" asked Toi.

Teco stared down the person in the car. *"Damn, who is that dude?"*

"Sure baby," responded Tyler, who parked the car on the curb.

"Teco, before you leave let me talk with you," said Toi with her hands on her hips.

"Sure, what's up?" asked Teco with an irritated look on his face. "Tyler's just an old boyfriend. You know how it goes."

"Well, I can't check you like you're mine," said Teco opening the car door and pulling out his Ray Ban sunglasses from the visor.

"How about we have dinner some time?" Toi asked Teco.

"I'll think about it and call you." Teco closed the door and started the ignition. Toi backed away not knowing how to ask Teco to stay, especially with Tyler at the house.

Teco slowly backed out of the driveway. As he pulled into the street, Teco looked at Toi, licked his bottom lip, and blew her a sensual kiss. When Tyler saw this, he looked to see Toi's response. Toi stood there still not knowing what to do. Tyler decided to walk up to the Benz and find out who was inside; however, he was too late. All Tyler saw was the rear license plate that read, "TECO."

CHAPTER 13

O nce Teco reached his townhouse, he headed straight to his bedroom and turned on the television to the 6 o'clock news, which was reporting an apartment fire. He needed to be at The Mirage by 7. He went into his walk-in closet and pulled out a gold satin shirt with a tie to match and a black pair of wide legged linen pants. On his shoe rack were the black silk woven dress shoes he decided to wear tonight. He knew he would stand out in the crowd. After he showered, he dressed and put the tie around his neck without tying it up. He grabbed his car keys and cell phone. Then he heard the television announcement. " . . . This is breaking news. The latest G-String murder victim has been identified as James Smith. He was a male exotic dancer in the D.C. area with the stage name of Shadow. His last performance was at the Royal Palace. Anyone with information related to this case is asked to call . . ."

Teco drove to The Mirage in a daze. He couldn't believe what he heard. This was the third dancer to be murdered. Perhaps dancing was just as dangerous as living on the streets. He made a mental note to be extra careful. As the valet attendant parked Teco's Benz, the owner of The Mirage walked out of his office smiling from ear to ear.

Tonight was ladies night and the club would be packed with gorgeous women with lots of money. The club owner stood by the front door as the ladies walked into the club. His ritual was to pick out the best looking female from the crowd and offer her free drinks for the evening. He made his claim early; because once the dancers performed, all bets were off for other men in the club.

As the owner scoped out the line, a knockout woman walked her fine ass through the door. She wore black stiletto heels and her calves were shaped to perfection. The skin tight red dress complimented her walk as her hand softly touched her inner thigh. The Mirage owner's eyes were glued to every bounce of her round bottom. Then he saw her magnificent face, which he believed Leonardo da Vinci would do anything in order to come back to life to paint. Then he said, "Hi Candi, drinks are . . . are . . . on me tonight. Meet . . . meet . . . me at my office after the show."

"Sure, I'd like that." She said and tapped him on his tight ass.

Before his body responded, the light bulb went off. *"I think Candi is that Burke person the detectives asked me about."* He immediately left the lobby and went into his office to find the business card. The phone rang 3 times and then the voicemail came on. He hung up and tapped his fingers impatiently on the desk for a few minutes. Then he redialed the number.

"Detective Troop, may I help you?"

"Hello, this is the owner from The . . . The . . . Mirage."

"Yes, I remember you. Any news?"

"That female you . . . you questioned me about . . . The one I said looked like one . . . one . . . of my customers . . ."

Trooper sat up straight in her chair and asked, "Yes, what about her?"

"That customer I talked about is here at the club tonight."

"Okay, thank you for calling. Keep an eye on her until I get there."

"Sure no problem."

Back at a table near the bar, Candi, Rasheeda and Yvette were having apple martinis. Rasheeda said, "Girl, Teco ain't shit . . . . He left my ass at the IBEX when they were shooting the other night." Tears formed in Rasheeda's eyes.

"I told you he was no good from the beginning. That's why you should have left his ass, when he became a dancer," said Yvette defiantly.

"I stuck by him when he was connected to that shit in Philly. When he came to D.C., he was talking like a thug. Now I have him speaking the King's English." Rasheeda said wiping the water from the corner of her eye with her left middle finger. She added, "I was his woman when he was catching the bus. Vette, didn't you see his car when he came over? Now, he has the balls to tell me that he has his own crib . . . ."

"Damn girl, he got it like that?" asked Yvette passing Rasheeda a small cocktail napkin to dry her tears.

"I was the one who put his ass on the map when he started dancing. I bought him his first outfit," said Rasheeda taking another sip of her apple martini.

"What kind of car does he have?" asked Yvette.

"A black Benz," said Candi. Rasheeda and Yvette looked at Candi astonished that she knew the make of the car.

"It has leather seats and wood paneling," said Rasheeda blowing her nose.

"Girl, stop lying," said Yvette.

"I rode in it last week," said Rasheeda.

"You mean to tell me that he had the nerve to let you ride in his Benz to the club, but couldn't drive you home?" asked Yvette who crossed her arms.

"Duh, there were bullets in the air. Who is going to wait on your ass to give you a ride?" asked Candi. Rasheeda and Yvette gave Candi a cold look.

"Hell, I should key his shit," said Rasheeda angrily.

"Girl, you better be careful because a man will kill you over his mobile dick," said Candi. Then all 3 of them laughed.

Rasheeda felt better; however, she wasn't going to let it go that easily. "I'm looking for his ass to come into the club tonight . . . ."

The way Rasheeda and Yvette's chairs were positioned at the table, only Candi could see Rising Sun, who walked into the club already in character. Candi's eyes were on him like a hawk ready to swoop down and take him to her nest. She licked her lips to taste the sweet residuum of the apple martini.

When Candi overheard the word "Detective," she immediately turned around and saw 2 detectives and 1 police officer at the bar.

"I'm Detective Brown and this is my partner Detective Troop," said Swoosh to the bartender. "We are here to speak to the owner about the G-String Murders. You might have known the victims as Polo, Ebony Wood, and Shadow . . ."

Candi's heart started to pound in her chest. *"Oh Shit! I have to get out of here. They will know by now that I've been with all 3 of these guys. I've got to vamoose from this joint."*

The bartender looked at Trooper's badge. "He's in his office waiting for you." Trooper and Swoosh headed in the direction of the office.

Candi stood up almost knocking the table and drinks over. "Girl, what the hell is wrong with you?" asked Yvette.

"I've got to run," said Candi taking the last swig of her apple martini.

"Sit down. We just got here," said Rasheeda.

"Later," said Candi, who pushed one man so hard that his beer spilled on his shirt. Candi saw Toi, who was working as a bar waitress; however, Candi didn't speak and accidentally stepped on Toi's foot.

"Damn Candi, where you going so fast?" asked Toi.

Candi said, "Shh!!! Be quiet Toi." Candi ran out of the club, got into her car and hit the gas. She never saw the black Town Car, which was tailing her.

Back inside the club, the owner, Trooper, and Swoosh walked out of the office. The owner said, "Candi is sitting with her friends." He pointed to the table. "Shit! She's gone."

"I thought I asked you to keep an eye on her," said Trooper.

"Sorry Detective, my . . . my . . . my liquor order was late and I had to make a call. I gave them complimentary drinks. I thought that would keep . . . keep them occupied for a while."

"Damn!" exclaimed Trooper. "Is Teco Jackson, a.k.a. Rising Sun, here tonight?"

"Yes, he . . . he . . . he should be here. He's performing tonight. Let's go over to the . . . the table where Candi was seated." They walked up to the table and the owner said, "Hey . . . hey ladies, where did Candi go?"

"She left like a bat out of hell," said Rasheeda taking a sip of her drink with her pinky extended.

"Officer!" yelled Trooper. "Please go with the owner outside and see if you can find Twyla Burke."

"What next?" asked Swoosh.

"Let's find Teco Jackson before he leaves the club. We can't loose both of them."

Pressing their way through a crowd of women at the opposite end of the bar, Swoosh and Trooper found Rising Sun as the bartender passed him a drink. Trooper asked, "Excuse me, Teco Jackson?"

He turned and faced the two badges and asked, "Yes, how may I help you?"

"We need to talk to you in private," said Trooper.

"Sure come with me." They followed him to a private lounge area. The peach walls with a horizontal black stripe in the center were appealing to the eyes. Rising Sun picked up the remote and clicked off the big screen television, which was built into the wall next to an empty wet bar. Then he put his drink on the S-shaped glass table. They immediately noticed that his body language transitioned from Rising Sun back to Teco Jackson. Trooper was impressed, because going in and out of character was extremely hard for some professional actors. "Okay you have 15 minutes because I have to get dressed for the show." Teco took a seat and crossed his legs like a smooth brother with class.

Swoosh spoke first. "Can you please state your name?" Trooper was analyzing Teco's facial expressions to see if he showed any signs of guilt. However, she found him to be quite relaxed and even charming. His eye contact was strong.

"I am Teco Jackson; however, my stage name is Rising Sun."

"How long have you been dancing?" asked Swoosh.

"I started this year."

"Where were you this weekend?" asked Swoosh.

"I was in Asheville, North Carolina doing a show. Is this an interview or something?" asked Teco scratching his head and smoothing his waves back out. He sat on the edge of the chair.

"Mr. Jackson, we are investigating the G-String murders. Are you familiar with the case?" asked Trooper.

"Only what I've seen on television or heard around the clubs," said Teco with a concerned look.

"Do you know this woman?" asked Swoosh pulling out a photo of Twyla Burke from the surveillance cameras at the Quality Inn.

"Yes, I've seen her around . . . ."

"This is a picture of a business card that was taken off of Robert Anderson, whom you might know as Ebony Wood. Can you tell me how he got it?" asked Swoosh passing Teco the picture.

"Sure—"

"Do you mind if we tape this conversation?" asked Trooper pulling out a tape recorder from her bag.

"That's fine with me," said Teco with the look of innocence. "Ebony Wood liked a dance move that I performed and asked to see how I perfected that move. He requested a business card before he left the club that night. Am I a suspect?"

"We have no reason to believe you are a suspect at this time. However, we did want to speak with you. Would you feel better going down to the station?"

"No need. What else you got?" Teco leaned back in the chair.

"Did you know Twyla Burke, a.k.a. Candi, from Conshohocken?" Teco's eyes lit up. "Did you ever sell drugs in West Philly and the Conshohocken area?" asked Trooper.

Teco sat at the edge of the chair again and rubbed his hands together, because they were getting sweaty. "Hell no, I don't know Candi. Why do you think that?"

"Records show that Twyla Burke's family is known for selling drugs in the same area you testified about during the trial of Mujaheed Bashi Fiten."

Teco stood up infuriated at the mention of Bashi. He wanted Bashi's memory to be about all the good things Bashi did to take people off of the streets and not about the drugs. "I said I don't know her. Believe me, I had no problem turning in Bashi's killer whom I knew and I sure don't have any alliance to Candi to protect her ass."

"Calm down, Mr. Jackson," said Swoosh. "Have a seat. We are just asking a few questions. D.A. Brown told us that you were extremely helpful in the Fiten case; and he told us that you would be helpful to us." At the mention of D.A. Brown's name, Teco sat down. Swoosh continued, "We're just trying to piece together a puzzle. We have information that leads us to believe that Candi is looking for someone who snitched on something that happened in Philly. Do you know if you are the snitch that Twyla is after?"

Teco was having heart palpitations and his breathing became short. "Are you kidding me? I turned in Gail Indigo Que. I don't know anything about Twyla what's her name. And trust me, if I knew I would tell you."

"Mr. Jackson, I am a good judge of character. After speaking with you, I don't think you are a suspect. However, I think we should take you into protective custody," said Trooper.

"Are you serious?" asked Teco rubbing the sweat from his forehead. "I am not going to be held hostage by you or Candi. Your concern is unjustified. It's a coincidence." He stood up and added, "I've started my life over. I have a legitimate job, a car, a home. I don't even smoke nor sell drugs anymore. I don't need any damn protection. I need all of you to leave me the hell alone." Teco stormed out of the room almost knocking over the brown drink tray, which Toi was holding.

"What's wrong with you?" asked Toi.

"I've got to get dressed," said Teco with an austere look on his face.

"Let me walk with you and we can talk. You have to change your mood before the show. You're acting like Teco and not

Rising Sun." Toi said putting down the tray and racing down the hall to catch up with him.

Back in the private lounge, Trooper asked Swoosh, "What do you think?"

"I think we need to watch him a little harder. What about you?"

"Well, he didn't give any incriminating responses that would link him to the crimes. However, we will keep an eye on him. I think it's more than a coincidence. He's known as a snitch on the streets of Philly. I just don't understand why these innocent people have to die. Is Twyla Burke weeding out Mr. Jackson?"

Trooper and Swoosh walked around the club observing the patrons. All the women were seated waiting for the next act. Trooper wondered if Rising Sun could pull it together for his performance. She heard the M.C. say, "Testing . . . Testing . . . We have a special performance for you tonight. Our next dancer is rising to the #1 position across the D.C. area. Women dream to be with him. Men want to be him. Laaadies put your hands together for Risssing Sunnn!" The lighting crew took the stage to black. Out of no where, a ball of fire went 5 feet into the air while producing a loud bang. The fire lit up the room; and Rising Sun ripped off his shirt in the glow. "Let's Get it On" by Marvin Gaye sounded throughout the building. All the ladies rushed towards the stage singing the lyrics and waving money in the air.

CHAPTER 14

After leaving The Mirage, Candi's breathing was shallow as she tried to decide which direction to travel. Observing her surroundings, the clear night sky made the stars and moon illuminate like a celestial art show. Through her rearview mirror, Candi saw what appeared to be the same black Town Car, which tailed her before. *"Damn! Now what do I do?"* For sure, she knew going back to her apartment was out of the question. A Washington Metrobus a few blocks ahead was in the same lane; and Candi decided to quickly pass the bus and cut a hard right onto the upcoming street. A Marriott hotel was in the same direction across the horizon. *"If I can loose this car, I'll check-in at that hotel for a few days. I need time to think about my next move."*

After making the right turn, the Town Car was still following her. *"Shit!"* Candi's left eye was twitching as she contemplated on her next maneuver. The Town Car pulled up close to her bumper; however, when she looked back again into the rearview mirror, she saw the Town Car make a right turn into a BP gas station. *"Whew! That was too close."* A block away Candi pulled into the Marriott hotel's parking garage. Rushing inside the lobby, Candi almost tripped on the carpet just as she reached the front desk.

"Hello, do you have a vacancy tonight?" asked Candi adjusting her shoe back onto her foot. She liked the fresh bouquet of purple orchids and pink lilies, which sat on top of the wood veneer counter. She reached into the class bowl and pulled out a peppermint. On the wall behind the Front Desk Clerk where clocks displaying several time zones around the world. The ambiance of the room appeared to calm Candi down.

"Yes, we have rooms. How may I help you?" asked the Front Desk Clerk, who was smiling as if she hit the lottery.

"I need a suite for 1 week. Is that possible?"

The clerk punched the keys with precision. "Miss, are you okay? You seem out of breath."

"I'll be fine. I just need to get out of these heels and into my room as soon as possible."

"Sure, here we go. I have a room with a king size bed, sofa bed, conference table, and wet bar. How does that sound?"

"Fabulous," said Candi breathing a deep sigh of relief. She also observed that she was the only guest in the lobby.

"Your name?"

"Kendra Blake."

"How will you be paying?" Candi reached inside her purse and pulled out a wad of cash.

Thirty minutes later, the driver of the Town Car was still parked at the BP Station and dialed 411 on the cell phone.

"411 Info, may I help you?" asked the operator.

"Yes ma'am. May I have the Marriott hotel in Crystal City, Virginia?

"Sure, I'm connecting your call. Thank you for calling 411 Info."

The phone rang 5 times before a male hotel operator answered. "Thank you for calling the Marriott Crystal City. How may I help you?"

"Yes, please connect me to a hotel guest named Twyla Burke."

"Just a minute sir." Elevator music played Beethoven's 5th Symphony for 2 minutes. "I'm sorry. We don't have a Twyla Burke registered with us."

"Are you sure? I just saw her pull into the hotel parking lot over a half hour ago."

"Hold on, let me call the front desk . . . . We have no Burke's listed," said the operator.

"Okay, thank you."

The driver of the Town Car drove into the Marriott parking garage and scanned for Candi's car, which was on the third level. Getting out of the Town Car, the driver popped the trunk where there was a black bag with all kinds of high tech military equipment inside. To the right of a covert 38" gun case was a small silver padded trunk that contained a handheld tracking scanner with a 2 inch display terminal. The device sounded after Crystal City Virginia was entered on the keypad. Chirp! Chirp! Within minutes, black, green and yellow lines appeared on the screen. Next to the handheld device was a magnetic transmitter with an antenna. The driver put on latex gloves to clean the transmitter off with a white cloth. Confirming that the coast was clear, the driver slipped under Candi's car.

◊◊◊◊◊

The next week, Teco lined up a set at a new club called the Oak Tree in Oxen Hill, Maryland. Seeing the advertisement for his performance on the side of a Metrobus and in windows of upscale salons made his ego soar. There was no way he was going to be late. So, he arrived early in order to meet with the manager before his set.

Walking into the club, Rising Sun headed to the bar, which was straight ahead. To his right, the stage and dance floor were outlined with white lights. To the left, he saw people getting hors d'oeuvres from the buffet line. Outside was a huge 2 level deck, where couples sat at 2 chair dinner tables. After reaching the bar, Teco nodded at Trooper, who was speaking with one of the waitresses.

Trooper was on this mission of her own and knew that Swoosh would be livid with her if he found out she was investigating solo without backup. Because Rising Sun was performing tonight, Trooper was hoping that Twyla Burke would show up; and if she did, Trooper was ready to take her ass down. Observing that an unrecognized female was sneaking up behind Rising Sun,

Trooper placed her hand on Sunshine because she knew that Rising Sun was still a potential victim.

"Rising Sun can I take some pictures of you?" asked the female fan.

"Whoa! Next time don't walk up on me like that." She really scared him shitless. "Sure, you can take the picture," said Rising Sun taking the toothpick out of his mouth. When she started to take picture after picture, he said, "That's enough." Trying his best to get away from her, Rising Sun headed for the manager's office to sign in for the evening. He never expected to see Rasheeda, who walked up to him out of no where.

"Teco, you are nothing but a dog." Rasheeda said with her hands on her hips.

"What are you talking about?" He asked trying not to look upset. The ladies in the club turned around when they heard Rasheeda's loud voice. Even the people at the buffet bar stopped putting food on their plates to focus on who was the female raising havoc.

"You're nothing but a freak ass dog worth nothing." Rasheeda said as she rolled her eyes.

"Rising Sun, you can freak me any time!" screamed a woman at the buffet bar. Rasheeda couldn't believe what she heard. She realized that she couldn't say anything to embarrass him at the clubs, because the women would protect his ass.

"Rasheeda, I think you need to chill out, because you're really lunchin'.'" As he walked away, she was right behind him. The bouncer was observing the entire scene and asked, "You're Rising Sun right?"

"Yeah, that's me," said Teco.

"You want me to handle this for you?"

"No, she's my old girl. She'll be alright."

Rising Sun proceeded towards the manager's office until he heard a voice say, "I thought you told me that you didn't need any protection." He turned around and was very shocked to see Detective Troop following him.

"So, is this business or pleasure?" He asked with a sexy smile.

Trooper took a few steps back and said, "Well that all depends."

"And what might that depend on?" asked Rising Sun with charisma.

"Let's see . . . . If I end up arresting one of these women for harassing you, then it's business. On the other hand if I don't, then I guess I'll enjoy the show." When she patted him on the back, he was trying to decide if the touch was cordial or sensual. She was a very difficult woman to read.

"Well, get a front row seat," said Rising Sun to Trooper. Rasheeda kept her eyes on Trooper and Rising Sun as she sat back down at the table with Yvette.

"Girl he looks good tonight," said Yvette.

"I wonder why he dresses more sophisticated. He looks like he is making some good money now," said Rasheeda hoping that her charade didn't tick him off.

"Girl, I did't think dancers made good money," said Yvette.

The M.C. walked onto the stage with the microphone as the medley of "How Deep Is Your Love" sung by Luther Vandross played in the background. In a deep sexy voice the M.C. asked, "Laaadies, are you ready to see some beefff?"

"Yeaaah!" At their response, The M.C. did a smooth James Brown dance turn on stage. On cue, the ladies screamed and waved money in the air.

Trooper was on the prowl searching stealthily for Twyla Burke. With no luck, Trooper posted in the back of the club where she could also watch the show.

"Okay, Laaadies! With no further ado, let's bring on our first dancer, who is climbing the charts to the #1 position in the dance clubs across the east coast. Put your hands together for Risssing Sunnn!"

Trooper still couldn't believe how the women actually desired to have Rising Sun. As he danced, the women reached for him. Rising Sun was surprised to see that Rasheeda was at the edge of the stage to tip him. The D.J. did a smooth transition from the medley to the song "Uh Ah" by Boyz II Men. The ladies threw money onto the stage.

On cue with the chorus, Rising Sun reached into the audience for a lady, who was wearing a black body suit and a long black skirt that flared at the bottom. After he led her on stage, she bent gracefully backwards. Rising Sun put his hands on her waist and lifted her into the air. When she pointed her toes like a professional ballerina, the audience immediately knew that she was a part of his performance. As she came down from the air, her body wrapped around his left side, then to his right side, and finally through his legs. After she limberly stood up, she snatched off his pants and with soft ballerina hands in the air exited the stage.

Trooper finally realized what the women saw in Rising Sun. He was more intimate with his performances than the other dancers. His eye contact seemed genuine. She even wished that she were the woman in the flowing skirt, lifted by a strong handsome man who knew how to elevate a woman and not let her fall.

The M.C. continued, "Ladies, if you want Rising Sun at your table, put your hands in the air!"

As hands went up all over the place, Rising Sun looked in the front row for Trooper; and when she wasn't there, he felt disappointed. Dancing from table to table to collect tips, he reached the back of the club where Trooper was standing. This time on cue with the chorus of the song, Rising Sun took Trooper's hands and glided them across his six pack. Trooper looked into his eyes for the first time and her heart began to ache like never before. She needed a man in her life; and here was this dancer giving her his undivided attention. She couldn't believe what she did next. Trooper said, "I have to go. I have a meeting with my boss in the morning." Then she ran out the front door with tears in her eyes.

Rising Sun was unsure for a split second if he should run after her or stay and finish his act. So he made Trooper the finale of his performance. He stood in the center of the spotlight and took a bow. Then he ran into the dressing room to put on his pants and shirt. When he reached the curb to look for Trooper, he could hear the M.C. announcing the next dancer. Rising Sun looked to the valet attendant for the answer, but the question wouldn't come out.

CHAPTER 15

"*T*eco *you know I love you . . . . You're the only man for me. You give me everything that I desire in a relationship. Please don't leave me alone . . . . " She reached out her hand but Teco seemed to fade away into thin air. She ran closer and closer to him; however, every time he drifted farther and farther away. She couldn't fake it any longer and fell to her knees. Trying to catch her breath, she managed to say, " . . . Teeco . . . Please don't leave meee . . . . Teeco . . . please." . . .* A jolt of electricity seemed to go through GQ's body; and she woke up out of her sleep. Sweat was pouring down her chest. *"Shit, why am I having these dreams about Teco?"* She put her hand on the pillow and it was soaked; then she felt her hair, which was damp.

GQ went into the bathroom. From the window, she saw 2 workers on the telephone pole. *"Are these men looking into our crib?"* She then saw an unmarked car parked beside a white van. *"Where in the hell is the telephone company truck?"* She looked closer; and the white van's tags read G-1974. She knew immediately that this was a government plate. *"Shit! What the hell is Gwen doing? I better get out of here. I'm on parole."* GQ picked up the phone to call her sister. She heard a double click. *"Damn, the phone is tapped. I didn't get out of the Pen to get banged back up for some bullshit."*

GQ threw clothes into her suitcase and did a quick double check to see if everything was packed. Then she remembered an important item. Under her bed was a black box. GQ entered the 3 digit combination and examined the contents before putting the black address book into her suitcase.

She found a pencil and a piece of paper. The note read, "Gwen, we need to talk. When I woke up, the Feds were outside the crib. Don't use the house phone. It's bugged. Meet me at the Sheraton on Chestnut Street. Love you, GQ." She put the note by the phone and left the crib ready to face any drama that came her way.

Stepping outside, GQ scanned the neighborhood, which was lined with row houses, also known as Strawberry mansions on this side of North Philly. The normal hustlers and drug users were no where to be found, because of the sting operation that was set up a few blocks away. Thank goodness that Gwen's front yard was no larger than a 1 car garage, because GQ needed to move quickly without being seen. Though Gwen left her car for GQ to drive, GQ followed her instinct to walk to the bus stop instead. Walking 3 city blocks, GQ waited 10 minutes before the SEPTA 23 bus came. She boarded the bus and dared to look back until she took a seat. When she sat down, she looked back towards the house and thought, *"I wonder if they will follow me thinking that I'm Gwen?"*

She needed to clear her mind and figure out what she was going to do, because going back to the streets was not an option. As GQ stepped off of the bus, she looked up at a clear blue sky. The heat from the sun warmed her face; and she reached into her purse to pull out a pair of Gucci sunglasses. The hotel was a few city blocks away; and she wondered if Gwen received her message.

When she arrived at the large atrium in the hotel lobby, she saw that the check-in line was extremely long. GQ needed to rest her feet and decided that the black leather sofa was calling her name. Business attire appeared to be the dress code of the day. The guests in the lobby wore business suits and carried either brief cases or computer backpacks. Looking down at her white t-shirt and jean pants, GQ reached into the front zipper compartment of her suitcase and pulled out a blue casual blazer. She slipped it on, looked up and saw her guest. "How did you get here so fast?" asked GQ.

"When Travis D. got home, he hit me on my hip. He's at the crib now," said Gwen. With the blazer on, GQ stood up and gave her sister a big hug. "Is everything alright?" asked Gwen.

"Things are not right. I'll explain when we get into the room," said GQ walking towards the front desk. After checking in, they walked into the elevator, which was decorated with beautiful red and yellow oriental wallpaper. GQ pushed the button to the fourth floor.

"Were you followed?" asked GQ who was rolling her large black suitcase down the hall.

"No, you're scaring me."

"You should be," said GQ opening up the door to room 421.

"Why are you tripping?" asked Gwen who walked into the room and sat in the chair by the desk.

"What do you mean why am I tripping? You must think this shit is a game," said GQ putting her purse on the bed. Gwen couldn't believe she was being chastised by someone who just got out of prison.

"Have you been sleeping with Travis?"

This was a question that Gwen didn't expect for her sister to ask so soon. However, the look on Gwen's face gave GQ the answer. Gwen said, "Gail, it's not what you think . . . . I . . . I . . . Sis, it wasn't like—"

"Don't sis me. Did you sleep with him?"

"Yes, already. Yes . . . But—" GQ gave her a galling stare; and tears rolled down Gwen's face.

"How could you be with my man? You've crossed the line that sisters don't cross." GQ sat down on the bed.

"Well, you're all I have; and when you got locked up, we thought . . ."

"You and Travis thought what? Gwen, if you weren't my sister I would kick your ass. Don't let my new look fool you." When Gwen stood up ready to fight, GQ looked at her and said, "What the hell are you standing up for? Girl, sit your ass back down." Gwen sat down with her hands folded across her chest. She didn't want to hear anything else from GQ. "Here, clean your face," said GQ passing Gwen some tissue.

"Gail, you had a life sentence, so I needed to find a way to take care of us. So I asked Travis to teach me what you use to do . . . Besides no one on the block knew I was your identical twin. It was easy to run things once you left. You know how these fiends are. They don't care."

"Have you paid any attention to the letters that I've been sending you?" Just because GQ was born eight minutes earlier than Gwen, GQ always thought that she was suppose to play the big sister role.

"Yes, I read all of—"

"Reading them and understanding them are 2 different things. Let me ask you this. Did you know that the Feds are watching the house?"

"You mean you've seen them," asked Gwen throwing the tissue into the small trash can.

"See, this is what I'm talking about. You are so caught up into the hype that you can't see because of the smoke and mirrors. Travis should have taught you how to see them."

"This is where you can come in and help us," said Gwen trying to get GQ's approval.

"Who is us?"

"Travis D. and I still have a few workers on the block. We've done good for ourselves. Since—"

"Since what? I love you; however, I refuse to go back to the Pen for anyone. Haven't you heard? The streets can kill. Look at what happened to me? It's only by the grace of God that I'm here talking to you now. I love you for what you did for me—"

"What happened to the gansta GQ? I looked up to you, because you were the only female who was respected on the streets. You put those fake ass hustlers on the block in check. Now you act like you have never—"

"Listen, when mommy abandoned us, the state separated us into different foster homes. No one wanted a 16 year old girl. So I bounced around a lot. Bashi took me off of the streets. Because of Bashi, I was never a prostitute and I was never raped. Bashi protected me. That's the difference; you don't have to be on the streets." GQ stood up mad as hell. Her sister's unawareness of what the streets will do was causing her blood to boil. So she decided to share something with Gwen that would demolish the GQ gangsta image for life. "Look, let me tell you what happened to me. I'm about to tell you something that I've never told anyone." GQ patted the side of the bed as a signal for Gwen to sit beside her. "The night Bashi was killed . . ."

"What? What?"

" . . . I was in the house but I don't remember everything that happened. All I can remember is . . ." Tears filled GQ's eyes. " . . . There was a knock on the door and I was hoping it was Travis. However, when I opened the door, it was Candi."

"You mean Candi the dope fiend?" asked Gwen looking intently into GQ's eyes.

"Yeah, her parents run a lot of big time businesses. Candi was next in line to run the prostitution ring; however, she rebelled against her mother and hid out at a crack house in Conshohocken. She didn't want her parents to know where she was located. So even though she was a crack head, Bashi protected her. The only person in SB who didn't know her was Homicide." GQ went to the round brown tray by the television and opened the bottled water. "Back to the day that Bashi was killed, I never knew that Candi found out where the SB crib was located in Mount Airy. As Candi stood at the door, all I saw was a man's hand coming from the side; and then I felt brass knuckles. It knocked me out. See this scar?" asked GQ pulling her hair back and pointing to the faded scar above her left eyebrow.

"Why didn't you say something?" asked Gwen as GQ poured the bottled water into 2 glasses.

"Let me finish. When I woke up the next day slumped over in the corner by the living room playpen sofa, I knew something was wrong. I went up the stairs to Bashi's room; and there were blood spots on the stairs. In Bashi's room was a large piece of missing carpet. There were cleaning bottles all over the room, like someone was trying to cover up something gruesome . . ."

"Oh Snap!" exclaimed Gwen covering her mouth with her right hand.

"Back to your question, I wasn't going to say anything about Candi because Teco, I mean, Homicide, told me that he could protect Bashi better than I could protect Bashi. I wasn't going out like that." GQ passed Gwen the glass of water.

"So why did you take the fall for something you didn't do? Why didn't you turn in Candi and find out who the man was?"

"I wanted Candi for myself. I don't do no snitching. Candi was just lucky that I couldn't find her. In fact, no one has seen her since." GQ rubbed the rim of the glass with her index finger. "Homicide was locked up when I got my SB spot back. When he got out, I had to keep it gangsta or I would have lost credibility on the streets. I was the one who was to protect Bashi, not Homicide." Gwen put her arm around GQ. "That's why I need to find Candi and that snitch Teco. Do you understand my position now?" asked GQ.

"Yeah. But why would Candi want to kill Bashi, if Bashi helped her out?"

"Even before I got locked up . . . Even when I was in the hospital after the police chase, I played every scenario out in my head about what could have happened to Bashi that day. Nothing I come up with makes sense."

"I hate to tell you this," said Gwen looking GQ in the eyes.

"What?"

"Remember you said you heard that Homicide was in D.C.? I also heard Candi is in D.C." Gwen removed her arm from around GQ and took a sip of water.

GQ's eyes widened. "Are you serious? I have got to get to D.C." GQ said walking to the window.

"That's exactly why I have to grind the streets. You don't have a job to be traveling all over the place. You know better than anyone how good the money can be for us," said Gwen standing to her feet.

GQ looked out of the window and said, "After I settle the score with Homicide, I'm walking away from this street life. It's not too late. Come start a new life with me in New York. I got a call from Karlyn Fashion Recruiters to show them my portfolio this weekend. Travis is not good for you or me. We both deserve better."

Putting down the glass of water, Gwen walked towards the door and said, "I'm sorry. I can't get out of the street game right now. I'm running shit as the new and improved GQ, Gwen Que." Gail turned around to confront her twin sister; however, the door sounded a loud click. She knew that ultimately their lives were headed in different directions.

GQ picked up the hotel phone and dialed the number in her black address book. "Hello, this is Gail Indigo Que, I'm calling to confirm my meeting on this Saturday with your Karlyn Fashion Recruiter."

The receptionist said, "Yes Ms. Que, we have you down. However, we had an appointment cancellation. Can you come into New York tonight for an appointment in the morning?"

"Yes, I can be there."

"Since we are asking you to accommodate our schedule, we will cover all travel cost. I look forward to seeing you in person tomorrow."

GQ did a Cinderella spin in the room. She was going to start a new life; and for the first time, she would be staying the night at a hotel without drug connections.

◊◊◊◊◊

Trooper and Swoosh were looking over the final report before putting their John Hancocks on the paperwork. As Trooper organized the contents of the folder in chronological order, the door to Captain Wicker's office flew open and banged the wall. As Trooper and Swoosh looked into his office, there were 2 heavy built men in black suits seated around his small conference table.

"Detective Troop and Detective Brown, you are wanted in my office, now," said Captain Wicker. Trooper knew the only logical explanation was that the Feds were getting involved in the G-String murder case. Her frustrated look was a sign that she wanted to demonstrate that things were indeed under control. However, she knew that was far from reality. Captain Wicker added, "Have a seat." One of the 2 FBI agents pulled out a small handheld tape recorder. Trooper and Swoosh eyes locked together as if they were sending subliminal messages on what they were going to say in the meeting. "Do you have my reports?" asked Captain Wicker.

"Yes sir we do," said Swoosh pushing the folder to the center of the table. The Captain picked up the folder and briefly shuffled through the paperwork. Then he passed the folder over to the 2 FBI agents.

"Detective Brown and Troop, we are with the FBI. We have an annual budget exceeding $6 billion, which provides us with the most sophisticated methods in crime prevention as well as advanced investigation techniques in order to assist our local law enforcement agencies, which is what brings us here today. Are we on the same page?" asked FBI Agent Mullis with the Drew Carey haircut and styled glasses.

"No," said Trooper not wanting any help with the case.

"What about you Detective Brown?" asked FBI Agent Rozier with a shining dark chocolate bald head.

"I have an idea. How about you fill us in," said Swoosh trying to be a bit more diplomatic than Trooper.

"We, meaning the Bureau, have the right by way of authority to take over this case because it potentially crosses state lines into Pennsylvania. Before we do that, we decided to talk with the 2 of you."

"It's all in our report," said Trooper looking at the folders.

FBI Agent Rozier unwrapped a piece of chewing gum and said, "Well tell us who is your lead suspect."

Trooper leaned forward in her chair and said, "Twyla Burke, a former residence of Conshohocken, Pennsylvania. Her DNA was found at each murder scene of the 3 male exotic dancers. We have 2 angles. The first angle is based on a crime of passion theory. Twyla Burke is known to have a sexual addiction. She dates handsome male dancers. When they no longer satisfy her fetish, she knocks them off. For the second angle, we are working to tie back the murders to a connection in Philadelphia. Detective Brown and I have spoken to a Teco Jackson, who is from the area and who is also a male exotic dancer. We have reason to believe the G-String murders are a possible camouflage for the actual target, who is Teco Jackson. Jackson was a snitch for the Bashi Mujaheed Fiten murder case. This would be a crime of revenge for Jackson turning in a Gail Indigo Que. Teco Jackson, Gail Indigo Que, and Twyla Burke are all from the West Philly and Conshohocken area. This is no coincidence." Trooper leaned back in her chair because she was actually pleased with her response to the FBI Agents.

"We have surveillance on Gail Indigo Que, who was recently released from prison. Did you know that she was out, Detective Troop?" asked Agent Mullis. Captain Wicker shot Trooper a scolding look. Not having this information was giving the FBI even more reason to take over the case.

Swoosh said, "We get your point now. I know we need to work together on this case. However, you don't have the relationships we have with the local businesses and local police offices. You need us for the field work on this side of the tracks. Agreed?"

FBI Agent Mullis said, "Yes, we agree. Actually, I'm quite impressed with the initial report from you and Detective Troop. I didn't know that you actually spoke with Teco Jackson already." A smile came across Captain Wicker's face and he winked at Trooper.

FBI Agent Rozier asked, "What about Twyla Burke? Where is she?"

"She is street smart. So far, she has been able to elude authorities; however, I'm confident we will catch her. Her sexual addiction will drive her back out to the clubs," said Trooper.

"Very well," said FBI Agent Mullis. Both FBI Agents stood and extended their hands to Trooper and Swoosh. Mullis continued, "We will give you our report on the surveillance of Gail Que. We have bugged her house and put a tracking device on her car. She was seen on the streets of West Philly this afternoon with her partner, Travis Delgado. Gail Que isn't very bright to be hitting the streets again, especially since she is on parole. The second she violates parole, we will bring her in for questioning."

After they shook hands, Trooper walked out of the office with a look of agitation. She knew that the FBI was out to take the G-String murder case from under their Homicide Division. As she pulled out her office chair to sit down, Trooper's telephone rang.

CHAPTER 16

"**H** ello, this is Detective Troop."
          "Hello Detective. I was just cleaning out my car and came across your business card—"

"Let me guess. You couldn't resist giving me a call right?" asked Trooper smiling from ear to ear.

"You're a great detective," said Teco who reached for the white lemon scented trash bag in order to throw away the Burger King wrappers.

"I'm glad you think so." Swirling the telephone cord between her fingers, Trooper decided that she liked his telephone voice better than his in person voice.

"Why would anyone think otherwise?" asked Teco.

"Actually, that's a long story . . . ."

"Okay, I'm not driving. I can hear you out. So, I'm all ears." He sat down behind the driver's seat to focus on their conversation.

"No, I can't discuss. It's work related. Plus, you're—"

"I'm what? Do I still need protection from someone?"

"That's a good question." She said picking up a round colorful stress ball and squeezing it tightly.

"Okay, come meet me at the Corner Bakery in Tyson's Corner and we can talk about it," said Teco with a player smile.

"That will work." Trooper leaned back in the chair trying to decide if this meeting was business or personal. She wanted to interview Teco about his connection with Gail Que. However, the memory of her hands on his chest at the Oak Tree dominated her thoughts.

Within the hour, Teco and Trooper pulled up in Tyson's Corner at the exact same time. The atmosphere at the Corner Bakery was quaint. The glass case displayed cookies and a large variety of pies. They found a booth near the back and sat down. Trooper said, "You're very good with listening. I like that about you. I needed to get away and talk with someone other than my partner." Trooper reached for the menu, which was behind the box of napkins. She looked at him as if she desperately needed his help.

"What should I call you?" asked Teco.

"Call me Hanae." She said with a casual smile. Trooper's thoughts were centered on her inability to crack the G-String murder case and her boss's reaction at the FBI meeting.

"Hanae, I sense that you have more on your mind than what you've told me on the phone."

"I do have a lot on my mind. But this meeting isn't about me. I still think you are in danger," said Trooper.

"I'm telling you. I'm not," said Teco leaning forward with his arms resting on the table.

"Tell me this. How did you get caught up in the streets?" After Trooper asked this question, a blond hair eighty-year old man carrying a green Halloween bucket with candy inside stepped up to their table.

"Would you two love birds like a piece of candy?" asked the man in an endearing tone.

"Sure. Thank you sir," said Teco reaching inside for the individually wrapped butterscotch candy.

"No thanks," said Trooper, who was looking totally baffled as to why Teco would take candy from a stranger.

"Have a great day," said the elderly man who went to the next table.

"See this is exactly what I mean," said Trooper leaning forward so that no one could hear. "You can't trust everybody you meet. Besides, it's springtime, not fall. What if the candy is poisoned?"

"Which candy are you talking about? Candi, the female or the old man's candy?"

Trooper was intrigued by his question and said, "I'm talking about—"

"May I take your order?" asked the waitress.

"Sure, we will have two ham and cheese sandwich combos with orange soda; and for dessert, we'll have the Snickers Pie," said Teco with confidence.

"Okay, got it," said the waitress, who turned and walked away.

"I'm very impressed," said Trooper smiling. "How did you know my favorites?"

"I'm a great detective myself," said Teco putting a white napkin onto his lap.

"Let's get back to my original question. How did you get caught up in the streets?"

"Is this being recorded?" asked Teco.

"No. I'm genuinely interested. I want to know how you came to know someone by the name of Gail Que."

Searching for her sincerity, Teco looked into Trooper's eyes. "I'll give you the Readers Digest version. When my father passed away, I became homeless. After a few years of roaming the streets, Bashi Fiten took me into his home. Before me, he also took Gail Que, GQ, and a guy we call Cap off of the streets. We all lived together in Mount Airy. It's that simple." Teco said as the waitress returned with their lunch.

"You can't get off that easy," said Trooper as Teco signaled for them to bow their heads to say grace. Afterwards Trooper continued, "Where were the adults in your life after your dad passed away?"

"My mom loves me a whole lot; however, I was too much for her to handle. My best friend is Bernard Gordon. Everybody calls him Fatboy. His dad, Mr. G. came the closest to being a father figure after my pops died. Mr. G taught me a lot about life; however, he couldn't afford to feed another mouth." Teco placed the napkin in his lap.

"Why do you think it was hard for you to walk away from the street life?" Trooper asked putting the straw in her drink.

"Lack of direction and goals. One day I want to open up a center for underprivileged young men from the ages of 16 to 21, a place for them to go and map out a plan. The big time drug dealers are the primary ones mapping that plan for young gangstas who run the streets. Don't you agree?"

"True. So, why did you think GQ killed Bashi?" asked Trooper taking a bite of the sandwich.

"The signs were all there that she was the killer. It's in the case file. I'm sure you've read it by now. I hear you're the best detective in D.C." Teco smirked and took a sip of his soda.

Trooper took a moment to swallow the potato chips and said, "Sure, I've read the file. But I really want to know why you turned in GQ?"

"Let me put it this way, I owed a lot to Bashi for taking me off the streets. My loyalty was with Bashi and not GQ." Taking a bite from his sandwich, Teco decided that Trooper was indeed concern about him.

"By the way, did you know that GQ is—" Trooper's cell phone rang; and she picked up. "This is Detective Trooper." A concerned look came over Trooper's face; and she stood up to leave. "Teco, we will have to continue our discussion later. My apologies . . ." Before Teco could say another word, Trooper walked out of the door without taking her Snickers Pie.

When Trooper stepped onto the curb, she felt the rain coming down; however, the sky was bright blue and clear without a single cloud. She reminisced back to the time when her grandmother said that this was a sign that the "devil was beating his wife, which meant that everything appeared well on the outside; however, the devil's wife was crying on the inside." Trooper felt this was analogous to her lunch conversation with Teco. In retrospect, she wished she told Teco about needing his help to nail the G-String killer. Letting the department down was not an option.

As she drove into the police parking lot, she saw that Swoosh's car was already parked in his assigned space. She walked into Captain Wicker's office and saw Swoosh seated at the small conference table. "Have a seat Detective Troop. I'm sorry that I didn't tell you two what was about to happen at the FBI meeting earlier," said Captain Wicker, who was pacing the floor. "Please understand that I was told not to . . . . My hands were tied." He walked over to the window and looked at the parking lot while placing his hands into his pants pockets. "One thing that I do know is that I have one unbeatable team. You two have done very well. The FBI was impressed with your initial report. They too say that this is a tough case to crack given that The Paradox is giving us these mixed messages." Trooper wondered why Captain Wicker couldn't look her in the face as he talked. "So, take the rest of the day off and get back onto the case first thing in the morning."

Captain Wicker turned around and Trooper said, "You know that we work around the clock; and just when we finally take our shoes off to rest, here comes the call."

"Okay, take a long break," said Captain Wicker in a jovial voice. They all laughed; and Swoosh and Trooper left the room.

Before Swoosh could sit at his desk, Trooper asked, "So what are you going to do for the rest of the day?"

"I think I'll go shoot some ball," said Swoosh moving his hands in the air as if he were shooting a basketball. "And you?"

"I'll be at the Boys and Girls Club. I haven't seen them in a while."

"Okay, tell our team that I said hello."

"No, why don't you come shoot ball with them and tell them yourself," said Trooper with a serious expression.

Swoosh looked at her beautiful brown eyes and said, "You know that I like a good physical game to take off some tension."

With frustration, Trooper said, "Any excuse will do." Then she walked away and left the building thinking about Teco. She couldn't put her finger on why she found him desirable. Was it his dark chocolate face with the tiny scar under his right eye or was it his rock hard shape? When she reached her SUV, she took a deep breath. Trooper pulled up Teco's cell phone number, which she programmed on her phone. For a split second, she thought to call; however, she put the phone back into her pocket.

Trooper pulled into the parking lot of the Palmer Park Recreation Center. She and some of the kids would sit on the stoop of the recreation center for hours waiting to see Sugar Ray; however, he never showed up. She remembered one of the little boys named Lil' G asking, "Why do they call it Sugar Ray's Gym if he is never there?" However, Trooper never gave a plausible answer to the kids.

Trooper parked the SUV and put Sunshine in the glove box. As she walked into the gym, the kids screamed, "Trooper! Trooper! Trooper! Trooper!" They were all over her like bees on honey. She knew that her hands were full with over twenty children. She went to the office to sign-in on the volunteer sheet.

Diane, the Recreation Center Director said, "Girl, I know that look. What's on your mind?"

"I don't know if I can take any more of this shit . . . . The FBI had Swoosh and I in the office." Trooper said as she picked up the ink pen.

"What did they want?" asked Diane.

"They were talking about taking over one of my high profile cases."

"That's why I left the department 5 years ago and came to work with the kids," said Diane with a concerned look. "So did they?"

"No . . . Well, they haven't said anything to us specifically about taking it over—" Trooper's cell phone rang and she picked up. "Hello . . . Teco?"

"Hello, I was wondering if you were all right, because you didn't seem okay after lunch." He was now at home in his master bedroom packing his clothes.

'Thanks for asking. Are you working tonight?" Trooper really enjoyed watching Teco perform.

"No . . . I have a show out of town—"

"Oh really? Where are you going?"

"Philly; but I will be back this weekend. Hopefully, we can get together."

She paused for a minute; and there was nothing between them but stillness. "I don't think you should go back to Philly because GQ is—"

"Hello . . . Hanae . . . Are you there? Hello . . . Hello . . ." Teco looked down at his cell phone and the battery was out of juice.

With a panicked look, Trooper looked at her cell phone and saw there was full battery power. She redialed Teco's number and it went straight to voicemail. Waiting a brief moment, she tried the number again. Since he didn't answer, she hopped into her SUV and popped the light onto the top of her car. She needed to tell Teco that GQ was out of prison before he left D.C. *"What am I doing? I know I shouldn't be going after Teco without Swoosh. Teco is a part of an ongoing investigation."* At that moment, Trooper didn't care. She liked Teco; and she wasn't going to let him leave D.C. until she knew for sure he wasn't a target of The Paradox.

CHAPTER 17

. . . *C*andi walked up the back alley and stood behind Bubble's neighborhood bar in Conshohocken, Pennsylvania. As she walked in the darkness, she wanted a hit of crack. Her hands were shaking and she knew what needed to be done in order to get another hit. There was no other way to get money because her parents cut all of her funds off until she agreed to go to a rehabilitation center. Looking like a zombie, Candi walked up to him and asked, "Hey Cap, can I work something off?" Cap was a runner for the SB Crew with Teco, a.k.a. Homicide, and GQ. They all worked the block for Bashi. Cap hung out with Candi off and on after he was put down with the SB Crew.*

Good at the street game, Cap played the big boy part and said, "Shit, it's almost time for me to leave." Candi walked up to Cap and put her arms around his neck. Pressing her body against him, he felt her firm ass. She gave him a sweet kiss and put her hands down his pants. "Yeah, we can do this." He said and followed Candi in the alley to where a 1988 Cutlas was stripped and abandoned. He leaned back on what was left of the back fender. Candi lifted up his shirt and circled his nipples with her tongue. Slowly she planted kisses down his chest until she reached his zipper. When she went down on her knees, he moaned deeply and put his hand gently on the top of her head. Just as he closed his eyes, somebody hit Cap on the right side of his temple knocking Cap out. POW! Candi moved aside as Cap got kicked all in his face and on his upper body. The assailant went into Cap's pockets and took all of the SB money; and what dope he found, he threw over to Candi who ran out of the alley . . . .

Candi woke up in a cold sweat from her nap. No matter how hard she tried, she constantly relived that chilling night when

Cap got beat down and was left for dead. She felt her heart, which seemed to jump out of her chest. Candi turned on the night stand light in her suite and looked around, because she thought she felt someone's presence in the room. She got out of the king sized bed and went into the bathroom to put a cold cloth on her face.

Deciding that she wanted to shave her legs, she looked into her cosmetic case and realized that she didn't have a razor. Candi walked back to the phone and dialed the front desk. "Hello, do you have a complimentary razor I can have? . . . Okay, I'll be right down." She put on some straight legged jeans, a black fitted t-shirt, and slipped on her black Burkenstocks. On her way to the elevator, Candi was starting to feel guilt-ridden all over again. She thought rehab would end all of her guilt trips; for some reason, the dreams of what actually happened back in Conshohocken played over and over in her head.

Positioned well to see the hotel revolving glass door as well as the elevator, the driver of the black Town Car was seated on one of the hotel lobby chairs. When he saw the Washington Post on the console table, he picked it up pretending to read. As he glanced over to the front desk, he saw Candi standing there. The Front Desk Clerk passed her the razor and shaving cream.

"I'll be damned. I can't allow her to see me . . . . Be cool Soulja, be cool." He thought and listened intently to what the clerk was saying.

"Thank you for the razor," said Candi.

"You are welcome, Ms. Blake," said the Front Desk Clerk who didn't know Candi was checked into the hotel under an alias.

As Candi passed by his lobby chair, he lifted the newspaper and closed his eyes hoping that she wouldn't see him. Until the coast was clear to follow her, he decided to think about Candi and his initial mission five years ago.

. . . *"Candi, I need your help. I plan on taking out the whole SB Crew; and I need you."* He said as they walked down the block in Conshohocken.

"What are you talking about? I'm finished with doing shit for you. That was dead wrong what you did to Cap and now you are talking about messing with the whole SB crew?" They passed an old lady with

long gray hair who was sitting on her porch. When Candi waved hello, the old lady gave her a disapproving look for walking with a thug. Then Candi heard the old lady break out into a hymn singing, "What can wash away my sins? Nothing but the blood of Jesus . . . "

As they continued down the street, he said, "Look . . . you don't have to do anything but roll with me to the SB crib. You knock on the door; and I'll do the rest—"

"Bashi got that crazy ass bald headed dude that don't take no shit from nobody living there now. Hell no! I ain't down with that shit. You crazy." When they arrived at the crack house, Candi immediately went to the coffee table and put a piece of crack onto her shooter.

He smacked Candi's hand causing her shooter to smash into the wall, breaking the shooter into pieces. "Let me tell you something. You started this mission with me and you will finish it. Let me handle Homicide. This is the plan and you won't be high when this goes down!"

Her fingertips were numb and she looked at him in amazement not knowing what to do next. He continued, "Dig this. SB will come for street retribution for me beating down Cap. SB will be ready to hold their own street court hearing. If SB don't find anyone on the block, they'll push on to Norristown and that's where I'll take out the whole crew. When they drive through tomorrow, I'll be sitting in the cut waiting for them to drive pass me. I want you to post up at the phone booth at the Main Street Tavern. When I signal to you that they are coming, you call the police, describe the black Bronco, red Cadillac, as well as the blue Jetta and tell them that there are mad drugs inside."

"How do you know that SB won't come for us tonight?" asked Candi reaching for some more crack; however, he snatched the crack off of the coffee table before she could get it.

"Look . . . Candi, you need to pay attention."

Wanting another hit of crack, Candi asked, "All I have to do is make the phone call right?"

"Just listen. I want you to wait until you see them get arrested; then we'll jet." . . .

"Sir, Sir, May I see the Washington Post after you finish," said a female hotel guest, who brought his attention back into the present.

"Sure." He looked at her, folded up the paper, and practically threw the paper in her face. The hotel guest looked at him appalled by his actions.

When he saw that Candi was gone, he made a mad dash out to his car and opened the trunk to get a piece of equipment. Then he found a pay phone around the corner of the lobby entrance. Positioning himself so that no one could see around his huge frame, he put the telephone voice changer onto the receiver. After, he pushed the woman's voice indicator; he dialed the hotel number.

"Marriott Crystal City, may I direct your call?"

"Do you have a Blake listed."

"Yes ma'am. Do you have a first name?"

"You know, she is a business associate and never told me her first name," said The Paradox speaking into the voice changer.

"I have a Jim Blake and another guest named Kendra Blake."

"Connect me to Kendra Blake, please." He said reaching for the handkerchief in his front shirt pocket to remove the sweat from his brow. The lobby music played soft jazz, which he enjoyed hearing until Candi said, "Hello."

"Hello Ms. Blake?"

"Yes," said Candi taking off her jeans in order to get ready for her shower.

"We want to know if you need any other complimentary items." He said looking around to make sure no one was walking up to use the other pay phones.

"No, I'm straight. Thank—" Before she could complete her sentence, Candi heard the dial tone.

The Paradox was becoming more and more vexatious at the fact that Candi was smart enough to evade the police. He removed the device and went back to the car. When he sat down behind the steering wheel, he reached into the glove box and pulled out a zip lock bag with the black G-String inside. He knew that Candi couldn't go too much longer without sex. After rehabilitation, a person's sexual appetite usually gets stronger.

Drugs no longer suppress the intensity of sexual desire. The Paradox convinced himself that Candi would be going to a club somewhere in D.C. tonight.

Therefore, he retrieved and turned on the high frequency transmitter. The Paradox acknowledged that a few more things needed to be taken care of before he headed back to Philly. Patience was the key to staying out of sight until then. The transmitter started to beep which meant that Candi was on the move. "Yes! Here we go!" He exclaimed as Candi's car headed towards the garage exit ramp.

She turned the radio on to 95.5 Jams and Prince's song "Let's Go Crazy" was playing. Her head bobbed up and down to the beat; and she believed the song was a confirmation that she was going to have a great time tonight. As she crossed the highway overpass, the black Town Car kept a 3 to 4 car distance. After the 45 minute drive, she pulled into the parking lot of Kendonna's, an upscale male exotic dance club. Candi circled the parking lot to see if any detectives or police were around. She pulled into a parking spot way in the back.

The Paradox waited in the Town Car for Candi to enter the club, before he found a parking spot near the front. A makeup case was on the passenger seat and The Paradox pulled out the fake beard and mustache. *"Okay, there we are. I'm looking like a new man."* He walked to the back where Candi's car was parked and switched tracking devices because the battery would be getting low soon. He put on a sheath shoulder harness and carried a boot knife just in case action called for it.

Inside the club, Candi went to the bar, which was positioned center of a rock wall. To the left, there was a nude statue of a man and woman holding each other as they danced. Water ran from the top of the statue's heads to their feet. The gold spotlight made the concrete couple look as if they were having a romantic evening. Searching for her date, Candi felt really racy because being neutered by the police was not going to happen. As she sat on a bar stool, a debonair man walked up to her and asked, "Hello . . . Candi, right?"

"Ummm . . . I see you've remembered my name. How nice."

"How could I forget your sweet name?" asked Kream, a male exotic dancer. Besides, every dancer knew that Candi was the best female tipper in the area. "So why haven't you called me?" He asked looking at himself in a mirror in front of the bar.

"Kream, to be honest I wanted to have a face to face conversation so I could see your mien. Tell me this, did you choose the name Kream because you like whip cream? You know whip cream is my favorite topping." She said softly rubbing her right foot against his left leg.

"Oh really, so can we hook up tonight?"

"Well . . . that all depends," said Candi looking into his hazel eyes.

"On what might I ask?" When her foot reached his knee he softly grabbed her thigh and held it in his hand.

"Are you dancing tonight?"

"Yeah, as a matter of fact I need to go so I can get ready."

When he released her leg, she said, "I like the way you take control. Let's see how well you beef up tonight."

"Damn, you're quite frank aren't you? I think you might want to . . . You know, come close to the stage so you can see my mien." He said whispering into her ear.

She smiled, "I think I just might do that." Kream walked away feeling as if he achieved a major goal.

For a moment, Candi liked the fact that her life was coming back together after rehab. Her mind, body, and soul were finally in sync. She refused to allow herself to be taken back to those streets. Always on point looking for the detectives in the club, she didn't want to go down for murders she did not commit. However, she knew that she must be the primary suspect. Candi was trying to figure out why the men she slept with were turning up dead.

Up on the balcony level, The Paradox watched Candi. A few months ago, he decided to use her new weakness of sex addiction to his advantage. He flashed back to one of the tactics, which he was taught while in the armed forces.

. . . "Once you kill mentally, the physical part is easy. The difficult part is turning it off. Men, do you understand?" asked the platoon instructor who trained them in the art of annihilating the enemy with their hands." . . .

"Sir, do you want a drink?" asked the waitress.

The Paradox looked at her in a daze and said, "Sure, I'll have a gin and tonic." He looked down at Candi who was sipping on a frozen strawberry daiquiri. He wasn't going to allow Candi to take away his freedom by snitching about what happened years ago back in Philly. The armed forces stripped him of too much already. The Paradox zoned out again.

. . . "Staff Sergeant! You have disrespected yourself, the corps, and your fellow brothers. For what you have done, you are hereby given a dishonorable discharge effective immediately. You will serve 2 years at Fort Leavenworth for stealing and trafficking military weapons." . . .

As the D. J. played Madonna's song "Holiday," The Paradox witnessed the club filling up with women. The waitress came back with his drink and said, "Hey handsome, here is your drink."

"Thanks." The Paradox took a sip and saw several dancers surrounding Candi. She was extremely beautiful and looked like she never did drugs a day in her life. This was not the Candi he last remembered. He sat back in his chair and drifted back to the last day that he and Candi were together.

. . . "Candi you started on this mission with me and I need your help again." They sat on opposite ends of the broken down red sofa in a Conshohocken crack house, which smelled like urine.

"Why are you putting me through this? First you said all I had to do was get Cap in the alley; and I did that. Then you asked me to set SB up with the po po; and I did that. I can't help it if only one of them got caught. I did what you asked me to do . . . . Now you want me to help you—"

"Candi, I just want you to show me where the SB crib is so I can buy us some powder; and we can get right, just you and me." He moved closer to Candi on the sofa.

"I've only been there once, when Cap took me after he first got put down with them." She said licking her powdered white lips.

"Does GQ know you?"

"Yeah, I met her once or twice on the block, when Bashi helped me after my fam kicked me out the house."

"Haven't I been treating you right?" He asked moving closer to her.

"Yeah, but SB don't play," said Candi displaying fear in her eyes.

"The main one we have to worry about is locked up since you called the police in Norristown. You know . . . "

"Who the bald headed one?"

"Yeah, Homicide." He said putting his masculine left arm around her shoulder.

Candi said, *"Homicide don't know me and I'm keeping it that way."* His right hand rested gently on her thigh. *"But . . . But . . . I don't know."* She said moving his arm from around her and standing to her feet.

"Look . . . Just knock on the door; and I'll ask them to sell me a half ounce." He said.

"Okay . . . I'll take you there if you give me a hit first." She asked reaching for his shooter.

He saw that Candi was twitching fiendishly and said, *"We're rolling out after you take that hit."* Then he went into the bathroom and pulled out his works. He put a metal bottle cap on the counter and placed the dope in the cap with three drops of water. He fired the bottom of the cap, which made the dope and water turn into an oily base. With a cotton ball in the base, the tip of the syringe rested on the cotton ball. He drew back 2 cc's, licked the tip and put it into his arm. *"Ummm,"* he sighed.

A few hours later, Candi pointed to where the house was on Williams Avenue in Mount Airy. They parked on the side street next to the SB crib. *"Okay, are you ready?"*

"Yeah, I guess," said Candi who was scared as hell.

He pulled out some money from his right pocket to play it off, so that she wouldn't punk out. Within his left pocket was a pair of brass knuckles and behind the waist of his pants was a 25 Smith & Wesson. They walked up to the door, where he stood to the right as Candi knocked 3 times. GQ came to the door and asked, *"Who is it?"*

"*Candi.*"

"*Hold on.*" *The locks turned and the door came open. GQ looked at Candi very strangely.* "*What are you doing here Candi? You know the rules.*"

Candi stepped into the house with GQ. "*I want to speak with Bashi.*" *Simultaneously, a fist made contact with GQ's face from the right side of the door never giving GQ a chance to react. POW! He hit GQ with a solid left blow, knocking her to the floor.*

Candi didn't know what to do next. He stepped into the house and slammed the door, making sure Candi was in the house with him. "*What the hell are you doing? Oh shit!*" *exclaimed Candi racing for the door.*

"*Shut your ass up before Bashi hears you.*" *He picked Candi up by her small waist and threw her onto the playpen sofa; then his huge hand slapped her. Ka-Pow!*

"*This wasn't a part of the plan,*" *said Candi sobbing hysterically and getting into a fetal position. Now ignoring Candi, he put GQ in the corner behind the playpen sofa. Candi glanced over the couch and saw GQ slumped over unconscious with blood coming from her forehead.* "*No! No!*" *cried Candi with tears streaming down her face.*

"*I said, shut the hell up.*" *He pulled out the gun and ran upstairs.*

Candi heard him arguing with Bashi about Homicide; so she ran up the stairs to see what was going on . . . .

"Excuse me, sir . . . Sir . . . Sir!" yelled the waitress, who thought he couldn't hear her because of the music.

"I'm sorry. Yes," said The Paradox now looking up at the waitress, whose black and rose bustier top made her appealing to him.

"Here is another drink. May I take this for you?"

"Yes, that will be fine." He said pushing the empty glass across the table towards the waitress, causing her to lean down so that he could get a better view of her top. After she walked away, The Paradox noticed that Kream was back at the bar and that Candi was sitting in Kream's lap, all up in his ear. Attracting handsome men came natural to Candi; and The Paradox despised these male dancers for taking Candi away from his world.

The Paradox remembered when he and Candi did everything together as a couple. After his dishonorable discharge from the military, he believed Candi loved and accepted him for his good attributes. Women admired how well he treated Candi as they walked down the street. Then when he and Candi experimented with drugs, their future was destroyed. For a moment, he was remorseful about tearing her life to pieces. However, if he couldn't have Candi, no other man would have her either. The Paradox wanted to go back to Philly, to a time before the drugs when they were happy.

CHAPTER 18

After Kream finished his set, The Paradox had Kream and Candi on lock. From Candi's body language, The Paradox knew that the couple would be leaving together and looked at his Swiss Army watch to time his exit. As he looked up from his watch, Kream and Candi stood up. The Paradox made a motion to move towards the door; however, Kream sat back down like a true gentleman. "Shit!" exclaimed The Paradox. When Candi walked to the ladies' room to touch up her makeup, The Paradox got up and walked through the crowd keeping an eye on Kream. After Candi came back, Kream gave her a kiss on her right cheek and whispered something into her ear. Still keeping an eye on Kream who went to the dancers' dressing room, The Paradox immediately saw the duffle bag in Kream's hand.

Before Kream reached the table, The Paradox rushed outside to get into the Town Car and kept looking back to keep an eye on the entrance of the club. He reached the car out of breath, but made it before the couple reached the curb. While tapping his fingers on the steering wheel, the only thing on his mind was taking out his next victim and exterminating Candi by driving her crazy.

Kream opened the car door for Candi and sat in the driver's seat of Candi's car. They drove by several hotels until Kream pulled into the Holiday Inn parking lot. Following suit, The Paradox waited in his Town Car until the couple walked to the front desk. Inside the lobby area, the grand spiral staircase led to a bar area. There were several guests having drinks and laughter filled the air.

Adjusting his disguise in the driver's mirror, The Paradox slipped on a light weight black trench coat and black tear drop hat. Just as the couple got into the elevator, the doors began to close and The Paradox yelled, "Hold it please!" Kream pushed the button and the doors came back open.

As The Paradox stood there with only Kream and Candi, his heart was shifting into overdrive. Kream faced Candi and penned her in the corner while kissing her on the neck. The elevator bell rang and the couple got off on the 2nd floor. The Paradox allowed the elevator door to barely close then hit the open button to follow them. Candi's left hand was now in Kream's back pocket as they strolled down the hall. When they reached the room, Kream passionately leaned Candi's back on the door as he pressed gently against her sexy body. With a player's move, he took out the key card and opened the door. As the door closed, The Paradox noted that they were in Room 216.

After waiting in the car for 2 hours, The Paradox went back to the second floor to finish them off. He walked past Room 216 once to see if he could hear anything. However, when he turned around to pass the door once again, the door unlocked. Just as the couple came out of the room, The Paradox tipped his tear drop hat so they could not see his disguised face. Kream and Candi strolled slowly down the hall to the elevators. Seeing Kream's duffle bag, The Paradox's blood pressure began to rise, because the window of opportunity was gone.

"Shit! Shit!" exclaimed The Paradox as he ran down the stairs to get to his car in time. A few minutes passed before the couple came out of the hotel. As Candi's car passed his Town Car, The Paradox pulled out behind them. Kream drove three city blocks until he pulled into the local Denny's parking lot.

The Paradox mumbled curse words, because having witnesses is never a part of the plan. However, he would have to make his move here. The Paradox parked his car directly across the street from the Denny's front door. He put on black gloves. Out of the glove box, he took the black G-String out of the zip lock bag and put the G-String in his inner trench coat pocket.

Inside the Denny's, The Paradox asked for a cup of coffee "to go." As he waited, he looked around stealing the chance to see what the scene was like. He was pissed off once he saw that Kream and Candi were placing an order with the waitress. The Paradox knew that formulating a Plan B in his mind was of utmost importance.

"Are you a biker?" asked the waitress at the counter.

"Why are you asking?" He asked while surveying the booth where Kream and Candi were sitting.

"You are wearing bikers' gloves and it's 80 degrees outside."

"Exactly." He said not wanting to disclose any other information. Then it dawned on him how he could orchestrate his plan.

"Here you go sir," said the counter waitress as she passed him the coffee and his change.

The Paradox walked past the booth where Kream and Candi sat. Then he spilled the coffee onto a nearby customer who exclaimed, "What the hell?!" The cup dropped, which splattered coffee across the floor.

Then a waitress asked the customer, "Are you alright? Let me get something to help you clean that up."

While everyone's eyes were on the customer's coffee stained shirt, The Paradox bent down to pick up the cup and threw the G-String inconspicuously under Kream and Candi's booth onto the floor. His heart was racing because, he was unsure if anyone saw him make that move. A bus boy came quickly up to him and said, "Let me get that cup for you sir. Do you want another coffee?"

"No, thank you," said The Paradox who turned away from the booth and walked out the door. From the window, he could see the bus boy mopping up the coffee. Kream and Candi were not fazed by the episode because they were still in deep conversation.

The Paradox got back into the Town Car and drove to the Exxon a few feet away. Parking in the back of the station, he popped the trunk and took out the 38" gun case. The Paradox walked to a wooded area, which would provide better cover and a clear shot to Denny's across the street. He pulled the zipper open and held the SKS rifle in his hand. Making sure all functions were in tact, he pushed the button to the laser sight system with a 500 yard range. The Paradox put in the SKS 30 round magazines. Getting into position, he pushed the laser button. From the 30mm illuminated scope, initially he saw Candi. *"Okay, yes, here we go."* When he moved the laser to Kream, the waitress came to the table. *"Shit, move baby move,"* thought the Paradox.

When the waitress left the table, Candi pointed to Kream's forehead and said, "What's that red dot on your face?" Everyone in Denny's heard a faint shatter of glass. When Kream slumped over, Candi saw blood and matter all over her clothes. She let out a sudden loud piercing cry. Some people hit the floor, while Candi and others ran out of the building to their cars. Tears rolled down Candi's face and she was acting psycho. She reached into her purse and couldn't find the keys. She screamed, "Oh NO! Oh NO! NO!" Then when she located the spare car key in the side pocket of her purse, she couldn't get the key into the ignition because her hands were shaking uncontrollably. Candi folded her arms across the steering wheel, rested her head on her hands and sobbed. Her eyeliner was running all down her cheeks. "Get it together! Get it together!" She screamed at herself. When she put the key into the ignition, she drove cautiously towards the Marriott in Crystal City trying not to go over the speed limit.

When Candi reached the hotel, she leaned against the steering wheel crying. As she started to hyperventilate, Candi willed herself to breath. She pulled out her overnight bag from the back seat and changed clothes in the car. When she saw Kream's duffle bag, she cried out, "Make this nightmare end! Make this nightmare end!" Beating the steering wheel with her fist, Candi felt hopeless. As she got out of the car, Candi fell to the ground because her knees were so weak. Nothing made sense. She thought about the other dancers and realized that she needed help.

Back inside Denny's, the night manager dialed 911; however, a police officer on foot patrol was already running into the restaurant. The officer pulled out his radio and said, " . . . requesting backup. We have a 10-27-1."

"One-nine-eight-eight-four, they are on their way. What is your exact 10-20?" asked the operator.

"I'm securing the perimeter. 10-4."

"That's a copy." The parking lot was now congested with police officers and detained restaurant customers.

As Trooper turned into the Denny's parking lot, her cell phone rang. "This is Detective Troop." She said trying to hear the caller.

"Hello Hanae, are you busy?" asked Teco, who heard a high pitch squeal in his ear.

"I wasn't a few minutes ago, until I got a police call. Oh! It's bad. Got to go."

"Trooper, is it another dancer?"

"I don't know and I sure as hell hope not." Then Teco heard the dial tone.

Before Trooper got out of the car, she made sure a new tape was in her mini-recorder. Several police were taking witness statements on the outside. As she looked through the shattered window, the victim was still slumped over in the booth. Trooper took a deep breath and exhaled. The uniformed officer pulled up the yellow crime tape so that Trooper could enter. Cameras flashed throughout the restaurant. As she took out the mini-recorder, Trooper saw Swoosh observing the victim's wounds. Immediately Trooper knew that the victim did not have his meal alone, because there were two plates of food and water glasses on the table. "Print that." Trooper said to Linda.

"What's up partner?" asked Swoosh.

"Same-O. Same-O. Who was eating with the victim?"

"We don't know; however, there is a sketch artist on the way to work with the witness."

"Where is the log sheet?" asked Trooper as she surveyed the restaurant. However, before Swoosh could respond a young male officer asked Trooper to sign and then he gave the log sheet to her. She scanned the list and saw that the G-String wasn't documented. Breathing a sigh of relief, she walked over to the window and measured the hole.

Analyzing the entry and exit wounds of the victim, she went outside. She pulled out a laser pen, put it up to the hole, and flipped the pen around. The laser followed a path that led to a wooded area across the street of Denny's. Walking back inside of Denny's she faced the window and the direction of the wooded area.

"Swoosh, did you walk the grid yet?"

He was talking to Linda, turned around and asked, "Walk what?"

"This . . . Come check it out." Swoosh and Linda followed Trooper outside.

"Based on the angle of the entry wound and the projection of my laser, the gun shot came from that direction." She said pointing to the wooded area and jogging across the street.

"Trooper can you wait?" asked Swoosh.

She looked back at him and said, "No, because I'm still mad at you for not going with me to the Boys and Girls Club. You could have gone with me to see the kids."

"Trooper, that's not fair," said Swoosh running across the street and pulling out his inhaler. Drivers honked their horns trying not to hit Swoosh, who picked up his pace to get to the other side. When he reached her, she pulled out her flashlight. She saw footprints and took one step when Swoosh exclaimed, "Wait! Trooper, stop!" He pulled out a pair of blue shoe covers and gave them to Trooper, who put them on.

"I'm still mad at you." She said following the path to the Exxon gas station. "Stop! Set your markers, look over there!" Trooper exclaimed while pointing Sunshine in the direction of gun shells.

"Do you need her? You know. Sunshine, the gun? After all, you are not in a good mood about me not going to the Boys and Girls Club."

"Oh, she decided to keep me company. I've got this."

"Yo, let's just wait for the lights." He said flashing a small flashlight in his face to show her that he was dead serious.

"Alright, I'll wait Swoosh." She said putting Sunshine back into the holster.

"Trooper, you know how I feel about my younger brother's death. He was at that exact same gym playing ball. Then he came out and got shot because of crossfire between 2 street gangs. When I see those boys, I can't stay focused. That boy, Lil' G, reminds me of him so much," said Swoosh leaning up against a tree.

"How's that?" She asked pulling out a Snickers bar.

"He's so smart and loves motorcycles. He plays ball just like my brother. That kid has promising skills."

"See, this is exactly why you should come down and help him out. He's a good kid." She said taking a bite out of her candy bar.

"Can we talk about this later?" Swoosh waved his flash light to signal an officer a few yards away.

Trooper rolled her eyes at Swoosh and said to the officer, "Get Linda from CSI over here."

The Paradox watched all of the action from inside his Town Car a few blocks down the street. He really didn't like Detective Trooper, who was already investigating the wooded area. *"Is she that smart? Or am I getting sloppy?"* He couldn't believe that his mission reached another level this quickly. *"Damn, why didn't Candi stay at the hotel? I should have been more patient by waiting another night for another dancer. Now what Soulja?"* The Paradox gripped the steering wheel hard. He knew that one more faux pas could ruin his plans in framing Candi. *"Why are they going back and forth across the street?"* Needing to see what was going on, he removed the disguise and took off the trench coat as well as the hat.

When he reached the road block an Officer said, "Sir this road is closed."

"My daughter called me to pick her up from Denny's. She was hysterical. I have to go get her," said The Paradox.

In a stern voice the officer said, "Sir, if you will, you can go right over there." Following the officer's index finger, The Paradox saw the group of witnesses.

"Thank you, sir. Is anyone hurt?"

"Can you please go over there?" asked the officer.

The Paradox walked down the street to the group of witnesses. He elbowed his way to the front of the line and pulled out the same press pass he used at the U.S. Capitol lawn demonstration against male exotic dancers.

"Sir, you can't—" When The Paradox held up the press pass, the officer with the witnesses flagged him to go to the press area to join the rest of the reporters.

"Is it bad?" asked The Paradox to a reporter.

"Well, as far as I know the victim didn't make it. They say that one of the witnesses saw a red laser light come through the window."

"Could that be possible?" asked The Paradox.

"Now a days anything is possible."

When a CSI investigator called for Detective Troop, all eyes were on her. However, The Paradox was too far away to hear what was being said.

"Make sure that this shell casing reaches the lab ASAP," said Trooper as she walked back across the street. When Swoosh joined her midway, The Paradox moved closer to the rope to hear their conversation. An officer stepped out of the restaurant and passed Trooper an evidence bag.

"You know that the Feds will be all over this," said Trooper passing the evidence bag to Swoosh, who looked inside.

"I agree. They will want to understand the tie back to Philly, especially with Gail Que out of prison.

"Yeah, this has to be connected to the Fiten case," said Trooper who walked into Denny's.

The Paradox was fighting back the panic in his eyes. *"Damn! How in the hell did GQ get out of prison?"* His master plan was disintegrating right before his eyes. When he looked through the restaurant window, Trooper put on plastic gloves and pulled out the black G-String with the note from inside the evidence bag. At that moment, he wanted the G-String back. He was ticked at Detective Troop for being so brilliant to tie this back to Bashi Fiten so quickly. The Paradox decided that both GQ and Trooper needed to be eliminated. He needed to calm down. So, The Paradox closed his eyes and saw the Philadelphia skyline in his mind.

CHAPTER 19

The sunrise came out boldly, as if it were ready to cast judgment upon the Philly streets. Sitting in the Sheraton hotel room looking out of the window, GQ was in a daze as the sun cast a beautiful amber glow throughout the grayish blue skies. This was the perfect time of the morning to put her skills to work by adding to her fashion portfolio. Her mind drifted back to the uneventful trip to New York where she met with the Karlyn Fashion Recruiter. Though her fashion portfolio showed much promise, GQ was instructed that she needed formal training before they would represent her work to clients. Two pigeons cooed and flapped their wings on the ledge of the window, which was distracting and caused GQ to come out of the trance.

After receiving Gwen's call to go with her to the Hunk Mania club, GQ decided to design a new style G-String to sell to the dancers. Picking up the Dick Blick sketch pad and a graphite pencil, her right hand glided on the paper. After 1 hour of working the instrument of creation, GQ pulled the lead away from the paper and there it was, a new style G-String with suspenders. She placed the pad on the easel and stepped back to view her work. A smile formed on her face. She went to the closet, pulled out the portable sewing machine, and placed it on the desk. Then she retrieved brown fabric to transfer her design from paper to cloth.

Before she began sewing, she reached for the Yellow Pages to find a local Fashion School. The phone rang 3 times before the receptionist picked up. "The Art Institute of Philadelphia, how may I direct your call?"

"I'm interested in taking some fashion classes. Can you send me some information?" asked GQ as she threaded the bobbin.

"Sure, may I have your full name?"

"Gail Indigo Que, and that's Q. U. E."

"Ms. Que, would you like for me to set you up an appointment with Mr. Gordon? He is one of our Admissions Counselors."

"Yes, that would be wonderful!" exclaimed GQ with new hope about her future.

"Okay, please hold." As the silence lingered, GQ made the first stitch in sewing the G-String.

"Ms. Que, are you still there?"

"Yes, I'm here," said GQ stopping the sewing machine so that she could hear the instructions.

"Mr. Gordon says that he can see you at 1:30 tomorrow afternoon. Do you know where we are located?"

"Yes, you are down the street from the Sheraton where I am currently staying. Ma'am, you have a blessed day," said GQ with excitement.

"Why thank you Ms. Que and I'll see you tomorrow."

GQ hung up the phone and looked at her sketch. Finally, she was following her dream. If she could find her niche, something that made her different from the rest, then she could break out strong into the fashion industry. This G-String design was better than all of the others.

◊◊◊◊◊

Driving two and a half hours from The Chocolate City to The City of Brotherly Love, Teco reached over and tapped Toi on her left thigh. "Toi, Toi, we're here." This was Teco's first trip back to Philly since Bashi's criminal trial three years ago. When Legend offered him the opportunity to dance at the Hunk Mania club, Teco jumped at the chance without thinking of the ramifications, especially since Trooper told him that he was known as a snitch in Philly. Regardless, he couldn't wait to show his homies how well he was doing. Teco continued, "Before I hit the inner city, I need to stop and clean the dust off of my car."

As Toi gained focus from her nap, she put her seat in the upright position and thought, *"Men and their toys."* While Teco drove down Rhode Island Avenue, Toi looked at an airplane in the sky with a banner, which read "Greek Fest at the Plateau Saturday." Toi asked, "What is the Plateau?"

"It's a huge park called Fairmont."

"Is this what Jazzy Jeff and The Fresh Prince rapped about? You know the song . . ."

"Summertime," said Teco driving through the automatic car wash near Pennrose Park Plaza.

"Yeah, that's it." As the blowers dried off Teco's car, he gave her the details about Greek Fest.

"I would like to go," said Toi as Teco drove towards City Line Avenue.

"Do you mind if I visit some of my friends?"

"No, I don't mind." She said reaching into her purse to get her lip gloss. Teco couldn't wait to introduce Toi to his best friend, Fatboy. Memories ran through his mind of the fun he shared with Fatboy back in the day. "Why are you smiling so much?" asked Toi.

"This is my old hang out," said Teco reaching Mount Airy.

"Who lives here?" She asked as she applied the powered makeup to her face as Teco parked in the driveway.

"My best friend, Bernard Gordon, and his family. I can't wait to see his dad, Mr. G. Stay in the car."

"You're going to leave me out here while you visit your friends?"

"No. I'm just checking to see if they are home. Chill." Teco knocked on the door twice before he heard several locks release.

"I be damn!" said Mr. G., who yelled to his wife. "Jean! Come down here! Our prodigal son is home." When Ms. G. came down from upstairs, she couldn't believe her eyes. Mr. G. added,

"Come here boy. Damn, you look good." Then Mr. and Mrs G. gave Teco a big hug.

"I have a friend in my car. Let me get her." Teco walked out to the car and told Toi to come into the house.

"Boy, I have taught you well. Who is this princess?" asked Mr. G; and Toi blushed at Mr. G.'s compliment.

"Toi, this is Mr. G, Fatboy's dad; and this is Mrs. G." Mr. G. led Teco to the dinner table as Toi and Mrs. G. sat down in the living room.

"Son, where did you find her?" asked Mr. G. patting Teco on the back.

"She found me first . . . . Where's Fatboy?"

"He moved out a while back to a place in North Philly. He's at work now though. Let me call him." Mr. G went to the green phone on the kitchen wall and looked at Teco with pride to see that Teco wasn't strung out on drugs. "Hey son, I have a surprise for you. Hold on," said Mr. G. who passed Teco the phone.

"Hey Man . . . I just got into town . . . My bad, I didn't know you were in a meeting . . . I'll get your number from your dad . . . Later."

Mr. G asked, "So, what's up with Ms. Toi?"

"She's my road manager."

"Your what? Are you a rapper or something?" Mr. G. rummaged through a kitchen drawer looking for a pen and paper.

"No," said Teco smiling. "I'm D.C.'s number one male exotic dancer."

Mr. G. looked at Teco waiting for the joke and when Teco didn't say another word, Mr. G. burst out into laughter. "No shit?"

"For real Mr. G, I'm here to do a big show at Hunk Mania. So how is Fatboy doing?"

"He's doing well for himself. Come with me. I have something to show you," said Mr. G. who passed Teco Fatboy's cell phone number on a torn sheet of paper. Teco followed Mr. G. into the garage, where Mr. G. pointed to a 1978 Cutlas in mint condition.

Not knowing if Mr. G. was going to ask him to help work on the car, Teco said, "You need me to change out of this white linen suit and help you with the car?" In the past, Teco was the one to always help Mr. G. do chores around the house, while Fatboy was in the house sleeping.

Mr. G. said, "No son, you look good. I was worried about you once you left Philly and didn't know if you would get caught up in the system down there in D.C. We need more male role models in the neighborhood. You were born a leader. I saw that in you." Mr. G. fumbled with the engine, accidentally smudged motor oil on the right cheek of his face, and continued, "Man, I thought I was training you to be a mechanic. But I see you are a pretty boy now." They laughed.

"Mr. G., I want to thank you for helping me out when I was out running the streets—"

"Hold on, I wanted to do more, but—"

"You gave me what I needed at that time." As Teco told Mr. G. about the male exotic stage life, Mr. G. continued to work on the car.

"Boy, tell me about those G-String murders in D.C."

Teco looked at Mr. G. in total shock. "How did you know about them?"

"It's all on the news up here. It's been reported that the G-String murderer has ties back to Conshohocken. You better be safe. I hope it's a coincidence that you are a male dancer and this thing is tied to Conshohocken, one of your old stomping grounds." Mr. G. made a final adjustment to the engine and let down the hood to the car. Teco passed Mr. G. a towel to wipe his hands.

"Listen, don't worry about me. I'm safe."

Mr. G. wasn't buying Teco's answer and asked, "Do you remember what I told you when your friend Blue overdosed on drugs and died?"

In unison they said, "Always do what you always did; and you'll always get what you always got." Mr. G. smiled.

"I know Mr. G. I know. Trust me. Those words convinced me to get off the streets. I have another one for you. 'See it for what it is and see it for what it's worth'," said Teco remembering the similar conversation with his own father.

"Damn, I've got to remember that one . . . . And living a life on the streets wasn't worth much was it, son?" asked Mr. G., who embraced Teco once more. As Teco and Mr. G. walked back into the house, Mr. G. kept repeating, "See it for what it is and see it for what it's worth."

◊◊◊◊◊

GQ sat in the Admissions Counselor's office at the Art Institute of Philadelphia. She was trying her best not to overhear his telephone conversation, which interpreted their meeting. So instead, GQ focused on the décor of the room. Behind the desk was a terrific view of the city. On the walls were pastel art drawings of Rosa Parks, Martin Luther King, Jr., and Nelson Mandela. To the right was a book shelf, which held a Bose stereo system and speakers. Just as she turned back to look at the cherry wood executive desk, the Admissions Counselor said, "My apologies Ms. Que, I had to take that call . . . . Where were we? . . . Okay, I find that it's a beautiful thing that you want to be a fashion designer; however, we have a problem."

"And what might that be?" asked GQ.

"This is the second week of classes and it might be tough to catch up—"

"Mr. Gordon, I need these classes . . . . Can I be honest with you?" She asked not knowing if she should tell him the details.

"Sure you can." He said intently.

With great eye contact and conviction, GQ said, "I just got out of the penitentiary and I refuse to go back. This has always been my dream. You see my fashion portfolio before you. A few weeks ago, I met with Karlyn Fashion Recruiters on 7th Avenue in Manhattan. They say that I have raw talent. I'm just missing a few of the fundamentals."

Mr. Gordon looked at GQ as she poured out her heart; however, there was something very familiar about her. "Karlyn Fashion Recruiters. Very impressive." He said.

"How much are classes for this semester? I'll pay cash in full."

"Not having to go through the financial aid process cuts down the application processing time. Just know that you will have to work hard to catch up on the work you've already missed."

"Whatever I need to do is fine with me. I owe you. Thank you so much."

As Bernard Gordon pulled out admission papers and put them in a folder, he looked at GQ with an inquisitive stare.

"Are you alright Mr. Gordon?"

"Yes, I'm fine. Have we met before?" Her hazel eyes were exquisite.

"I was thinking the same." She said.

"Have a seat in the waiting area to fill the papers out or you can bring them back with your payment." He said standing with his hand extended. GQ shook his hand and walked towards the door. "Ms. Que . . ."

"Yes." She said turning around.

He looked into her almond-blue eyes again and said, "Please tell no one about your late admission; and welcome to our school."

She put on her sunglasses and said, "Mr. Gordon my word is my bond, Strictly Business. Thank you." When she walked out of his office, she breathed a sigh of relief.

"*Strictly Business . . . Strictly Business . . .* " Mr. Gordon sat in his office trying to figure out why "Strictly Business" was such a vivid phrase. Drumming his hands on his desk, he exclaimed, "Damn! That's the SB Crew name, Strictly Business." He hopped out of his executive chair to see if she was still in the lobby. However, when he opened his office door, she waved at him and did her Cinderella spin as the elevator doors closed.

CHAPTER 20

When Teco hit City Line Avenue in Philadelphia, he called Fatboy. The phone rang four times and went directly into voicemail; so he left a message. Toi was pointing to the hotel where they would be staying. The Valet Attendant opened the door for Toi and said, "Welcome to the Westin hotel." Teco stepped out of the car feeling like a big time celebrity. The only other time he felt like this was when he was put down with the SB Crew, who took him to Atlantic City on his first major shopping spree. In spite of that, the SB life was behind him now; and better things stood in his future. "Any luggage sir?" asked the Valet Attendant.

"Yes we have 5 bags in the trunk," said Teco, who released the latch.

"Sir, here's your ticket." After Teco put the valet ticket in his pocket, he gave $50 to the attendant, who said with a huge smile, "Thank You sir." Teco allowed Toi to lead the way to the front desk.

As Toi checked into the hotel, Teco checked out the lavish layout of the lobby. The cathedral ceiling and the white column pillars made Teco feel as if he were in another country. The marble floors looked so slick that he was surprised that guests weren't watching their steps. The artwork on the walls reminded him of an art exhibit. *"Damn this is tight."*

A few minutes later, Toi tapped Teco on the shoulder. When he turned around, she gave him his key card with a smile and said, "Our suite is 331."

"Thanks." He said giving her a kiss on the forehead. "When can we go see the club?"

"Can we just relax a little before we get to business?" asked Toi.

He looked at her with his left eyebrow raised, "I thought this was a business trip . . . . I guess we can chill." Teco was dispirited because he wanted to get a feel for the stage at the club before dancing tonight. Once the elevator stopped the bellhop stepped off making a left to take them to their suite. Then Teco's cell phone rang. "Hello, this is Teco."

"Yo, homie. What's up?" asked Bernard Gordon, a.k.a. Fatboy.

"Fatboy!" Teco burst out into laughter. "Man, what's up with you?"

"I just checked my voicemail. My dad says you're doing good."

"Well, I'm doing okay for myself. Look, Greek Fest is tomorrow. Let's hook up."

"Yo, I need to talk to you about something."

"What's up? Fatboy, hold on . . . ." Teco held the door to the suite open for Toi. "Yo, you there?"

Fatboy said, "Yeah, meet me at noon. Guess what female came into my office—"

"Hello, hel—" Teco looked at his cell phone and saw that he didn't have reception in the room.

"What's wrong?" asked Toi.

"That was my homie, Fatboy. The line dropped when he was going to tell me something. Maybe he wants to be a dancer. No . . . he said something about a female. Well, I'll see him tomorrow."

They walked into a 2 bedroom and 2 bathroom suite with a huge living area. Toi smelled the fragrance of roses as she and Teco stood by the wooden sofa table. Before Teco could put his things down, she blocked the doorway to his room. "Would you like something from the wet bar to drink?" She asked.

"No thank you . . . . Excuse me. I need to make a quick call. I'll be right out," said Teco closing the door to his room. He went to the phone beside his bed to call Trooper. The phone rang three times but there was no answer; therefore, he left a charming message with the number to the room.

Teco grabbed the remote and pushed the button. An ABC newscaster said, "Some time last night a male exotic dancer was shot and killed in a Washington, D. C. restaurant. The AP reports that the murder still appears to link back to ties in Philadelphia. However, this has not been confirmed at this time. We will keep you informed as we get additional updates . . . ." Teco turned up the volume not believing what he heard. Even though he was glad that he was in Philly, he would feel better once he knew Trooper was safe since she was the lead detective on the case.

Deciding that he needed to be in a good mood to dance tonight, Teco turned off the television and shifted his thoughts to being in a meaningful relationship with Trooper. Here he was in a hotel suite with a drop dead gorgeous woman like Toi; however, he no longer wanted to be known as the "playa" who always "dipped out." As he thought about holding Trooper in his arms, the hotel phone rang. "Hello."

"This is Detective Troop."

"Hello Hanae, are you busy?"

Trooper smiled at the sound of his sexy voice. She was surprised how turned on he made her feel. "I'm working on a case, but I can talk for a minute or two." She said while sitting at her police station desk.

"I wanted you to know that I made it safely; and I'm looking forward to a second tryst."

"Is that right? So, I guess you called yourself checking in? She asked playfully.

"You said you wanted to provide me some protection." He said lying down on his back.

"I did indeed. Do you still need protection?" Trooper asked biting on her bottom lip.

"Yes, I'm terrified without you near," said Teco trying to entice her. "I also want to know that you are safe. I just saw on the news that—"

"Teco, I've got to go. Call me later. Bye." Detective Troop looked at the Caller ID and the incoming call said "Candi." Trooper picked up the phone and said, "This is Detective Trooper speaking . . . . Hello?"

"Yesss." Candi said trembling beside her car in the Marriott Crystal City hotel garage.

"Are you hurt?" asked Trooper trying not to sound confrontational in order to keep Candi on the phone. Trooper signaled for Swoosh to trace the call.

"Nooo. Not yet," said Candi, who was crying as she tried to clearly speak into her cell phone.

"Good, because I won't let anything happen to you . . . . Twyla, we know who you are. Just give me a chance to talk with you please?" After setting up the trace, Swoosh looked at Trooper with sheer excitement, because they were finally speaking with Twyla Burke. Trooper continued, "Candi, where are you?"

"When can we talk?" asked Candi, who was finally composing herself. Trooper's voice was putting her at ease; and Candi began to feel like she was going to be given a fair chance.

"Tell me where you are and I'll come to you," said Trooper.

"No, no, I'll set the place and time when I call you tomorrow."

"Let's meet at a public place tonight if that will make you feel better. My partner and I are headed over to the Classic."

"Whoever is following me will be there tonight. He will think that I'll be there. It's as if he is setting me up."

"Who is setting you up Candi?"

Click! There was a dial tone. Candi saw a black Town Car come into the garage and she hunkered down beside her car. She knew she had to leave immediately. The car passed by and headed to the upper level. So, Candi quickly hopped into her car because this was the perfect time for her to leave and go back home to Philly. As Candi pulled out of the garage into the street, she dialed her mother's number.

"Hello," said Candi.

"Twyla, what have you been up to? Hit me back on the red line." Mrs. Burke knew that the phone was tapped. The Burke family had a separate telephone system which was for emergencies only. Candi realized that she was jeopardizing her mother's prostitution business by calling.

"Mommy—"

"Are you okay? The FBI has been posted by the house for weeks. They even came by to question me. They say it's tied to some of your doings here in Conshohocken." Mrs. Burke took a seat on the red, blue, and tan plaid sofa in her office.

"They said Conshohocken?" Candi asked almost dropping the phone.

"Yes and they asked me about some hood rat named GQ. I'm glad you don't know her. I'm going to ask you one more time. What have you been up to?"

"Mommy, I swear to you—"

"Girl, don't be swearing. Baby, you know I wouldn't tell you anything wrong. Go to the police wherever you are. I believe you are a good person caught up in a bad situation." Candi burst out into tears and her mother didn't know what to say next.

"Mommy, I didn't do any of it. I am innocent."

"I believe you. That's why you have to go to the police." Mrs. Burke said convincingly.

"I'm going to talk with them tomorrow."

"No, Twyla, tonight . . . Do you hear me?" asked her mother, who got up to look out of her office window. She wanted to see if anyone from the surveillance truck down the street was approaching the house.

"After I talk with them, may I come home?"

"Of course, baby."

Candi wiped the tears from her eyes and tried to focus more clearly on the road. She was so busy thinking about what she was going to say to the detectives that she never saw The Paradox tailing her car. He followed Candi into a gas station parking lot and saw her talking on the cell phone.

"Hello, this is Detective Troop."

"Can you meet me at my apartment tomorrow—"

"Candi, I would like to see you tonight. We really need to talk. The waitress at Denny's identified you as the female who was with the victim."

"I know, but not tonight. How about in the morning?"

"What's the address?"

"I'll tell you tomorrow." Candi wiped her face and touched up her makeup. Deciding tomorrow was soon enough, Candi headed back to her apartment to pack her clothes for Philly.

"Hello? Hello?" asked Trooper, who turned to her partner.

"What happened?" asked Swoosh.

"She hung up. Any luck on the trace?"

"Nothing. We only traced it to the switching station and never made the trace to her phone," said Swoosh disappointed.

Trooper put on plastic gloves and pulled out the evidence bag with the note which was tied to the black G-String.

"The notes just spell out the colors of all the G-Strings. Does it spell out anything else? It has to." She said, pushing backwards from her desk.

"Trooper, you will want to see this," said Swoosh. Trooper walked over to Swoosh's desk. He continued, "I just got this email. Check it out."

The note read, "YOU HAVE SEVERAL COLORS. HOWEVER, YOU ARE MISSING TWO."

"Damn! That means there may be 2 more murders. We have to figure this out fast," said Trooper pulling out a Snickers bar.

Rubbing his forehead, Swoosh said, "That's not all I'm concerned about. Why is he emailing me and not you?"

"Why does that matter?"

"Because I'm not a dancer, and it makes me think he doesn't trust you any more. That's not good."

"Well, nothing this killer does makes sense to me. I'm going to call it a night," said Trooper. Her muscles were tense as hell; and she needed to find a way to relax. On the ride home, she turned on some smooth jazz; then her cell phone rang.

"Hey sexy," said Teco.

"Hi there. I'm sorry I hung up on you. Something urgent came up." She said rubbing her neck as she waited at a red light.

"You don't sound good. Are you okay?" Teco was at the club and "Give Me The Night" by George Benson was bumping in the background.

"Yeah, I'll be alright. Hearing the concern in your voice helps."

"Listen, I have to go get dressed for my set. I'll be thinking of you as I dance."

"Oh really?" She asked smiling.

"Why are you surprised?" He asked entering the dressing room and acknowledging the other dancers with a subtle nod.

"I like that you will be thinking of me." She said as she pulled into her driveway.

"Well, I have to jet. Talk with you soon."

"Night." Trooper was still stressed. Having a man like Teco in her life would serve her well, because no man ever called her up out of the blue to check up on her. Because she worked long hours her ex-husband left her over a year ago. In fact, work still consumed her. As she sat in her driveway the crime scenes flashed back and forth and side to side in her mind. Trooper let out a deep exhale. Even opening the car door seemed to be hard work for her.

When she hit the top steps inside her two-level home, she went straight to the bathroom to turn on the shower. Before she left the bathroom, Trooper started to take her clothes off. By the time she reached her bedroom, she was in her birthday suit.

She went into her walk-in closet and reached up to the top left shelf to pull down a black box. After placing the box onto the marble bathroom countertop, Trooper turned on her CD player to "Cause I Love You" by Lenny Williams. Lighting several lavender and thyme candles throughout the bathroom, Trooper cut off the lights. Then she stepped into the shower. The hot water flowed over her figure eight body from head to toe. She smelled the lemon verbena fragrance of the shower gel.

As the steam kissed her face, Trooper closed her eyes and heard Teco's voice, *"Hey sexy . . . sexy . . . sexy . . . I will be thinking of you when I dance tonight . . . tonight . . . tonight . . . "* Trooper *turned around and let the water massage her lower back. She felt Teco come from behind and press his body sexily against her. As he placed his hands on her hips, Teco turned her around. Then he put her hands on his chest. He moved her hands lower . . . lower . . . There was no G-String and no need for him to use a strap to beef up. "Umm . . . Hanae . . . " Their bodies merged. "I love you. I love you. I love you."* The song ended, and Trooper opened her eyes.

Trooper cut off the water and put on her white waffle spa robe. The aroma from the candles and shower gel seemed to relax every muscle. Changing CDs, she turned on the "Elixir" smooth jazz CD by Fourplay. She sat down on a small purple cushioned bench in the bathroom and softly rubbed body oil all over her wet body. Her skinned glistened. Moving to the bathroom counter, Trooper opened the black box. Holding Pleasure in her hand, she knew all remaining stress and tension would dissolve away, because Pleasure sometimes put her to sleep. Sliding the button to the on position, she watched the gold tip haze up from the steam in the bathroom and sighed with relief.

CHAPTER 21

C andi felt the warmth of the sun on her face from the window. Looking at the clock, she couldn't believe that 8 o'clock in the morning came so quickly. She awoke thinking about all of the victims. Even the person following her in the Town Car was unnerving. She was starting to agree that this was related to the death of Bashi Fiten. Then the cell phone vibrated which scared the shit out of her.

"Hello."

"Candi, I know you are trying to leave town. Are we meeting this morning?" asked Trooper.

"Yes, I live at Rosewood Village Apartment 322."

"Do you mind if I tape our conversation?"

"No, I don't mind."

Trooper pushed the button to the recorder. "These dancers . . . Are you the one killing them or having them killed?" asked Trooper, who was also waiting for the judge to approve the search warrant.

"Detective Troop, I haven't killed anyone. It's a long story." Candi said crying with her right hand on her forehead.

"Okay, tell me so that I can understand." Trooper said trying to calm her down.

"You won't understand." Candi moved to the bathroom to get a cold hand towel to wipe her face.

"Listen Candi, whoever is doing this is making it look like—"

"I know, but I didn't do anything to hurt my friends. Remember, I was the person eating with Kream when he was shot. I didn't pull the trigger . . . ." She said walking to the living room.

As Trooper and Candi spoke on the phone, The Paradox got out of the Town Car. From the trunk, he pulled out a portable sound amplifier and a multi-element microphone, which he put into his pocket. The earpiece was in both ears. Then he pulled out his Beretta and put the silencer to the tip of the barrel. As he approached the apartment building, he turned on the amplifier. The Paradox scaled the fire escape to a 3rd floor exit door. After closing the door, he put a wedge at the bottom so that no one from the outside could enter. Candi's apartment was 2 doors from the exit; and he stopped in front of her door to listen.

" . . . I use to be on drugs real bad when I lived in Conshohocken, outside of Philly. I should have told the police the evil things I saw; but I didn't." Candi said pacing in the living room.

"I see." Trooper emptied the pieces of colorful cloth from the envelope onto her office desk. "Go on."

"At first I was in love with this guy. Then I started using drugs with him. I became very dependent . . . ." Outside the door, The Paradox could hardly wait to hear Candi talk about the love they shared.

"Did he love you?" asked Trooper trying to establish motive.

"Yes. However when I became an addict, he used me as a decoy to hurt people. I never touched a soul; however, I should have reported him when he killed Bashi Fiten."

"You mean Gail Que didn't kill Bashi Fiten?"

"No, she didn't. However, she was there when Bashi was killed. My ex-boyfriend knocked GQ out before killing Bashi."

"Where was Teco Jackson?" asked Trooper.

"Who is Teco Jackson?" asked Candi, who went to the kitchen to get a glass of orange juice because she was feeling dizzy.

Trooper leaned back in her office chair. Somewhat relieved that Candi didn't know Teco, she asked, "Do you know him as Homicide?"

"I don't know Homicide. However, my ex-boyfriend was arguing with Bashi about Homicide . . . then he . . ." Hearing Homicide's name caused The Paradox's temperature to rise.

"Candi? . . ." asked Trooper. Swoosh walked up to Trooper and passed her the search warrant.

"I'm here," said Candi sitting down on the living room couch with the glass of juice in her hand.

Looking over the search warrant, Trooper passed Swoosh a piece of paper with Candi's address and signaled for Swoosh to get officers over there. "Why is he killing dancers?" Trooper asked Candi.

"He hates other men around me. He is extremely possessive." The Paradox smiled that Candi still knew how much he cared about her.

"He references a snitch. A note he left says, 'I despise a snitch.' Who is the snitch?"

"I can only guess. There was a lot of talk on the streets about who killed Bashi. Before I left Philly, I told my ex-boyfriend that I was going to the police and tell them everything that he did to the SB Crew and Bashi; however, my threat didn't phase him one bit. Back then, he was more afraid of being caught by that guy name Homicide and the Young Black Mafia crew than he was of the police. So, I guess he figured that I would eventually be the snitch, because he knew sooner or later that I would talk." Just the sound of the word snitch made The Paradox press his muscular shoulder against the door.

"Who is your ex-boyfriend?"

"My ex-boyfriend's name is B—"

BOOM! The front door flew open and 2 shots were fired from The Paradox's Beretta. He snatched the phone from Candi's hand.

"Burke! Burke!" yelled Trooper, who stood to her feet.

"Hello Detective Troop," said The Paradox calmly.

"Who is this?" She asked demandingly.

"It's all your fault that my beloved Candi is dead. Those men didn't deserve her love." He said placing a red ladies G-String with a note in Candi's hand.

"You know this has nothing to do with your love for Candi. Looks like you knocked off a key witness," said Trooper in a hostile voice.

"My, my, my, did I hit a nerve, Detective? Did you figure out my puzzle yet?"

"Well I have a riddle for you," said Trooper placing her hand on her gun.

"Okay, I'm listening."

"What's too bright to look at in the broad daylight?" She asked trying her best to calm down and not let him feel as though he was getting the upper hand.

"Hummm, I must think about that; however, I have to go now because I hear sirens coming. Your friends are on the way. Tell me the answer the next time I buy you another drink at Club Classic."

Click. "Hello? Hello? . . . Swoosh, we've got to go!" exclaimed Trooper.

The Paradox looked around the room for any evidence that might lead Trooper back to him; however, Candi didn't have one single thing of his, which in a way ticked him off. He kissed Candi on the cheek and ran down the stairwell and into the car. As The Paradox drove down the street, he saw 5 police cars headed towards the apartments with the lights at full blast. Deciding the heat was too high in D.C., The Paradox decided to pack up his belongings.

When he arrived at his temporary residence in Southeast D.C., he drove to the backyard and parked beside his Chevy Astro van. The Paradox looked around to see how much he needed to transfer between cars; then he unlocked the door to the mini van. He thought it would be best to abandon the rental Town Car, which he stole weeks ago from the Avis parking lot. After he wiped down the Town Car for prints, he took out a full sized mirror to review the plan with himself.

"You need to start focusing on your next mission, which is not as easy. I can still count on you. Right?" asked the voice in The Paradox's head as he looked at his reflection in the mirror.

"Yes, Yes, I'm your man. I despise a snitch . . . . I despise a snitch . . . . Detective Trooper made me kill the only woman I loved and ultimately made my precious Candi talk. Now Detective Trooper must die!" The Paradox exclaimed holding the mirror tightly.

"Who else is a threat to us?" asked his alter ego.

"GQ was no risk to me in prison. Now that she is out, she can destroy what's left of my life if she remembers everything that happened the day I killed Bashi."

"Okay Soulja, 2 more then you're done. Remember to take your tools."

"I can't take everything. Now what?" He asked putting the mirror down in order to rummage through the trunk of the Town Car for the parts he needed.

"You know what you have to do?"

"Yes, it's done," said The Paradox taking the tools to the front of the house.

He looked around to ensure no one was watching and walked up to the front door. Measuring the length of the threshold, he pulled out a roll of green trip wire. He placed two 12 gauge security control devices next to the door. Then he rigged his contraption to be explosive. His mission was drawing him back to the streets. When he heard the next door neighbors pulling up in their driveway, he sprinted to get into the Astro van. There was some unfinished business in Philly with the woman whose eyes were simply exquisite.

◊◊◊◊◊

When Trooper saw Candi sitting there dead on the chair, Trooper asked, "How did he beat me to her?"

"Did you say something?" asked Linda.

With latex gloves on, Trooper knelt down beside Candi to examine the note, which was attached to the red G-String.

As she studied the attached note, Trooper was distracted by the chirp on her radio.

"B1 to T1," said Swoosh to Trooper.

"Go ahead," said Trooper.

"We've found something on her car," said Swoosh.

"I'll be right there." Trooper took this opportunity to egress out of the apartment. The hallway was full of badges so Trooper decided to exit down the fire escape. When she saw the door was jammed. She looked to the closest officer and said, "This is the way he got in." She turned around and rushed down the stairs to the first floor. Breathing quite heavily she exhaled deeply and looked at her watch. *"Eighteen seconds. This is the way he left."*

Swoosh walked up to Trooper and asked, "What do you think about this?" He held up a clear evidence bag with a little black box.

"Is that what I think it is?" Trooper asked looking around at the onlookers.

"Yep, it's a tracking device. And guess what?" By Trooper's expression, Swoosh knew that she couldn't fathom what was coming next. "When they found it, Candi's car was on a tow truck. The red light was flashing, which got my attention. After CSI removed it, that's when I saw the reflection of a finger print." Swoosh said looking as though he hit the lottery.

"We just might find her," said Trooper.

"Who? Candi is dead."

"Not Candi. We will find Lady Justice." The lights from the police cars were making the streets look like a club scene. The only thing missing were the dancers.

"I'll have them trace the serial number on the device. It might just help us out," said Swoosh.

Just as Trooper decided to go back into the building, Linda came out and said, "We have a print off of this wedge by the fire escape."

"Let's head back to the station." Trooper said to Linda.

Within the hour, Linda and Trooper were sitting in the lab waiting on the finger print results. The room looked sterile; and the white walls gave Trooper an eerie feeling. She didn't understand how Linda could work in a room with little character. Linda asked, "Okay, what do you want to see?"

"Show me the G-String murder weapons for each case."

Linda punched the computer keys with determination. "Okay . . . right there." WHITE, PINK, YELLOW, RED and BLACK displayed underneath each G-String on the screen.

"Okay, drag and drop all of the letters in the words out here on the screen. Can you spell out the name—" Before Trooper could finish her sentence, Linda displayed the name TWYLA on the screen. Trooper added, "Do you see any other names as it relates to this case?" When Linda displayed TECO, Trooper's heart dropped. She felt as if someone hit her in the gut. "Shit! I knew it!" Trooper exclaimed as the room seemed to close in upon her. "I'm headed back to my desk."

"You okay Trooper? You don't look so good," said Linda with a concerned look on her face.

Trooper never answered and left out of the lab. After getting off of the elevator, Trooper saw Swoosh sitting at his desk. "Booh-Yah!" exclaimed Swoosh as a balled up piece of white paper went into a trash can several desks away. When he saw Trooper, he said, "You know, for some reason, The Paradox wants you on his back."

"Why do you say that?"

"Before you got up here, Linda called me and told me the news about the names in the G-String colors. Linda's concerned about you. So am I."

"Well, The Paradox sure has my attention." Trooper said as Linda walked into the room.

"I have all of your reports back," said Linda smiling. Passing Swoosh 7 folders she continued, "Open the last folder."

"Oh, look at this . . . interesting," said Swoosh rocking in his office chair.

"What?" asked Trooper walking over to Swoosh's desk. "Don't tell me The Paradox is white."

"The fingerprint is from a white male; however, this guy owns an Army Navy store."

"Let me guess. He's from Philadelphia," said Trooper.

"Right again," said Swoosh as if he were a television hostess on a game show. "From the report, it looks like he has no ties with Twyla Burke or the SB Crew."

Linda said, "The Paradox wants us to put the puzzle together. Right? Okay, jot this. The Paradox is from Philadelphia or Conshohocken and so is Twyla Burke and Teco Jackson."

"Why do you think Teco Jackson has something to do with the murders?" asked Trooper defensively.

Swoosh replied, "How about this motive? . . . With these guys dead, Teco is now the #1 dancer—"

"No way, I don't believe he has anything to do with these murders. He was out of town during 2 of them. He has an alibi. Remember?" Trooper asked in an irritated voice.

"You don't have to be in town to hire a hit," said Swoosh.

"Before you open your big mouth you need to listen to my taped conversation with Candi," said Trooper trying not to curse Swoosh out.

"Damn, you don't have to be so oversensitive. I already know that you've had lunch with Mr. Teco Jackson," said Swoosh leaning forward in his chair and looking like he scored 3 points. Linda backed up knowing that the sparks were getting ready to fly.

"Are you following me?" asked Trooper with her arms crossed.

"When my partner starts having lunch with a possible murder suspect, hell yeah, I think its time I have my partner's back. Every time you see Teco Jackson, I see how you look at him. Then you go to the clubs investigating without me and—"

"What I do on my time off is my business!" Trooper exclaimed. Linda smirked because this was a good sign that Trooper was finally getting a life outside of work.

"Well, I had him followed. Miss I know how to handle my personal life," said Swoosh sarcastically. "Did you know he's back in Philly?"

Linda felt as though Swoosh was interrogating Trooper. His line of questioning was annoying both Linda and Trooper.

"Yes, of course." Trooper said emphatically.

"Well my new buddy FBI Agent Rozier faxed me these pictures," said Swoosh who took out the sheet of paper from his drawer and tossed it onto his desk. "You might feel differently about your boy, Teco, after seeing this."

"Since when have you become buddies with Rozier?" asked Trooper feeling her blood pressure rise and snatching the paper off of Swoosh's desk. There were several clear photo shots. The first photograph showed Teco opening the car door for Toi at a house in Mount Airy. Trooper scanned through the pictures until she reached the last picture of Teco sporting a huge smile as he escorted Toi into the Philadelphia Westin hotel. Trooper went back to her desk chair and plopped down. She didn't know whether to strangle Swoosh or to strangle Teco.

CHAPTER 22

G Q put ten of the G-Strings into a small bag and went to the club, Hunk Mania. Wanting to see if there was indeed a market for this style of G-Strings, GQ needed the money and also wanted to get her name out there. Radio station Power 99 was playing an old school jam "Rock the Bells" by L. L. Cool J as GQ traveled in her new Ford Tempo, which she bought on the low-low. Her spirits were instantly lifted. When she pulled into the parking lot of the club, she saw that the line circled 2 city blocks. GQ attributed this to a huge college crowd celebrating The Greek a day early.

When she reached the front door, the bouncer asked, "GQ, what's up?" She looked at him really crazy because she didn't know him. Then he asked, "Do you have any powder and weed?" Not knowing how best to respond, she smiled; and he let her go directly into the club. The entrance hallway was narrow. The walls were painted black with sparkling silver stars, which made GQ feel as if she were going to have a party experience out of this world. Then the club opened up into a huge space. She immediately saw the stage and 2 dance cages on each side. To the far right, the bar was outlined in white lights. On the wall was a neon sign that read, "HUNK MANIA."

The first dancer she saw, GQ asked, "Excuse me. May I speak with you?"

"Sure baby girl." The dancer said causing GQ to blush. "What can I do for you?" As "Love You Down" by Ready For The World blast through the speakers, he could hardly hear; so he grabbed GQ's elbow and led her to the pool table area of the club.

She continued, "I have this new style G-String; and I wanted to know if you or the other dancers would be interested in making a purchase."

"Let me see what they look like." He said looking into her hazel eyes.

As she was pulling one out of her bag, a guy walked up and whispered into her ear, "I need 2 bags of weed. Meet me at the bathroom in 15 minutes." Before she could respond, he walked away. Trying not to display a concerned look on her face, she handed the dancer the G-String.

He inspected the G-String and said, "Damn, I've never seen one like this before. How much is it?"

"$25." She said pleased that he liked her design.

"Do you have blue?"

"Yes, I do," said GQ pulling a blue G-String with suspenders from her bag.

"Do you have any business cards?"

"Here are a few for you." She said with a smile.

GQ sold all the G-Strings before the show. However, everywhere she turned somebody asked her for some drugs. She finally realized that they thought she was Gwen, which pissed her off. So GQ decided not to stay long, because she didn't want to get caught up in anything to violate parole. As she walked to the exit, the club was so crowded that she felt as if she were swimming up stream. As she continued towards the door, someone squeezed her ass. When GQ turned around to see who touched her, Teco walked through the door with Toi. He shoved his way through the crowd trying to make it to the dressing room. From a side view Teco saw GQ. He thought, *"Damn, I must be seeing shit again . . . . like when I was back at the IBEX in D.C., the night of the shooting."*

"Teco, did you hear me? Once I introduce you to the owner, you are own your own!" Toi screamed over the loud music; and Teco's cell vibrated in his bag.

As Toi led the way downstairs, she and Teco passed a few offices until they came to a door with a MANAGER sign in gold letters. She knocked.

"Come in," said Tye, the club manager who buzzed the door to open for them. "What's up baby girl? I see that you made it. How is your brother, Legend?" Tye asked Toi.

"He's fine. I brought you one of Chocolate City's finest, Rising Sun." She said.

Teco looked at the manager and gestured his head, "What's up?"

"Have a seat," said Tye pointing to 2 burgundy executive leather button chairs. "I hear that you guys have a lot of action going on in the Chocolate City with those G-String murders."

His comment took Toi and Teco by surprise. Teco said, "Yeah, we have to be on our P's and Q's. Plus, they have D.C.'s number one detective on the case."

"Right, I saw her fine ass on the news earlier today," said Tye; and Toi rolled her eyes. Tye continued, "Legend told me that you are a native of Philly."

"Born and raised," said Teco.

"Well, glad to have you here at the hottest spot in Philly." Then Tye pulled out some papers. "Toi, sign here." He said pointing to a line on the document. They all stood up and shook hands. Then Toi showed Teco the direction of the dressing room.

Putting his bag down, Teco noticed a dancer holding a blue G-String with suspenders. Because this style was not in D.C. yet, he wanted to purchase one. "Who makes those G's?" asked Teco.

"This female was selling them."

As Teco put baby oil on his chest, his cell phone vibrated again in his bag. "Is she still here?" asked Teco.

"If I see her again, I'll tell her that you would like to see her."

"Thanks man. Is the money good at this club?"

"Yeah, they like to see a real good show." He said putting on the G-String and pulling up the suspenders.

The stage manager came in and said to Teco, "New guy, 2 minutes to places."

The M.C.'s voice could be heard in the dressing room from the sound system, "Okay, Laaadies! We have a big treat for you. For your entertainment pleasure, we have with us the #1 dancer from the Chocolate City. If you have crossed over the burning sands to be here, it's well worth the journey because tonight the CITY . . . OF . . . BROTHERLY . . . LOVE welcomes home Risssing Sunnn!"

The club became pitch black. A white strobe like flickered insanely on stage as red, blue, green and yellow lights came from behind the strobe. The sound of thunder came from the background; and smoke covered the stage floor.

A computerized voice said, "You have now been sexualized by the Exotic Zone!"

Gliding on stage wearing a fuchsia and black rhinestone long cape, Rising Sun hit center stage. He dropped to one knee with his head down towards the floor and his cape sparkled from the spotlight. The thunder stopped rumbling and the fog cleared the stage as Babyface's song "When Can I See You Again," started to play. Women were magnetized to the stage as Rising Sun's torso popped to every beat of the music. Around and around his waist moved as he went lower and lower to the ground. Then he leaned his body back as if he were going under a pogo stick. After swaying back up with the music, he leapt through the air and landed flat on the floor. The women came closer to see him grind his body and to throw money on him. He smoothly stood up, struck a pose and took off the cape.

With the sound of an airplane landing, Toi's voice came over the loud speaker, "Ladies, this is the time which you've been waiting for. Please fasten your seatbelts and get ready as Rising Sun lands the beef in your lap!" The sound effects went BOOM! A black G-String trimmed in fuchsia displayed what every woman in the club wanted to see and to feel.

He navigated the crowd well. "Rising Sun come over here!" yelled a lady sitting at a nearby table. When he reached her, Rising Sun knelt down and kissed the back of her hand. As he stood up, she tipped him. The music ended and he left the stage while women cheered and screamed his name.

After his set, he was soaked with sweat and tired as hell. In the dressing room, he drank 2 bottles of spring water to cool off.

He didn't hear the phone in his bag vibrating because the M.C. came over the speaker system announcing the next dancer.

Tye came into the dressing room with a huge smile. "Man, you are a bad dancer, Mister; and the women loved you. I've got to get you back here soon so you can rock this place."

"Any time," said Teco as he shook Tye's hand.

"Look all drinks are on the house. I'll see you downstairs at my table. You can't miss it." Tye walked out of the door leaving Teco to get dressed. After Teco put all of his tips in his Crown Royal bag, he freshened up in an adjourning bathroom.

As he walked out of the bathroom naked, Toi walked into the dressing room. The other 3 dancers in the room acted as if she wasn't there because having a woman in the dressing room was not unusual. Toi's eyes immediately saw that Teco wasn't wearing a G-String. With her hand over her mouth, she said, "I see you've been holding back on a sister. You don't need to beef up after all. Well, I think I better leave."

"You can stay. I was just getting dressed." As he put on his shirt and tie, Toi told him that several women in the club were lined up outside to greet him. After he pulled up his pants, he placed a hand full of business cards into his pocket.

The dancer with the new style G-String said, "Yo, here is the business card of the female I was talking to earlier." Teco took the card, which read "Fashion Trends by Indigo." He added the card to the others in his pocket and put on his suit jacket.

While Teco sat in the VIP section with Tye, Teco couldn't help but notice these 6 guys dressed in red and white jumpsuits spinning red and white canes throughout the audience. Teco made a mental note to add the canes as a prop for one of his upcoming performances. Toi was talking with several ladies, who kept giving Teco the eye. "Excuse me Tye, I have a lot of ladies to mingle with," said Teco who pulled on the end of his cuffs making sure his cuff links could be seen. As he walked through the group of women, a female said, "Excuse me. May I speak with you?" For some reason, her voice was familiar. Teco felt her tapping him on his right shoulder and turned around. His toothpick almost fell out of his mouth when he saw his ex-girlfriend Rhonda, who was smiling at him with that "oh so" sexy look. She added, "Don't just stand there. Give me a hug."

He did as she requested and asked, "Did you enjoy my performance?"

"Yes I did. I still have that hotel room reserved for you." She said rubbing her hand up his arm.

Teco laughed and swiftly removed her hand. "Not tonight. I came here for all the ladies. I'm a professional male exotic dancer."

"So Mr. Rising Sun, what are your plans while you are in Philly?"

"Well, tomorrow I'm going to check out The Greek Fest. Then I'm headed back to D.C. with my road manager. As a matter of fact, let me introduce you to her."

"That's okay. I have to run," said Rhonda with no interest in meeting Toi.

As Rhonda walked away, Teco took his cell phone out of his bag and saw that there were a few missed calls. As he was scrolling through the list, the phone rang.

"Hey man, need your help," said Legend.

"What's up?" asked Teco.

"There is a big ladies convention in Atlanta; and the dancers who were supposed to perform called and cancelled. The show is tomorrow night; and they will pay us double."

"Word?"

"Yeah, you guys get some rest tonight. I have 2 plane tickets for you and Toi on a 1 o'clock flight tomorrow afternoon. I'll meet you guys there."

"Got it." Teco ended the call. Continuing to scroll down on his cell phone, he saw 10 missed calls from Trooper; however, there was no voice message. So he dialed her number.

"You have reached the voicemail of Hanae Trooper, please leave a brief message at the tone." Beep.

"Hey sexy, I'm just leaving the club here in Philly. I just saw your number on my cell. I'm headed to Atlanta for a show. Call me back. I miss you," said Teco in his bedroom voice.

Toi walked up to Teco and asked, "Are you ready?"

"Let me call Fatboy before I forget. . . . Damn!" exclaimed Teco.

"What's wrong?" asked Toi. Teco didn't respond because he was leaving Fatboy a voice message that he wouldn't be able to meet him at Greek Fest at the Plateau tomorrow.

"Did Legend call you?" asked Teco putting his cell phone on his hip.

"Yes he did. Do you have an outfit to wear tomorrow night?"

"I'm set." Because people where pushing Toi around as they left the building, Teco put his arm around her waist and pulled her close to him to insure she wouldn't get trampled. Across the street, FBI Agent Rozier continued to take pictures of Teco and Toi for Swoosh.

CHAPTER 23

T oi and Teco met Legend by the Hertz Gold marquee board. They put their luggage into a pearl colored Infiniti J30. Then Legend took them to an area called Buckhead, which is the Beverly Hills of Atlanta.

"Teco, they also call Atlanta the Black Mecca of the South," said Legend.

"Yeah, I think I've heard something like that. Are we going to have time to go by the King Center?" asked Teco.

"Yes, every dancer I bring to Atlanta asks me that question."

"That's because he is one of our forefathers."

As they pulled up to Lenox Square mall, Teco's phone vibrated for a brief second and stopped. "Man, we must have bad coverage around here," said Teco seeing that he lost cell reception.

"Nah, you need to get a new phone. Mine works fine. I got it here at this mall," said Legend.

"I can dig that. I do need a new phone."

As they walked into the mall, Teco went to a pay phone to check his cell phone voice messages. Trooper's message said, "There's no need for me to tell you who this is. I've tried calling you for the longest. I need to talk with you. It's very important. I got your message that you are in Atlanta. Call me back with your return flight information. I'll pick you up from the airport when you get back to D.C." Teco wondered what Trooper wanted to talk with him about.

After an hour, Teco's hands were full with bags. His purchases were all top of the line gear from Polo to Gucci. Teco saw a beautiful necklace with a diamond "X", "O", and a heart pendant in the window of Mayors Jewelers.

"Hey, I'm going into this jewelry store," said Teco, who believed this necklace would be the perfect gift for Trooper.

"Okay, meet us in the Louis Vuitton store. I need some luggage," said Toi.

As Teco walked in, a female jeweler said, "Sir I'll be happy to valet your bags for you in order for you to relax and shop. Is there a special gift you are looking for today?"

"Yes, I'm interested in the necklace in the window with the "X", "O", and the heart."

They walked towards the window; and she said, "Why yes. It represents hugs, kisses, and love. This is a great gift for someone you are getting to know. It's not too formal and not too casual."

"Perfect, I want to buy it." After she placed the necklace in a red velvet jewelry box, Teco paid and walked towards the Louis Vuitton store. Just as he came to the Starbucks, someone asked, "Teco, is that you?"

When he turned around, there was Lisa Turner who was also a witness at Bashi's murder trial. "How have you been?" asked Teco.

"You have time to chat for a minute? I wouldn't mind catching up." She said with a big smile.

"Sure," said Teco as he pulled out a chair for her at a Starbucks wooden table.

"Wow, you look great." She said looking at his muscular arms.

"Do you remember our night together before we testified at the trial?" He asked while noticing that she wore a low cut top, which displayed her plump cleavage.

"Actually I think about it often." She looked at his chest and remembered how he flexed his muscles.

"Do you remember asking me to dance for you?"

"Don't laugh; but when I get stressed out at work, I think about your dance moves. I remember the passionate kisses you planted on my neck and the way you picked me up and put my legs around your waist—"

"Well you don't have to dream anymore. Come see me tonight. I'll be at the 20 Grand Club tonight."

"You are lying." She said with desire in her eyes.

"No, I'm serious. I enjoyed entertaining you that night; and I became a male exotic dancer."

"I just heard on BET News about some male exotic dancers being killed in D.C."

"I dance in D.C. and know the lead Detective on the case."

"Wow, I'm surprised. I never thought that you would be fraternizing with the po po." She said laughing.

Teco chuckled and said, "Let's just say, I'm helping her out like I did D.A. Brown at Bashi's trial."

"So you owe me for starting your dance career." She said moving her foot softly up his pant leg.

"Well, I guess so." The sexual innuendos were too much for him, because his pants filled with desire; and he wanted to sleep with Lisa again. Teco decided it would be best to find Legend and Toi before things went too far. He wanted to see if being in a meaningful and monogamous relationship was the life for him; and he wanted that life to be with Hanae Troop. He added, "Listen, I've got to run and get ready for the show. I hope you can see me perform tonight."

Disappointed that he didn't respond to her advances, she said, "I'll try."

As Teco walked down the mall hallway, Legend walked up to Teco and said, "Let's jet. We need to get over to the club."

Several hours later, Legend and Rising Sun stood stage left at the 20 Grand Club. There were 500 ladies in the audience. They were the last act; and the other dancers from Atlanta kept the ladies pumped up throughout the night. The atmosphere in the room was electric and the M.C. exclaimed, "Laaadies! We love to give you something new every time. We have promised you a Chocolate City treat. To mix it up, we have 2 flavors milk chocolate and dark chocolate. Put your hands together for '2 The Hard Way!'"

Everyone in the club clapped and a few ladies even whistled. "Whoop There it Is" by Tag Team played; and there was a loud BOOM! The sound was like a bomb dropping onto the red Georgia clay. Legend came onto the stage doing back flips and hit the ground just as the sound effect made another loud BOOM! Legend stood there in an erotic pose with the lights sparkling off of his blue and green outfit.

There was yet another sound effect of a bomb dropping; and when it hit, there was a bright flash with a puff of smoke. BOOM! Once the smoke cleared there was Rising Sun in a blue and red outfit striking a pose next to Legend. Then the lights went out. Boosh!

The M.C. continued, "I would like for you ladies to let go and let '2 The Hard Way' give you what you've come here forrr!"

The lights came back on and there stood Legend and Rising Sun each wearing a black cape. The audience screamed and several ladies tried to grab them both off the stage. Legend did a swift spin causing the cape to spread open; and Rising Sun followed Legend's lead. As they spun around, their capes fell to the floor and the music came to a complete stop. Boom!

Fog filled the air. When it cleared Legend was no longer on the stage and Rising Sun held his pose ready to dance for the ladies. "Trading my Life" by R. Kelly played; and the cheers were deafening from the 500 women.

◊◊◊◊◊

The next day, Trooper ate a Snickers bar as she waited for the plane to taxi. The door to gate B7 opened; and Trooper leaned against the wall so that Teco wouldn't see her right away. As passengers deplaned, the gate area started to become full with people. There was no sign of Teco; therefore, Trooper looked at her watch. When she looked up, there he was coming off of the plane with a man and the woman in the Philly pictures. Trooper's heart jumped an extra beat; and she couldn't believe that he never saw her standing by the wall. Walking behind him until he passed the security gate, Trooper said, "Mr. Jackson, I have some questions for you. You need to come with me down to the station." Then she flashed her badge as Legend watched Trooper grasp Teco's arm.

"Hanae, what's up?" He asked with a bright smile trying not to appear embarrassed. Her hand demonstrated that she was for real about going down to the station. Then she walked in front of him to stop him right there in the hall. "Jackson, don't make me cuff you."

Legend looked at Teco with a smirk and thought that Teco and his girl planned a role playing stunt, which was kind of cool. Trooper dressed in a nice navy blue business pant suit with a white button down shirt. Legend immediately admired her stance.

Trooper stared at Toi with her right eye brow raised, because she still couldn't figure out how Toi fit into the picture. The last set of pictures of Toi and Teco at the Hunk Mania club made Trooper's blood boil. Though Candi said that she didn't know Teco, Trooper was insistent on finding out once and for all if Teco put a hit out on these dancers to advance his own career.

Toi returned Trooper's stare by sucking her teeth. "Rising Sun, you aren't going to introduce us to your girl?" asked Toi.

"His girl?" asked Trooper sounding confused.

"You have to be his girl because he ain't giving it up for nobody else," said Toi in a sarcastic manner.

Teco decided to break the tension and said, "Detective Hanae Troop, this is Jimar Wilson my partner for out of town performances; and this is our business road manager Toi Wilson, Jimar's sister."

Trooper kept her guard up and said, "Nice to meet you. I'm investigating the G-String murders. I'm taking Mr. Jackson in for some routine questioning. Here is my card if you have any information regarding the case."

"Oh, you are the girl who Teco has been bragging about as the #1 Detective in D.C. I've seen you at Club Classic," said Toi looking relieved, because this meant Teco was still available.

"Rising Sun, we'll holla at you later . . ." said Legend turning towards baggage claim. " . . . Detective Trooper, don't hurt my boy." Trooper looked at Legend with the "cop look" that says, "Mind your business and move on."

CHAPTER 24

When Trooper and Teco reached the airport curb, she stood behind Teco, pushed him against the car and said, "Put your hands on the hood."

"Wait . . . wait . . . what the hell is this Hanae?" He asked trying to turn around.

As she frisked him she got close up to his left ear, "You know what this is Mr. Homicide."

"So you are bringing up my past now?" At first he was tolerating her treatment of him. Now she was going too far. Trooper didn't reply. Opening the back door, Teco got into the car; and Trooper put his bags in the trunk. As she started the car, he said, "Hanae talk to me. What do you need to know?"

"Are you murdering these men to become the #1 dancer in D.C.?"

"Hell no," said Teco leaning forward and looking through the bars in the police car. "Why would I kill somebody? I have natural talent. I don't have to bump nobody off to be #1. I don't want it like that." He leaned back in the seat mad as hell.

"So, you expect me to believe that this is all a coincidence? Candi said that someone in Conshohocken is behind this. And that person knows you."

"If someone else is behind this, why the hell am I in the back seat of this car?"

She ignored his question again and said, "Seconds before she was killed, Candi mentioned someone whose name begins with a "B." Who was the last person, whose name begins with a "B" in Conshohocken did you argue with before Bashi was killed?" Teco looked baffled.

There was a call over the car radio, "T1, are you there? Copy," asked Swoosh.

"Yes B1, I'm here. Go ahead," said Trooper.

"We have the address where the transmitter was shipped. It's a house outside of Southeast D.C. We're on our way up there with a full SWAT team."

"Don't go in until I get there. What's the address?"

Teco couldn't believe what he was hearing. Trooper put on the sirens and the flashing lights. When she pressed down on the gas pedal, Teco grabbed his seat belt because she was flying through traffic as if she were in the Daytona 500.

"Hanae . . . Hanae! Do you hear me? I have nothing to do with this shit! If you are not going to let me go, then read me my rights!" He was frustrated beyond belief. However, she suspected that Teco had nothing to do with the murders. This was her way of making sure and protecting her heart.

When they arrived at the rundown house in Southeast D.C., Teco was in total shock. There were cops everywhere. "What the hell is this?" He asked as Trooper parked the car across the street from the house.

She turned around and said, "Stay right here."

"Hanae, this is crazy!" Sweat was popping from Teco's brow. He felt as if he would never put the street life behind him. Then he remembered his dad's advice. *"See it for what it is and see it for what it's worth."*

Each member of the SWAT team was covered from head to toe in tactical gear and helmets. As Trooper approached Swoosh, he gave her a disapproving look. "Why is Teco Jackson in the back of your car?"

"I was on my way to the station to question him when I received your call." She said defensively.

"Well let him go. Teco Jackson is not a suspect. Our suspect lives in this house and is ex-military. The owner of the Army Navy store gave us a great deal of information about him."

"Hold up! When did you find this out?" asked Trooper.

"We tried to call you several times. Where was your radio?"

Trooper saw this as Swoosh checking up on her; and she didn't dignify his question with an answer. "I'll be right back." She said walking back towards the car as if she were going to kill someone. Teco just knew he was the target. Trooper opened the back car door and said, "Teco, I apologize for treating you roughly. I had to double check that you were not tied to these murders." She reached for his hand and Teco stepped out of the car. She continued, "It's come to my attention that you are no longer a suspect. If you give me a chance to make it up to you, I—"

FBI Agent Rozier walked up to Trooper and said, "Okay, it's your show."

Trooper surveyed the perimeter and saw several drivers who stopped in the middle of the road in order to see the drama unfold. Trooper exclaimed, "Get these cars out of here!" Immediately an officer ran to direct traffic. Then Trooper turned to the SWAT team and said, "Okay, let's get this asshole."

Rozier held up 2 fingers and pointed to the house. The entire SWAT team got into position. One group split to the left while another ran to the right. The third team went towards the front door with a battering ram. Rozier spoke through the radio, "All teams we enter on three . . . 1, 2, 3. Go! Go! Go!"

The officer with the ram hit the door once knocking the door halfway off it's hinges. When the door swung open there were shots fired. POW! POW!

"Oh shit!" exclaimed Trooper grabbing Teco by the arm as they hit the deck.

"Everybody stand down! We have gun fire! I repeat. We have gun fire!" shouted the SWAT team leader.

As Trooper motioned to get on one knee to stand up, the house went KA-BOOM! The explosion ripped the front of the house completely off. Teco took his entire body and shielded Trooper from the debris. When the atmosphere was quiet, Trooper looked up and saw blood coming from Teco's head.

"Are you okay?" She asked Teco. When he nodded, she looked around.

SWAT team members were scattered all over the ground. Some were missing body parts. The scene felt like an action movie; and Trooper prayed that the movie director would say, "Cut." However, this wasn't a film. Many of her comrades were down. EMT began doing triage.

Trooper looked for Swoosh who pulled out his inhaler and was headed towards her car. "You guys okay?" He asked taking a puff of the Albuterol.

Swoosh extended his hand to Teco, "Thanks man for shielding my partner. I should have been there myself. Let's get EMT to look at you." As Teco looked up, the skies were blue and the television helicopters looked like bees in the sky. He knew for sure that national stations were broadcasting this live.

As a paramedic checked Teco out, Swoosh pulled Trooper to the side. "I'll take care of the operations. I need you to get Teco out of here. If The Paradox is looking at us now, he will surely want to make his move on the next #1 dancer."

She ran over to the paramedics to check on Teco's status. They explained that he had a mild concussion and didn't need to be alone for 24 hours. When they found out that Teco was living alone, Trooper agreed to take Teco back to her house. As they were putting the steri-strips on Teco's cut, Trooper's phone rang.

"Hello Detective Troop. I think this is the first time I've seen you covered in dust," said The Paradox, who was in Philadelphia looking at Trooper on NBC News.

"Where in the hell are you?" Trooper asked observing her surroundings.

"You don't expect me to make this easy for you. Do you?"

She said, "I'm asking the questions. Did you find your snitch yet?" He didn't like Trooper's question and was hoping that she would conclude that the house episode was his grand finale. He constantly underestimated her skills.

Trying to throw Trooper off of his tracks, he said, "I'm tying up some loose ends. Maybe we can meet sometime . . . ."

"Hello? Hello?" Trooper stood there holding her cell phone. Everyone in law enforcement was doing their job. Crime scene tape was going up. EMT transported people to the hospital. CSI was walking the grid for evidence. Linda was taking pictures. Swoosh and Rozier sprinted with their guns drawn to what was left of the back of the house. However, Trooper knew if she didn't find out what loose ends The Paradox was talking about, more lives would be lost.

The next morning, Teco woke up in a strange place and sat up in a queen size canopy bed. The bedroom colors of mint green trimmed in tan made him feel peaceful. His attention was drawn to the 3-tier tray ceiling. He wasn't alarmed about his location, because the alluring scent of the expensive lavender therapeutic oils put him in a calm state.

Then Hanae sat down on the bed beside him. She was holding a glass of water and an aspirin. Teco thought he was dreaming until she said, "I'm sorry about what happened earlier today."

"I'm listening." Even though his head was throbbing, he decided not to say something stupid because he was finally in the bed of the woman of his dreams. The 1000 count sheets were so soft. If she were making up, her plan was working.

"All my life I've been driven to succeed. Every single case I'm assigned, I believe that I can snatch the perpetrator. I also believe that I have a great judge of character," said Hanae passing him the aspirin.

"What does this have to do with me?"

"I work long hours. I have no social life. Then I start falling for a man who is a suspect on one of my cases. That's a conflict of interest. However, I believe that you are innocent."

"So why did you treat me like a criminal earlier. I was ticked," said Teco trying not to come across too hard. He didn't want her to kick him out of her house.

"I was acting with my heart and not with my badge, to be frank." As he put the aspirin in his mouth, she passed him the water. "See, Swoosh faxed me these pictures of you and what's her name at the airport."

He put the glass on the night stand and asked, "Who? Toi?"

"Yes. And I must admit that I overreacted. I should have never thrown you around. If you want to press charges you—"

Before she could finish her statement, Teco reached over and grabbed her face putting his lips softly against hers. Teco's kiss was so mellifluous that she closed her eyes to go with his flow. At the end of the kiss, she bit down gently on his bottom lip. "Hanae, I accept your apology on one condition."

"What's that?"

"You agree to get to know me better."

◊◊◊◊◊

When Trooper left her home the next morning, Teco was still asleep. As she drove up to the house in Southeast D.C., she saw the smoke rising from the ashes left behind. Trooper couldn't believe whose car was already in the driveway and pulled up right behind him. The first object she saw on the ground was a smut covered sewing machine, which was too damaged to examine. Knowing that a fire scene is dangerous, she put on a blue medical face mask. Because this was an older home, there was a risk of asbestos. She made a note to be careful because of potential collapsing floors and falling beams.

Trooper walked to the back of the house watching her every step just in case she came across a piece of evidence. When she did reach the backyard, Swoosh was down on his knees looking at some tire tracks. "Damn I can't believe I beat you here this morning." He said without looking up.

"Yeah, whatever. What do you have here?" She asked ready to jump in and help.

"Tire tracks. There's a lot of build up. So, the neighbors probably didn't see what actually went down . . . Wait . . . Why do you have a glow on your face?" asked Swoosh looking closer into her eyes.

"I'm in a very good mood this morning. Thank you." She said smiling.

"Your eyes tell a more exciting story."

"Anyway . . . Do you want me to call CSI to lift those?"

"I've already called them. Thanks. If you look carefully at the tracks, you will see that the tread design is not simply a monotonous repetition of grooves and ribs. After careful inspection, we can compare the tread design with the makes and models of the cars that use different tires. Therefore, our computer database search will ultimately lead us to the make and model of The Paradox's vehicle." He said sounding studious.

"I see. You are paying me back for telling you about the history of fingerprints." They both laughed.

When Trooper looked around, she saw 2 little boys between the ages of 6 and 8 years old, who were looking over the wooden fence. "Be careful not to fall," said Trooper.

"We won't. We are standing on an upside down trash can," said the older brother.

"May I ask you a question?" asked Trooper.

"Our mama said not to talk to the po po," said the younger brother. "Are you a police woman?"

"No, I'm a detective." She said with a bright smile.

"Do you carry a gun like they do on television?" He asked picking his nose.

"I sure do. What's your name?"

"Mama said you can't tell her your name Jamal," said the older brother to the younger.

"Did that man burn up in there?"

"No Jamal. Did you ever see the man that lived in this house?"

"Yeah, me and my brother seen him. He is a black guy who is tall and looks like one of those wrestlers on television. Can I see your badge?" asked Jamal with bright brown eyes.

"Stop asking so many questions. I'm going to tell mama that you are talking to the po po," said the older brother, who hopped down and took off running. Jamal's eyebrows raised and his mouth flew open. The next thing Trooper heard were Jamal's feet hitting the dirt and the door to his house slamming.

CHAPTER 25

◊◊◊ 2 Months Later ◊◊◊

G Q got up from her assigned draft table. A lot of females in the class took a liking to her off the jump. She could inspire anyone, because she was taught by Bashi to always be a leader. Only 2 students in the classroom knew that GQ was released from prison a few months ago. One of the students was Francene, Mr. Gordon's sister. When Mr. Gordon came into the classroom, everybody looked up except GQ.

Mr. Gordon walked over to the female fashion instructor, who was writing in a green records book. He gave her a piece of paper and turned to leave the room.

"Bernard!" Because he knew the voice was his sister, he continued to walk out the door. "Fatboy! Fatboy!' exclaimed Francene.

GQ looked up. *"Fatboy . . . Fatboy . . . damn, why does that name sound familiar? Oh hell no, that can't be."* She stared harder at him as he turned around and went to Francene's drafting table. GQ turned back to her work to add the finishing touches on the outfit she was designing for an upcoming contest. Then he walked over to GQ's table.

"Ms. Que." He said in a formal voice.

"Hello, Mr. 'Fatboy' Gordon." She said with a smirk knowing Fatboy was her ticket to his best friend, Teco, a.k.a. Homicide.

"Is this your contest entry?" Everyone in the class turned to see if GQ would show her piece to him, because she was holding her design close to the vest.

"Yes, it is. As a matter of fact I've just finished it."

"May I see?" He asked. GQ was the leading designer in the entire school. Only attending college for 2 months, she was the most dedicated of all the other students. She held up her black coat dress design to the light, knowing that everyone wanted to see.

"Ah snap!" He shouted putting his hand over his mouth in excitement. "Excellent. Do you have more fashion designs?"

"Sure."

"Bring them to my office. There are distinguished guests at our college today. I would like for you to show them your work. Do you have your portfolio with you?"

Reaching into her bag, she said, "I have one right here."

"I like that you are always ready for business. Follow me."

GQ walked into Mr. Gordon's office as if she were the owner of the fashion school. Her presence was strong; however, her look was soft. She wore a business jacket and her hair was pulled back into a ponytail. Mr. Gordon signaled for her to take a seat.

"Gentlemen," said GQ nodding. The men in the room where taken aback by her beauty.

"Ms. Que, we would like to talk with you about a business proposition." This was new to GQ, because the only propositions she received on the streets were all illegal. "My name is Frontino Lefébvre. I'm the owner of an exclusive clothing line in Paris. These are my assistants and designers. May we look at your magnificent work? Is your agent coming to our meeting?" He asked with a deep French accent.

"Mr. Lefé . . ."

"Lefébvre"

"Mr. Lefébvre, I'm sorry but I don't have an a—"

"Wait! Excuse us for just a moment," exclaimed Mr. Gordon who pushed away from his desk and took GQ's arm. In the hallway, he looked into her eyes which appeared to be almond-blue and said, "Ms. Que." His speech was rushed.

"Call me Gail."

"Okay, Gail, these guys didn't come here to have a cup of latte. I don't know what I'm about to get my self into . . . ." He took a deep breath. " . . . but I'm willing to be your agent for 10% providing that you take their deal."

"You have got to be tripping. I don't know what kind of deal we are talking about yet."

He looked at her with a proud smile. "You will once we go back into the meeting and close that door behind us." With a flummoxed expression, she looked at the wood paneled door. He continued, "Look, several graduates from our college are working with top fashion designers. We can work out a way for you to continue your education in Paris. Gail, I'm down with you on this. How do you say it? Strictly Business." They shook hands and walked back into the office to commence their meeting. After he sat down, Mr. Gordon said in a business tone, "Gentlemen, I'm representing Ms. Que as her agent. She is ready for her presentation."

"Very well. Shall we continue?" Mr. Lefébvre asked looking at GQ, who passed him the portfolio. They marveled at the design of her new G-String. She enjoyed seeing their nods and whispers of approval.

"Did you design the jacket you have own?" Mr. Lefébvre asked.

"Yes, I did. I think it's important for a designer to wear her own work."

"May we see, please?"

Mr. Gordon stood up to assist GQ in taking off her jacket. Mr. Lefébvre and his staff looked at every dart and seam as they spoke in French. GQ didn't know if they liked her work or not, because their demeanor was serious.

"Well made, I must say." One of Mr. Lefébvre's assistants helped GQ put her jacket back on. After several minutes of discussion, Mr. Gordon offered everyone spring water. Then Mr. Lefébvre said, "I understand you want to call your collection Fashion Trends by Indigo. For our market, we suggest a different name. Would you allow us to create an Indigo Signature Collection? We love your work."

She gasped. "Are you serious?"

"Ms. Que, we don't make an offer unless we already know the designer will accept. We'll offer you 1 million U.S. dollars with a 250,000 U.S. dollars signing bonus. You can work at the Philadelphia studio, which we are building as I speak . . ." GQ turned to Mr. Gordon, who was taking notes. Everything was coming at GQ so quickly that she didn't know if this was a good deal or not. Mr. Lefébvre added, "Or you can come to Paris with us tomorrow, because our new employees always start at the first of the month. It's totally up to you."

"The first of the month in Paris sounds . . . How do you say wonderful in French?" She asked.

"Merveilleux," said Mr. Lefébvre.

"That too," said GQ and everyone laughed.

"We can do this deal if Ms. Que can have separated rights for some of her future work," said Mr. Gordon

"Oui, Oui. Mr. Gordon, we'll send you the papers for Ms. Que's attorney to review," said Mr. Lefébvre.

"Thank you." She said not knowing exactly how to respond. GQ retrieved her portfolio and shook their hands. As Mr. Gordon stayed to finalize the details, GQ cheered as she went back to the classroom.

By GQ's countenance, everyone in class knew that the meeting went well. GQ exclaimed, "Listen everyone! I have something to say. Ssshhh! Ssshhh! I've just signed with a major company out of Paris. Everyone that graduates with me will have a job at Fashion Trends by Indigo. My word is my bond!"

The entire class clapped and gave GQ hugs. Mr. Lefébvre heard them as he waited for the elevator. Mr. Gordon stood at the door smiling, because this was a big boost for the college. When GQ turned around, she saw Mr. Gordon. He winked at her with his left eye and said, "I'll pick you up to take you to the airport in the morning."

GQ turned back towards the class and said, "Yo! Yo! Let's clean up. Let's go to Happy Hour at Labelle's VIP Lounge on South Street by the Landing. I can't stay long because I'm GOING TO PARIS!" GQ said as she did her Cinderella spin.

When GQ walked out of class, she looked at her cell phone which displayed 1 missed call. She hit the number 1 button, which dialed her voicemail. "Hello, this is Teco Jackson, a male exotic dancer from D.C. I received your business card from a dancer at Hunk Mania and would like to buy a few of your G-Strings in several colors. Please call me at . . ."

"Oh shit!" exclaimed GQ. "Homicide is a dancer?" She laughed. As the message continued, she took out a pen and small notepad to write down his number. After taking a deep breath, she dialed him back.

The call went straight into voicemail, "Greetings Ladies, this is Rising Sun. Did you know that *The First of the Month Show* is coming up at The Mirage? Come see me and all the other exotic brothers of D.C. I'm unable to speak with you right now; however, leave a message at the tone."

Finally Teco, a.k.a. Homicide, was in reach. For 3 years, she served time because of him. She was going down to D.C. for the final face off once and for all. As she walked towards the exit, she remembered that her trip to Paris was also at the first of the month. *"Damn!"* Then she recalled what Chi Chi, her former cell mate, told her a while back. *"GQ, your future is more important than revenge."* With over $1 million at stake, GQ decided to fully disclose to Mr. Gordon, a.k.a. Fatboy, that she was the GQ, formerly from the SB Crew.

CHAPTER 26

Trooper was trying her best not to think about The Paradox, who seemed to be AWOL over the last 2 months. Because there were no more G-String murders since Candi's death, Trooper actually appreciated the reprieve from Captain Wicker in allowing her some needed time off. Even Swoosh told her that his background check into Teco Jackson turned up only minor infractions because Teco's Philadelphia criminal records were sealed.

After Teco shielded Trooper from The Paradox's house explosion debris, many of the law enforcement officers felt that Teco earned their respect by protecting one of their own. Since then, Trooper and Teco met daily for lunch getting to know each other at the Corner Bakery in Tyson's Corner. A week ago Teco asked Trooper on an official date; and she was driving over to Georgetown to meet him.

As she gripped the steering wheel, Trooper felt the moisture in the palm of her hands. This was her first date since her divorce. She didn't know why she felt skittish, even though her mind and body showed a deep interest in Teco. Regardless, she decided to hold her equanimity because her reputation preceded her.

Driving to Georgetown, Trooper looked into the navy blue sky and witnessed a bright white crescent moon with stars bursting with light. Beautiful shady trees lined the streets. When Teco gave Trooper the address, she pretended not to know. She made a left on M Street and a double right onto South Street. Pulling into the 2 car driveway of Teco's townhouse, Trooper parked beside the Benz which sparkled like a black diamond. Inside, Teco was reading, *Black Tail*, one of his favorite magazines. Then he saw headlights from a car cast a contour shadow on the curtains of his living room wall. He wasn't expecting anyone other than Hanae; however, he went to the curtains to confirm that she was the guest outside. When he saw her car, all he could do was smile. Because he knew Hanae was extremely conservative, he slipped the *Black Tail* magazine under the sofa cushion. He went to his sound system and turned on the album "Just an Illusion" by Najèe. Then he took the wave cap off of his head and smoothed his wavy hair with his hand.

When she didn't come to the door within 15 minutes, he stepped outside. Hanae turned and saw Teco, who wore Dolce & Gabbana (D&G) brown linen wide legged pants with a half inch cuff, a brown leather belt with a D&G symbol, a Gucci white silk shirt and brown suede slip-on shoes by Kenneth Cole. Trooper liked the fact that he always looked dapper. As he approached, she rolled down the car window and looked into his sexy brown eyes as he rested his elbows on the roof of the car.

"Would you like to come in for a brief moment? I'm almost ready." He was trying to think of a way to make her feel more comfortable.

"Teco, I'd rather not. I don't want you to get the wrong idea about me—"

"Hanae, before we go on this date. I need you to think about something. You are Hanae tonight and not Detective Troop. I've enjoyed getting to know Trooper over the last 2 months. Tonight, I want to date Hanae, the beautiful woman that I know she is." He looked into her eyes to see how she was receiving his words and was relieved to see her smile. Teco continued, "I'm going back into my place to finish getting ready. When I come out, you let me know if you want to finish this night in the most romantic way with Teco Jackson and not Rising Sun." He blew her an air kiss and spent around on his heels in a half circle to go back into his townhouse. Then he heard her laugh when he stumbled over a crack in the sidewalk.

Teco ran up the steps to his bedroom and put on his diamond studded white gold Wittnauer watch and a spritz of Drakkar Noir cologne. Kneeling at his safe, he pulled out five $100 dollar bills and put them into his billfold. He took another look at himself and jogged back down the stairs.

As he emerged from the front door, Hanae could not believe that she was still sitting in the car. She put Sunshine in the glove box and a 38 snub nose in her purse, just in case The Paradox showed up.

As he walked to assist her out of her car, he unlocked his Benz car doors and turned on the interior lights with the remote. When he opened the door for her, he saw that she wore a beautiful Liz Claiborne light blue baby doll top with a matching wrap around skirt, which hit right below her sexy thighs. The Nine West 2 inch black slingback pumps set it all off.

He extended his hand; and she said, "Teco, before we go I want to share something with you."

"Sure, what's up?" She was unaccustomed to a man helping her out of the car and hesitated for a second as to how she was going to stand up without revealing too much of her legs.

"I understand your request. I'll try my best to relax; but you must realize that I'm a detective 24 hours a day and 7 days a week." As she spoke, he admired how her diamond earrings sparkled from the lights on the street.

"Let's just have a romantic evening." He said closing her car door and walking her to the passenger side of his car. She felt like a celebrity the way he catered to her every move.

Before Teco hit Wisconsin Avenue, he turned on an Old School CD and turned it to the "Fire and Desire" track by Rick James and Teena Marie. When they reached the Blue Alley, a well known jazz club, he turned off the car.

Hanae said, "Wait Teco. I want to finish hearing this song. Let me sing the rest for you." He turned on the car; and he noticed that her eyes were closed. She sung in a low tone.

Teco was surprised that she could actually sing. As the song came to an end, Teco leaned over to kiss her on the cheek. "Thank you. That was beautiful." They walked to the jazz club and there was a long line wrapped around the block. "Do you want to walk to the park until the line gets shorter?" asked Teco.

Hanae couldn't believe how easy he made it for her to relinquish control. As they walked, Teco palmed her hand. She noticed that she was becoming very comfortable around him. All kinds of things went through her mind. *"Does he treat women like this all of the time? Will he want a lifestyle that is worlds away from the street life? Can a man really change?"*

When Teco spoke, he broke her train of thought, "So what are you thinking about?" She noticed him swinging her arm.

"Am I falling for a thug?" asked Hanae.

"Whoa, Whoa, hold up. I'm not a thug. I'm more of a street guy."

She laughed, "How can you differentiate the two? Isn't it the same?"

"Hell no. A thug protects his or her hood and carries armor to insure no one steps inside their turf without permission. A street guy would rather be outside on the streets than inside the house and is always on the go." He smirked to see if she agreed with him.

"I'll have to give that some thought. I can see your point though." She said leaning her head softly on his shoulder. "So are you going to remain a street guy?"

"Let's put it this way. I've given up the illegal aspects of street life." Walking and talking, they passed a lot of small shops and came across this one adult novelty store called TABOO which piqued Teco's curiosity. He was always looking to improve his stage performance.

"Do you mind if we step in for a brief moment?" He asked stopping in front of the store.

Hanae looked at him as if he were crazy and asked, "For what?" The last time she was in a store like this was on her way home from divorce court when she bought Pleasure. She looked at the window display and there were two mannequins, one with a French Maid costume and another with a Naughty

Nurse costume. There were all types of massage essentials on display as well. "Teco, I don't think this would be a good idea for us to go into this store together." However, he already opened the door and gently pulled Hanae into the store by her hand. She continued, "I don't believe I'm in this store."

Teco walked to the counter with the glass case full of adult toys; and Hanae came and stood beside him. He put his arm around her waist.

"Which one would you like to see me use on stage?" He asked; and she blushed like a virgin bride.

"I am not answering that Mr. Jackson."

He moved his hand from her waist to her round derriere and said, "Come on. Help a brother out."

"I tell you what mister . . ." She said in a playful tone. "If you don't move your hand, I'll be doing some police paperwork tonight."

He threw up his hands as if he were giving up. "Okay, so you want to put a brother in hand cuffs. Would you rather go to the bondage section of the store?"

"You really would like that. Wouldn't you?" They laughed.

Hanae felt as if someone was watching them. When she turned around, she said, "Oh shit! Teco we need to go." He thought this to be her way of leaving the store without helping him find a prop for his performance.

"If you tell me what you like in the case, then we can go."

"Teco, I'm serious."

"So am I . . . Ms. Detective with the handcuffs." He said sarcastically.

The undercover cop started to walk in their direction. Hanae moved in front of Teco, rested her face on his chest and whispered, "Teco, there is an undercover cop behind us; and I don't want to be seen in here."

When she looked up into Teco's face, she knew he wasn't going to leave the store without an answer. She turned around, looked into the case and said, "Okay, this one and that one." Teco was surprised when she pointed to a love wand and a silver bullet. Then she took Teco's hand and led him out of the store hiding behind Teco's tall frame. Walking out of the store unnoticed, she hit his arm hard but playfully and said, "That was wrong for you to do me like that."

"I kind of liked knowing what you like." He said laughing. While they walked and held hands in Rock Creek Park, they stopped to sit on a bench to talk a little more. The night seemed to be just right, not too hot and not too cool.

"Do you see the Little Dipper in the sky?" She asked looking up.

"Okay, you are joking right?" He asked rubbing her soft hair.

"No, I'm serious. Look up." Hanae said lifting his chin with her fingers.

"I see it. The 7 stars that form a punch bowl spoon," said Teco pointing in the directions of the Little Dipper.

"I'm impressed." She said looking into his eyes, which reminded her of how he captivated his female audience.

"So, do you think you'll ever leave male exotic dancing to become a bodyguard?" She asked leaning her head slightly to the right to see his facial expression.

"A what?" He asked in a quick high pitch tone.

Being alone with him and having no other woman around really made her feel special. She maneuvered closer to his side. Even without her having Sunshine, there was something about him that made her feel well protected.

"A bodyguard. You protected me well when that house exploded."

"I'll be your bodyguard any time," said Teco putting his hand around her waist. He added, "I need to ask you something."

She was really happy to be on this romantic date with him. "Sure . . . What's up Teco?"

"Can we walk up on those train tracks?" He asked pointing to the top of a hill. She pulled away from him and asked, "For what reason?"

With boldness he said, "I was wondering if you would take a ride on the wild side."

"And do what?" She smirked.

"Are you into fulfilling fantasies?" Teco asked rubbing her side softly with his hands.

"My fantasies or yours?" She couldn't remember the last time she did something spontaneous just for the fun of things.

"Make love to me tonight." He said giving her a passionate kiss.

"On those tracks?" Before she said another word, he kissed her again.

He stood to his feet; and from a long distance, they could hear the train's horn blowing. "Come with me." Teco said extending his hand.

Though she was hesitating on the outside, on the inside her spirit was saying, "The last one to the top of the hill is a rotten egg." She looked into his bedroom eyes and he touched that button. "To be honest, I'd love to feel the wind of the train as it passes by."

As they walked, they could see the moon glistening off of the Potomac River. When they reached underneath the train overpass, Teco helped Hanae take off her high heel shoes. Then he planted soft kisses on her neck. They continued walking up a grassy incline and reached the 4 train tracks. The train was coming from the North tracks and they stood on the South tracks.

"Teco, you are the craziest man I know."

Without saying another word, he pulled her close to him and kissed her erotically. Hanae put her arms around his neck and was lost in the moment. However, she said, "Teco these rocks are hurting my feet."

He said, "So much for 'the Trooper'." Then they laughed.

Unzipping his pants, he put on protective gear. He eased her shirt up and lifted her up to his waist with one good pull. As he held onto her thighs, she wrapped her legs around his upper waist.

Kissing her on the neck, Teco said, "Ummm, Hanae. I want to—"

She said, "Shh! Don't say another word. Let me hear how you feel."

His hand pulled the right side of her thong to the left; and he entered into her world. She let out the most erotic gasp that he ever heard. They held each other tight in order to savor this unforgettable night. As the trained passed, he rocked from side to side; however, he held ground with his strong dancer legs. Teco worked his hips in a circular fashion, which caused his body to caress her sweet spot. She returned his "Umm's" with her "Ah's." The strong wind intensified their combined climatic moment. As he released her and lifted her down, his ardent kisses made her want him even more. She didn't have to think, because he straightened her skirt and her blouse. When he picked her up to carry her across the tracks to the grassy area, she leaned her head on his shoulder. Holding hands down the slight hill, he helped her put back on her shoes under the overpass.

"I'm hungry," said Hanae.

"Let's get some take out and go back to my place to freshen up." They walked back to the car; and he ordered food from a restaurant called Mitzi's on his cell phone. As he ordered, he asked her, "What do you want to have?"

"I am not picky about food. I'll let you order."

After they picked up the food and walked into Teco's townhouse, they ascended the stairs to the master bathroom. Teco turned on the shower for Hanae and passed her a towel. When she closed the bathroom door, he went downstairs to put the food in the oven to keep it warm. Just as he suspected, Hanae came downstairs fully dressed.

"Did you enjoy our adventure?" He asked closing the door to the oven.

"Umm . . . yes I did." She said giving him a kiss on the cheek.

"Well, make yourself at home while I go take a quick shower."

Hanae decided to set the table and put the food on their plates. She found it interesting how easily she moved around his kitchen. There were fried chicken breasts on top of Glover Family Farm grits, sautéed broccolini, and a micro salad of beef chips and thin sliced green apples drizzled with a touch of honey.

When he walked downstairs wearing black dress pants and a white shirt with a red tie, she asked, "Where are you going?"

"You don't think the night is over after we eat. Do you? I don't hit and run." Hanae laughed. There was nothing better than a man who knew how to please a woman.

"Teco this food is great."

With a smile he said, "I'm glad that you like it. I go to Mitzi at least once a week. That's all my budget will allow. Are you ready to go back to the Blue's Alley?"

"I know you are all dressed up; however, I think I want to stay here and listen to music. Your home is so comfortable."

"Why thank you." Teco said taking off his tie.

"Teco, can I tell you something?" She asked kicking off her shoes.

"Sure, what's on your mind?" He asked thinking, *"Don't leave me Hanae."*

"What we did at the tracks today . . . I've never done that with anyone before. I must say that I enjoyed myself. Did you?"

"I think I enjoyed having you wrapped around my body more than you did."

"I would like for us to be more than just friends." She said waiting for his reaction.

"Hanae, what about your career?" He asked in a very concerned tone.

"Please, let me worry about that. I can defend what we have. All I ask is the truth from you."

"And I ask the same of you."

Teco took Hanae's hand and led her into the living room. He turned on the song "All My Life" by K-Ci and JoJo. Then he said, "Shall we dance?" He took her by the waist and they slow danced to the music. She closed her eyes and put her arms around his neck. He squeezed her tight and vowed to never let her go.

CHAPTER 27

After the FBI reviewed the audio recording of Candi's confession that someone other than Gail Que killed Bashi Mujaheed Fiten, GQ's was exonerated. Unfortunately GQ could not be contacted because she received approval from her Parole Officer to receive an expedited passport in order to travel to Paris for a new job.

On the way out of the classroom into the night, GQ saw Mr. Gordon who offered her a ride to the Happy Hour celebration. When Gail walked through the revolving glass door, she saw a snow white super stretch limousine. She asked Mr. Gordon, "Where is your car?"

He replied, "Ms. Que of the Lefébvre Indigo Signature Collection this is for you."

"You didn't have to Mr. Gordon." She said stepping into the limo.

"Yes I did. I want to make sure you made it back safely from Happy Hour and get packed for your Paris trip tomorrow."

Parked one block away, The Paradox thought, *"Damn, I'm just in time. Look at GQ's fine ass in those high heels."* He was trying to figure out who was the guy with her. The Paradox loaded the 45mm handgun ACP 40-Round drum magazine. When he looked up, the limo was almost to the corner with its right signal on. "Shit!" He exclaimed. He practically threw the drum into the passenger seat in order to swiftly pull off to catch up with the limo.

For two entire months, The Paradox searched to find GQ. Finally, he decided to use his fake press pass to locate her. When he told GQ's Parole Officer (PO) that he wanted to do an exclusive interview with GQ, the PO sung like a canary. GQ's PO mentioned that GQ's conviction was overturned because they found evidence that another person killed Bashi Mujaheed Fiten. The PO even asked The Paradox to include this information in the news article, which infuriated The Paradox more. Because he lost so much time finding her, The Paradox knew that he needed to move quickly. The FBI and Detective Troop were closing in on him. Looking at the limo, the Paradox thought, *"Soulja, stay focused on your mission."*

GQ sat across from Mr. Gordon in the limo and said, "I have a surprise for you too."

"Oh really? What is it?" asked Mr. Gordon.

She pulled out a men's sweat suit made of soft material. "So do you like it? It's a sample that I'm going to propose for my Indigo Signature Collection." She said crossing her legs.

"Yes, I do. What type of material is it?"

She looked at him batting her hazel eyes and said, "Now you know I can't tell you that."

"I'm your agent. And you won't share design secrets with me?" He asked in a shocking as well as joking manner.

"Boy, I'm just playing with you. It's a special blend of velvet and velour, which I call vevelour."

"Okay I like this," said Mr. Gordon with a bright smile.

GQ turned on the 10 inch television inside the limo. She noticed that Mr. Gordon picked up a stack of legal papers and was reviewing them intently.

"This is CNN News. Just 2 months after the death of Twyla Burke, a.k.a. Candi, who was associated with the D.C. G-String murders, we just received news that Twyla's mother Ginger Burke passed away today of a heart attack. Ginger Burke owned several establishments in the Conshohocken area and was known as the queen of a prostitution ring called Special Touch." GQ's heart sank; and she looked out of the car window trying to figure out how she missed the news about Candi's death. Candi was the only person who could vindicate her from Bashi's murder. Tears filled her eyes, which now appeared almond-blue in the sunlight.

"Gail, are you alright?" He asked.

"Yes, I'm fine. I was just thinking about something." She said turning off the television.

"Is it something I can help you with as your agent or friend?"

She looked at him and asked, "My friend? Well, since you put it that way, yes you can."

"Okay, you have my undivided attention." He put the paperwork down and took her hand.

GQ took a deep breath and said, "Please don't get mad at what I'm going to tell you next." She said with a sincere look.

"I'm listening."

"We have a mutual acquaintance, your best friend Teco Jackson whom I call Homicide. And though I was accused of a horrible crime, I want you to know that I never committed murder." She said with tears rolling down her cheeks.

He put his arm around her and said, "I believe you when you say you didn't kill Bashi Mujaheed Fiten. Strictly Business."

She pushed him away and asked, "What did you say?"

"Gail, I've known that you are Gail Que, a.k.a. GQ, for several months. I even pulled your criminal record. After talking with your prison counselor, she explained that you claimed your innocence the entire time you were in prison. You might want to see this." He reached into his brief case and pulled out a court document which was dated several weeks ago.

"What's this?" She asked taking the paper from Mr. Gordon.

"It's the transcript of the audio interview of Twyla Burke by the lead female Detective on the G-String Murder case in D.C. Twyla Burke, Candi, confessed that you were not the killer. I thought you already knew."

"No! I never saw the paper or heard it on the news." Her next reaction was unexpected. Sheer hatred filled her eyes. "Why in the hell didn't you tell me that you knew I was GQ and that you found out weeks ago that I didn't kill Bashi?!"

"Gail, calm down." He said in a rational voice. "Look, you didn't tell me either that you knew I was Fatboy. So you haven't been up front with me either."

GQ started to gather her belongings to get out of the limo. Then she discovered that she didn't have her portfolio with her. She screamed at the driver. "Turn the car around! I need to go back to the school and get my things." As the driver drove them back to the college, GQ crossed her arms and didn't say a word.

When they reached the campus, Mr. Gordon said to the driver, "Charge my account. I'll take her home."

As she stepped out onto the curb, GQ said sarcastically, "The hell you will."

Behind the limo, The Paradox parked and rolled down the window to hear what the commotion was all about.

Getting out of the limo, Mr. Gordon exclaimed, "Gail wait!" They stood on the sidewalk within a ear shot of The Paradox.

"If you knew I didn't kill Bashi, you should have let me know weeks ago."

"I thought you saw the news." He said grabbing her arm as she was trying to walk away.

GQ said, "I've been busting my ass on this fashion line. I haven't had time to look at T.V. I need to go see Homicide in D.C."

"How will you find him?"

"He's dancing at *The First of the Month Show* at a place called The Mirage. I'm going to get his ass, because we were supposed to stick together like fam."

When The Paradox heard that Teco, formerly Homicide, was in D.C., he started to jump out of the car and kill GQ right then and there in order to shut her up. However, people were all on the streets. Then he remembered how he panicked with Kream; so he took deep breaths to calm down.

Mr. Gordon said emphatically, "You are leaving for Paris tomorrow. You can't go to D.C. Think for a moment Gail. Your new career is more important. Is this about settling a score?"

"Yes, it has everything to do with that; and I don't want you to be upset with me be—"

"Gail, why would I be upset with you?"

"Because Homicide is your best friend; and there are some things that I only can talk to him about." Several people looked annoyed as they maneuvered around GQ and Mr. Gordon on the sidewalk. The casual pedestrians slowed down to see if this was a lover's quarrel.

"Can you understand that I don't want anything to happen to you? You are getting on that plane to Paris. Do you hear me?"

"I'm going to the classroom to get my portfolio."

"I'll get my car out of the garage. Meet me right back here on the curb. I'm taking you home to pack." Mr. Gordon said taking his car keys out of his pants pocket.

"Fine," said GQ who stormed away into the building. She quickly gathered her portfolio and walked back outside.

Waiting for Mr. Gordon to pull his car around, she realized that he forgot to tell her the make and color of his car. So she pushed through the crowded streets and headed towards The Paradox's black Town Car to see if Mr. Gordon was inside. When The Paradox saw GQ approaching, he put on his black gloves and pointed the 45mm handgun at GQ. Just as The Paradox put his finger on the trigger, Mr. Gordon blew the car horn for GQ to get into his silver Volvo S60. *"Damn, that was close,"* thought The Paradox.

As Mr. Gordon drove down Walnut Street, The Paradox saw GQ open the sunroof. Simultaneously, Mr. Gordon saw the Town Car tailing him. When the Town Car began to increase its speed pulling right beside the Volvo, Mr. Gordon said, "Gail, I think something's up." Before she turned her head, bullets rang out making a thumping noise on the driver's side door. GQ screamed. Mr. Gordon pushed her head down towards the floorboard and mashed the pedal leaving the Town Car behind him. "Gail! Gail! Are you alright?"

"Yes! Yes! What the hell is going on?"

Mr. Gordon came to 59th Street and took a quick right, thinking he could loose The Paradox. He looked back into his rearview mirror and the car was not there. He pushed it 4 city blocks and took another right onto Market Street knowing that he was only 8 blocks from I-95. Out of no where, the Town Car rammed the passenger's side sending the Volvo flying 10 feet into the air. After flipping 7 times and then sliding 80 yards, the Volvo landed on the driver's side in the opposite lane.

Blood ran down the right side of GQ's forehead; and she tried to look over to see if Mr. Gordon was alright. When she smelled gas, she knew that she had to get out of the car. She reached for the seat belt release and let out a loud moan because of the excruciating pain. Her body fell onto Mr. Gordon's and she smacked him on his face, "Get up! Come . . . on . . . Get up!" He was unresponsive.

GQ crawled out of the sunroof. Just as she hit the ground, she heard footsteps and crawled several feet away from the Volvo. The Paradox walked across the street in his black trench coat and tear drop hat. He reached to pull out the 45mm handgun to finish the job; however, the Volvo S-60 exploded. KA-BOOM! The Paradox covered his head to shield his face from the shockwave. Turning around, The Paradox realized that the Town Car was totaled; therefore, he ran several blocks to the 60th Street Station to catch the SEPTA train.

GQ laid there trying her best to make sense of what happened. The only people she knew who would want her dead were Bashi's band of brothers, the Fiten Posse. Whether she was innocent or not, the Fiten Posse would always hold her accountable for the death of Bashi.

Three fire engines pulled up behind the car fire. Then an EMT truck came and put GQ onto a stretcher. With the red and white lights on, the sirens sounded as they entered the Pennsylvania Hospital ER entrance.

CHAPTER 28

As GQ stood at the Philadelphia International Airport ticket counter, she became more and more upset that her international flight to Paris was cancelled. She said to the international ticket agent, "The last 24 hours have been hell; and I really need to get to Paris to start my life over."

The ticket agent looked at GQ with curiosity. "Aren't you the lady I saw on the news last night in that horrible car accident?" She asked looking at GQ's visible stitches on her forehead.

GQ said, "Yes, and I left the hospital a few hours ago, packed my bags and have got to make it to Paris for a new job."

"Let me see what I can do." The ticket agent looked down at the computer screen as GQ stood there feeling as if her entire world was destroyed. The hospital wouldn't tell GQ the fate of Mr. Gordon, because she wasn't a relative. So she decided to follow his advice and go to Paris.

"Here we go. I can route you through Reagan International Airport."

"Okay. Anything to get me out of here."

"You've had a hard day. I'm upgrading you to First Class straight through to Paris. Here you go, enjoy your flight."

"Thank you so much." As GQ walked through airport security, The Paradox walked into the Philadelphia International Airport. He approached the domestic ticket counter and said, "Hello, I'm checking in."

"May I see your I.D?" asked the domestic ticket agent.

As he handed her the fake I.D., he said, "Yes, here you go." The Paradox looked around to see if he was being watched by airport security.

As she waited for the system to respond, the ticket agent stole the moment to look at this fine brother. He looked like a 6 foot tall body builder straight out of Muscle & Fitness Magazine. His pecan tan skin complimented his gray eyes. She wanted to ask him for his number; however, she said, "My, that's a nice ring you have on." Looking closer, she asked, "Does that say SB?"

At first, he was irritated by her question, but decided to go along with the flow. "Yes it does."

Seeing that he was not interested in small talk, she said, "Well, your bags are checked to Washington Reagan International Airport. Enjoy your flight."

The airplane was boarding when GQ reached the gate. The female gate agent called for First Class passengers. GQ handed the female gate agent the ticket and walked through the Jetway. When GQ reached the aircraft door, she moved to turn to the right; however, the flight attendant said, "First Class is to the left."

"Thank you," said GQ looking confused.

A few minutes later, The Paradox boarded the plane to the right. When he realized that he was on the last row in the middle seat, he became very agitated. He hoped that he could keep his temper under wraps until they landed, because he hated tight spaces and felt like there was no way to easily escape.

When the plane landed in D.C., the First Class flight attendant saw GQ's distressed look and asked, "Ms. Que., how may I help you?"

"This is my first international flight. Are we leaving for Paris on this same plane?"

"Well, we have a 6 hour layover here in D.C. You will have to get off; and 1 hour before the flight, we will re-board the aircraft. But don't worry, I'm working First Class and will make sure you enjoy your flight to Paris."

GQ sat there while all of the passengers deplaned. After she got up and gathered her carry-on bag, she found a nice quiet spot in the back of a terminal airport bar. All of the seats at the bar were filled with men, who were watching the ESPN Washington Redskins Preseason Special. There was only 1 table that was available; and GQ sat down. She took out her sketchpad to create an evening gown for her Indigo Signature Collection.

A man dressed in a business suit walked up to her and said, "Hello, I saw you sitting in First Class. You are the most stunning woman I've ever seen. I overheard that you are also going to Paris. If you like, I can show you around once we get there. Are you travelling with someone?"

GQ looked down at her sketchpad and said, "Yes, Dick Blick."

He walked away disappointed; and another man walked up to her and said, "Hey gorgeous, I'm going out on the town tonight and wonder if—"

She said, "I'm just leaving." Hearing the man talk about partying reminded GQ of Teco's performance at The Mirage. She pulled out her calendar and exclaimed, "Oh Snap! That's Tonight!"

"Pardon?" He asked as GQ packed up her carry-on bag. Then she ran out of the terminal area to catch a cab.

When she reached the curb, she heard, "Need a safe ride? Use our limo service." She walked over to a man who was dressed like a funeral director.

"Can you take me to this address please?" She asked showing him the piece of paper.

"Yes I can. I know exactly where it is." He said looking her up and down.

"How fast can you get me there?"

"I'll have you there in 30 minutes. That will be a flat rate of $75."

"I need you to wait for me an hour or so and bring me back to the airport. Can that be arranged?"

"Why certainly. How about I give you a flat rate of $200 for the evening?"

"Good."

He opened the black Town Car door for GQ as she looked at her watch. When he got into the cab, he radioed dispatch to let them know that he was booked for the evening.

◊◊◊◊◊

Excitement displayed in Teco's eyes about tonight's *First of the Month Show*. He played his performance song over and over to insure he knew every word. The club opened at 7 o'clock on the dot. Sitting in the parking lot, Teco looked at his watch; and it was 6:45. When he saw Trooper, he flashed his lights to get her attention. He liked the black Brooks Brothers pant suit she wore.

The Paradox looked in the direction of the flashing lights. This distracted him from watching the D.C. Homicide Division and the FBI, who were setting up the stakeout. He couldn't believe they were being so obvious. So, he put in an earpiece and tried to intercept their radio frequency. However, all he received was a high pitch squeal that almost hurt his eardrum. Becoming more and more perturbed, he furiously threw the earpiece in the backseat of the car.

In the surveillance van, Agent Rozier said to the team, "This is the biggest male exotic dance show this month. We haven't heard nor seen anything from The Paradox. We are very much expecting this asshole to show up. No one acts alone. Everyone must be in radio contact with our command post at all times." Agent Rozier looked at Captain Wicker and said, "Even you sir." Then he passed out earpieces.

Captain Wicker asked, "Detective Brown, will your partner be joining us?"

"Yes sir; she went to talk to Mr. Jackson because she thought it best that he knew he's being used as bait," said Swoosh trying to cover for his partner.

"Damn!" exclaimed Captain Wicker slamming his hand down on the table. "I'm tired of her compromising our mission by seeing Mr. Jackson."

Trooper got into the Benz to kiss Teco on the cheek; however, he was quicker than she; and he met her soft lips. "I'm working." She said and saw him reach into the glove box for something.

"Do you remember when I went to Atlanta a while back?" asked Teco.

"Yes." Trooper said looking in the direction of the officer in the unmarked car.

"Well, I got you something. I think the time is right to give it to you now." He said passing her the red velvet jewelry box.

"You didn't have to."

"I wanted to." She kissed him right then and there.

Trooper opened it and said, "It's beautiful."

As she looked at the necklace with a diamond "X", "O", and a heart pendant, he said, "Here, let me put it on you."

Do you know what it means?" She asked as he lifted her ponytail and closed the clasp.

"Yes, I do; and this is why I'm giving it to you." Teco reached in the backseat and presented to her a single rose. She thought the rose was the most vibrant color red she ever saw and not like the roses sold by the local street vendor. She smelled the sweet nectar.

He looked purposefully into Hanae's brown eyes and said, "I'm falling in—"

She put her right index finger over his lips and said, "Hold that thought until we can talk about it over some white wine later tonight. Keep the rose until I get off of work tonight; and we can use the rose petals in our bath."

"That sounds good to me. Hanae . . . tonight, please be careful," said Teco in a concerned tone.

"I will. I've got your back tonight."

"Only tonight?" He asked in a provocative voice. She smiled, got out of the car, and went back to the stakeout van. As Trooper entered the van, the surveillance team watched Teco get out of his car.

When the Paradox saw Teco, a.k.a. Homicide, he could not believe his eyes. His mind drifted back to the day when Teco was furious about him stealing drugs from the SB Crew. *"I bet you won't take nobody else's shit . . . . Will you? Say you sorry . . . . Say you sorry . . . . "* *Teco said leaving him for dead.* The Paradox watched Teco vanish into the crowd of women. *"I won't give Teco, Mr. Homicide, a chance to say he's sorry for how he humiliated me on the streets back in Conshohocken."* Then The Paradox lifted up his right index finger and looked at the SB ring that he stole the day he killed Bashi.

Inside the van, all eyes were on Trooper; and this made her feel uncomfortable. Swoosh pulled Trooper to the side and said, "The Captain is pissed that you are talking with Teco."

"Can I have a life?" As she spoke, Swoosh eyes shifted to the sparkling necklace and he raised his right eyebrow.

The driver opened the black Town Car door for GQ, who stepped out looking like a supermodel. Observing the camera monitors, Swoosh pulled out a photo of GQ for confirmation and said, "We've got company; and you will not believe who it is." Trooper and Agent Rozier fast paced it over to see, hoping that it was The Paradox.

"Is that who I think it is?" asked Trooper.

Swoosh said, "Gail Que." Trooper stepped out of the van and headed towards the club. Swoosh thought, *"Damn, GQ is fine."*

Before anyone could say a word, Captain Wicker asked, "Where is she going?" Swoosh didn't say a word because he didn't want the Captain to know that Trooper didn't have on her surveillance earpiece.

Turning back to the camera monitor, Swoosh saw GQ walking up to the ropes in the front of the line. She said to the bouncer, "I'm Gail Que, the new designer of the Lefébvre Indigo Signature Collection. How much is your VIP section?"

The bouncer asked, "Are you for real? My girlfriend read about that in USA Today. She is a fashion fanatic. Can she get your autograph when she gets here?"

"Sure." At first GQ didn't know how to respond, because she didn't officially start until she got to Paris. Mr. Gordon was right. Starting out with a major fashion designer was a major boost for her career.

"Can you stand over here please?" He asked; and GQ stepped aside.

Swoosh got out of the van. When he made eye contact with GQ, he spoke and she nodded.

After 15 minutes, the club manager came down wearing a suit with a nice black dinner jacket. "The owner sends his regards and asked me to make sure you have a great time this evening. I'm Ron. And you are?"

"I'm Gail Indigo Que. I recently signed with Lefébvre, a major fashion designer out of Paris."

She extended her hand for him to shake; however, he kissed the back of her hand instead and said, "I understand you want to be at a VIP table. Please join me at my table." They stepped inside and he pointed to the location. The VIP room was also called the Gush Room, because there were 5 large plastic tubes which extended from the floor to the ceiling. Each tube contained water, which bubbled from the bottom to the top. The tubes were positioned several feet apart in a circle around the VIP room. A different colored light was at the top of each tube. GQ scanned the room and couldn't decide if she liked the blue, red, green, yellow or clear tube the best.

"Why thank you. Do you mind if I look around?" GQ was determined to find Teco.

"No please do. I'll have the bar put you on my tab."

"Oh one more thing . . ." She said batting her eyes.

Distracting GQ's thoughts, the M.C. signaled for the lights to dim. The women in the audience were excited to see that the show was about to start. Then the M.C. asked, "Laaadies, are you ready to see the #1 dancer in D.C.?"

The women scream, "Yeaaah!!!" GQ turned around to see who was coming onto the stage.

"Laaadies, do you love him?"

"Yeaaah!!!" The women yelled and came rushing to the stage. The sounds of "I'm Going Down" by Rose Royce pumped through the speakers.

"Are you ready to see some beeeef?" The red, blue, and yellow lights created imaginary circles on the stage.

"Yeaaah!!!"

The #1 dancer came out on stage wearing a tuxedo with a black opera style coat with tails. GQ couldn't believe how handsome he was on stage. She smiled unconsciously.

"Without further ado, here is Risssing Sunnn!" With this announcement GQ's mouth flew open, because Homicide did not look like the same thug she knew 3 years ago.

From the corner of his right eye, Rising Sun saw a female walking up on the stage. He tried his best to tell her to get off of the stage; however, she kept coming towards him. Before she reached into her pockets, Swoosh was on the stage to guide her off. Even though she dropped the money which was in her hands, she tried to break away from Swoosh to touch Rising Sun. "Sorry baby girl, you can touch him later," said Swoosh.

There was a private bar and waitress in the VIP section. Tonight Toi was the waitress and said to GQ, "Yeah girl, every woman he meets has that same look on her face. What are you having?"

"White Zinfadel." GQ said not taking her eyes off of Rising Sun, who continued to dance. Rising Sun's coat tail flared open as he spun around. In the process he slipped his coat off and it floated in the air. When the coat touched the floor, money was all over the stage. His chest was bare; and he wore a brown G-String which gave the illusion that he wasn't wearing any clothes. The ladies cheered.

GQ looked around to determine where she wanted to sit. There were 5 tables in the middle of the room. When she saw the nice black leather couch, she took a seat and crossed her legs. In the far corner, men were playing a game of pool. Ron walked into the VIP section and said, "Are you having a good time Ms. Que."

She asked deceptively, "Who is that dancer on stage now? He would make a great model."

"That's my best dancer, Rising Sun. Would you like to meet him?"

"Sure that would be nice." She said taking a sip of her wine.

As Rising Sun came into the audience to charm the crowd, GQ looked at him like a hawk. Teco appeared to be a different person to her. Nothing about his demeanor reminded her of the old Homicide from SB. Somehow he appeared to be less arrogant. He looked like he finally had a home.

CHAPTER 29

As GQ walked to the restroom, Toi went into the dressing room and said, "Rising Sun, Ron would like to see you at his table once you're dressed."

"Sure, I'll be right there." He said, thinking that Ron wanted to discuss a business deal, which meant more money in the bank.

Rising Sun walked to the VIP section with a drink in his hand. "Hello, my beautiful ladies." He said reaching for their hands and greeting each one with a kiss.

Coming back from the bathroom, GQ approached Rising Sun from behind and took a seat. Since the club was dark, only the rays of light from the tubes illuminated the VIP section; and Rising Sun could only see a woman's face from up close. He leaned forward to kiss several women sitting down and kissed GQ as well. When he went to rise up, GQ pulled him back down to whisper in his ear. He licked his lips as if she was about to ask for another kiss; but instead she asked, "Isn't it Strictly Business, Homicide? We need to talk." Her voice was clear as ever. He jumped back bumping into Toi and knocking the tray of drinks over.

"Oh Shit!" shouted Ron who jumped up to help Toi. GQ looked at Rising Sun with her fist balled up. Something deep inside of her wanted to knock the shit out of him. Rising Sun's heart palpitated. As people turned to see what the chaos was all about, he got a much better look and could not believe his eyes.

"I'm sorry." Rising Sun said to Toi wanting to help her with the mess. The only thing he could do was walk away.

GQ stormed after him. Then she thought to double check her watch in order to see if she had enough time to settle the score. Unfortunately, GQ needed to run to the Town Car before she missed her flight to Paris. She felt like Cinderella who needed to reach the horse drawn carriage before it turned back into a pumpkin at midnight. Where was her fairy godmother when she needed her? GQ thought, *"Damn! I wanted to kick Homicide's ass for snitching and putting me away in prison for life."* However, GQ agreed with Chi Chi that a person's future was more important than revenge.

Trooper watched Rising Sun and wondered why his face was perplexed. His mind was racing a hundred miles per hour, because those ever changing colors in GQ's eyes were undeniable. Rising Sun ran up a flight of stairs to the D.J. Booth, where there was a 62 inch screen with a video feed of the entire club. He scanned the screen and saw Trooper walking the club trying to locate GQ. Shifting his attention to the VIP section, Rising Sun saw that GQ was gone. "What the hell? Where is she?" He asked aloud.

The D.J. yelled, "What Rising Sun? I can't hear you man!" Then the D.J. played "Baby I'm a Star" by Prince & The Revolution. Looking on the screen at the hallway entrance, he couldn't believe that GQ was no where to be found.

Downstairs, Ron ran to catch GQ. When he found her on the curb, he said out of breath, "Gail."

She said, "Ron, my driver is across the street. I'm sorry that I don't have time to stay, but I have to catch my flight to Paris. Thanks for everything."

When Ron looked up, he saw 2 black Town Cars and said, "No bother. I'm sorry for the mishap."

The Paradox was still sitting in the rental Town Car and rubbed his eyes. There was no way that GQ was standing over there; after all, she was killed in the car crash in Philly.

GQ said to Ron, "Tell Teco that I will be back."

Ron waited for GQ to get safely across the street. As he walked back into the club, he thought to himself, *"Hummm . . . I never told her Rising Sun's real name. I will ask him how he knows her."*

Meanwhile, Rising Sun was pacing the floor in the DJ's Booth. "I need to find her."

"Rising Sun, what did you say? I can't hear you!" screamed the D.J. as he played "Escapade" by Janet Jackson.

Rising Sun ran down the stairs. When he saw Swoosh, he said, "I'm going outside for some air."

Teco stood at the front door of the club trying to piece things together and reached into his left inside pocket for his car keys so that he could jet. That's when he saw the red dot on his jacket. Before he moved, two amber flashes came towards him. POW! POW! Teco fell to the ground. Pandemonium was on the streets. Even the people who were once in the club came out to see who was shot. Teco's female fans were hysterical. Swoosh ran outside and saw GQ facing in their direction.

Wearing the trench coat and black teardrop hat, The Paradox got out of the rental car as GQ got into the limo service car, which spun off. Swoosh hustled to an unmarked police car, got in on the passenger's side and yelled to the officer, "Go! Go! Go! Catch that car!" Pulling out his 9mm weapon, Swoosh was ready for any drama. The limo service Town Car was several blocks ahead and turned a right onto Capital Avenue to go over the bridge. When the unmarked police car reached halfway across the bridge, an unrelated car accident happened right before Swoosh's eyes and traffic seized. The Town Car was no where to be found. "Shit! Shit!" exclaimed Swoosh as he banged his pistol on the dashboard.

Back at the club, The Paradox needed to be quick about his next move. So, he ran to the front door of the club, knelt beside Teco and yelled at the crowd of bystanders, "Please, back up! Back up!" Looking into Teco's eyes, The Paradox took off the stolen SB ring, put it on Teco's finger and said, "Take this to the grave with you and give it to Bashi, you sorry ass mutha . . ."

Teco looked into The Paradox's cold eyes and wished he never stepped foot on the streets of Conshohocken. In his mind, Teco heard his father's voice, *"See it for what it is and see it for what it's worth."* Feeling the excruciating pain, Teco willed himself to live in order to start his life anew with Trooper. However, he didn't know if he would be able to continue breathing much longer.

The Paradox hopped up, because he saw Trooper running in his direction. As police officers tried to secure the area, Trooper's eyes locked with The Paradox. She remembered that he was the man who bought her the drink at Club Classic. When he bent a left around the corner, Trooper was right on his ass. They ran several blocks away from the frenzy and away from Trooper's police force backup. EMT sirens could be heard from a distance.

The Paradox took another sharp left into an alleyway, which was a city block long. Trooper saw rats running away from a three day garbage feast. The street lights illuminated the alley, because the tall buildings blocked the moonlit skies. Trooper was right on his heels and exclaimed, "Freeze! Put your hands up in the air!" The Paradox stopped running and slowly turned around. She put Sunshine to his temple. Suddenly, The Paradox matched her move by placing his 45mm gun to her forehead.

"I told you that we would meet again Detective," said The Paradox, who was enthused to have her in the alley alone.

"Yeah, you did," said Trooper never taking her eyes off of him. They started to walk slowly in a circle. As Trooper's legs crossed, she planted her heels slowly and carefully, so that she wouldn't trip over her own feet. The tension was electric as she glared into his gray eyes, which seemed to turn black as coal under the alley's shadows.

"Now you've met the Paradox in person." His smile was bright as if this were their first date; however, his lips quivered at the same time. She noticed the cut of an old scar on his upper right lip and wondered if Teco's fist put it there five years ago.

"So you despise a snitch? Guess what? You loved Candi and killed her before she could snitch and say your name, Bobby." Trooper relished the surprised look on his face.

"Are you calling me a liar?" He asked wanting to pull the trigger. "Are you saying I don't despise a snitch? You think your ass is so smart because you know my name." He said with a scowling look.

"Candi said you snitched on the SB Crew for selling drugs. So, do you despise yourself, Bobby 'The Paradox' Stephens?" She asked with confidence in her investigative work.

"Shut the hell up!" exclaimed The Paradox as sweat rolled down his face.

"Word on the streets is that Homicide kicked your ass back in Philly for stealing from the SB Crew. Is that why you shot him tonight?" She fought back any signs of vulnerability, because she didn't know if Teco was alive or dead.

"That's little boy shit! My mission is much larger!" He shouted; and Trooper never expected what came next. Out of nowhere, the back of his fist came down on Trooper's left jaw like lighting, while cutting her lip at the same time. Ka-Pow! As she was going down, she grabbed his black trench coat lapel to keep herself from falling. With everything Trooper possessed, she tried to pull herself up.

"What's too bright to look at in the broad daylight?" She asked with determination trying to shake off the dazed feeling.

"I never figured that one out," said The Paradox enjoying their game.

"Well meet Sunshine." Then Trooper pressed Sunshine against his throat and pulled the trigger. He flinched; however, all they heard was "click," because her gun misfired.

He hit Trooper with an open fist driving her to the ground and making blood come from her previous cut. As she lay there, he slammed his foot on her right hand, which held Sunshine. The Paradox kicked Sunshine several feet away. "Arrrgh!" Trooper roared out in pain. "You already destroyed the SB Crew. What else is left?" She asked.

As he knelt down beside Trooper, he said, "You will have to figure that out." The Paradox pressed the cold steel barrel closer to her third-eye; and she smelled his foul breath. Closing her eyes, Trooper willed herself to think of her last date and sweet kiss with Teco. She reached and held the diamond necklace in her hand. When she opened her eyes, she saw the shadow of The Paradox's trench coat and teardrop hat.

Trooper jumped up and reached in her pant's leg to retrieve her backup weapon, which was a 380 automatic pistol. She ran deeper into the alley after The Paradox; and when she reached the blue dumpster, two shots rang out almost striking her. Pow! Pow! However, she dove behind the dumpster, holding the 380 safely against her chest. "Give yourself up. There is no way out of this." She said peeking from behind the dumpster in order to locate The Paradox.

"Not true. Who knows? You might just find me in the Black Mecca of the South or Chi-Town or the Big Apple! How about the City of Syrup?" The Paradox saw a street and was relieved that he didn't have to go back to where the chase began.

Trooper heard his footsteps, ran behind him, and fired. Pow! Pow! Pow! Pow! Pow! The Paradox turned around to return fire and shot at Trooper three times. The last bullet struck Trooper, knocking her to the ground and making her almost twist her ankle. "Araagh, shit!" She yelled hunkering down behind 2 trash cans. Inspecting the wound, she sighed with relief to see that the bullet only grazed her left shoulder.

Trooper heard footsteps coming towards her, which caused her to aim her gun in that direction. She was overwhelmed with the flashlights shining in her face.

"Trooper! Hold your fire! Stand down!"

When she raised her right hand over her forehead to shield the light, she saw Agent Rozier, Agent Mullis, Captain Wicker, and other surveillance team members.

"Trooper you have gone against direct orders. You were clearly told not to pursue the suspect alone. Where is he?" asked Captain Wicker.

Agent Rozier helped Trooper to her feet; and she walked back to where Sunshine lay on the ground. She was so frustrated with herself for not killing The Paradox that she never answered Captain Wicker. Down by her feet was Sunshine and a brown ladies G-String with a note attached.

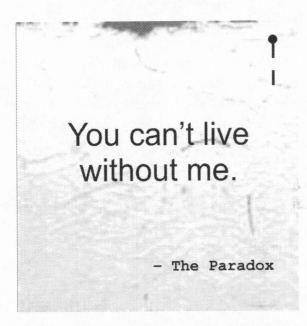

You can't live
without me.

— The Paradox

"Trooper, why didn't you call for backup? That was our agreed to procedure. Where is he?" demanded Captain Wicker.

"How is Teco Jackson?" asked Trooper, who knew that The Paradox turned their encounter into a personal mission.

"We don't think he is going to make it. They are loading him up now. Have you not heard a word I said? Where is The Paradox?"

Holding Sunshine in one hand and the G-String in the other, Trooper walked through the band of men. Captain Wicker could not believe that his most dependable detective was ignoring him. They all turned and headed back towards the club with Trooper leading the way. The crowd was thinning out and traffic was moving smoothly.

"Trooper, did you hear me ask you a question? I repeat. Where did The Paradox go?!" exclaimed Captain Wicker.

Coming down the street was the EMT ambulance. The red and white lights reflected off of street cars; and sirens filled the air. A host of women watched wondering if this was Rising Sun's grand finale.

Despite the sheer pain in her shoulder, Trooper flagged down the ambulance and said, "Let me in."

As Detective Troop hopped into the back of the ambulance, she saw her boss standing in the middle of the street with his hands in mock surrender. He really wanted to know what the hell was on Trooper's mind. Was she choosing her job over a life with Teco? Captain Wicker exclaimed, "Trooper! Trooper! Trooperrr!"

To be continued in *The Street Life Series: Is It Rags or Riches?*

SOURCES

The following book was used as a source of information on the background of forensic science.

Lyle, Douglas P. *Forensics for Dummies.* New York: Wiley, John & Sons, Incorporated, 2004.

If you wish to contact the author, Kevin M. Weeks, the email address is *info@thestreetlifeseries.com.* He looks forward to corresponding with you.